OKLAHOMA SKY

A Holder County Novel

JILLIAN NEAL

Photography by **GOLDEN CZERMAK / FURIOUS FOTOG**

Cover Model **MAVERICK WILLETT**

Edited by **HAPPILY EDITING ANNS**

Published by Realm Press

ISBN: 978-1-940174-51-8

Library of Congress Control Number: 2019918527

First Edition

First Printing – December 2019

CONTENTS

CHAPTER ONE

"I need a clean break," Callie Monroe reminded herself as she slowed her Honda behind an old truck with heaped hay bales in its bed. "Just a breather." She needed to put some distance between herself and Derrick. Nothing else had worked. It was better this way.

It was not at all the way her mother had done this. Callie had tried a dozen times to tell him that she wanted to end their relationship. Eventually, he had to understand. Once he got used to her not being there to remind him to eat, and he learned to pair his own socks, he'd be fine. She was tired of being the replacement for his mother's maids anyway. That wasn't what love was supposed to be.

Going back to the farm would be good. She missed her grandparents so much she swore the pain held a physical mailing address in her chest. The absence stung her throat. She pressed the accelerator harder, focusing only on seeing her grandparents, and not on having to live all of the awkwardness that would surely come when Derrick finally realized she wasn't returning to California. She just needed to rip the bandage off. Easing it away slowly was not working.

A few weeks back on the farm would give her a fresh start. That's all she needed. From there, she could plan her move to New York. On her own. By herself. She shoved those terrifying thoughts to the furthest recesses of her mind.

Stopped at one of the very few traffic lights in Holder County, the only consolidated city-county in Oklahoma, she used the seconds to wind her long blonde hair into a messy topknot with the band she kept on her wrist. Memories washed over her like a warm bath as she rounded the old square. Everything still looked the same, and that suited her just fine.

A small portion of the stability she'd always longed for slipped back into place beneath her the same way it had every summer when her grandfather had come to Tulsa to retrieve her. Cattle ranchers were still leaned up against the porch railings of Carraway's Feed Store. Three old dogs were lounging on the cool concrete platform in the shade of the old train depot, and the rusty water tower, that loomed in the distance, still declared its panther pride for Maxwell High in fading paint.

The red-brick courthouse stood proudly in the center of town. Its battlements and spires announced Holder County's pride of placement to all of Oklahoma, and the clock tower clanged the arrival of three o'clock.

When she was a little girl, Callie used to pretend the courthouse was a magical castle complete with a prince who would rescue her from her parents' endless arguments and the heavy hand her father wielded when his temper got the best of him.

But she no longer required a prince to rescue her. She could do that all on her own. Maybe.

Yep, it was good to be home. This was the best decision she'd made in a long time. With that mental reassurance, she turned off the square and headed to the outskirts of town. A grin lifted her cheeks as she passed the Lucky Strike. She secretly couldn't wait to hear her grandmother admonish the discreetly tucked pool hall and bowling alley where the waitresses wore slightly higher skirts and lower-cut tops than her nana thought appropriate.

She glanced at her Canon Rebel tucked in its case in the seat beside hers. She'd never photographed Holder County before. Somehow during her summer visits, she'd missed all of its comfortable grace and calming reassurance. In the throes of adolescence, the familiarity had become mundane. It was a backdrop for the play of life she often pretended she was really living. Since she'd never attended school in Holder County, she was forever an outsider. But she'd spent her summer days pretending she lived on the farm full-time and grew up the way all of the cattle ranchers' kids did. The appreciation Holder County deserved had slipped through her young grasp. She needed to capture those feelings through her lens before she set off again.

On one side of the two-lane, a few oil pumps, scattered every few yards, tried to coax begrudging oil out of the endless expanses of land. On the other, wind turbines rhythmically stirred the air high above.

Another few miles passed until she finally arrived where the blacktop ended. She turned down the gravel road that would eventually carry her all the way home.

Her grin had expanded to the width of her face when she pulled up in front of her grandparents' tiny two-bedroom house, and just like always, her nana was on the front steps awaiting her arrival. "There's my girl. I was getting worried."

Flinging herself out of the car, Callie raced up the steps. "I told you I'd be here before dark. I'm early."

"I know, but I worry about you. Scared me thinking about you driving halfway across the country without anyone to look after you. I'm so glad you're here, honey."

"Me too." Callie drank in her grandmother's hug like it was her life source. Perhaps it really was. She let her eyes trail over the redbud trees out in the field, and even knelt down to run her fingers over the cool concrete porch steps where she'd pressed her handprint when she was a little girl. "Where's Pops?" she asked her grandmother.

Nana's forehead creased and worry displayed in her kind eyes. "Oh...he uh, had a meeting at the bank in town. He'll be back in time for supper. Let's get you in and settled."

"Is everything okay?" If her grandparents needed money, her bank accounts weren't going to be of much help. She couldn't exactly ask Derrick's family for money since she was effectively leaving him, but she'd think of some way to take care of her grandparents.

"It's fine. Everything is fine," Nana assured her. For a woman who prided herself on never lying, Callie was pretty sure she'd just told a whopper.

After Callie had her suitcases and camera equipment shoved in her old bedroom, she joined her grandmother at the ancient kitchen table and once again reveled in how little had changed since she'd left for California.

Nana plied her with herbal tea and studied her cautiously. "Was Derrick okay with you traveling alone? What's he going to do in California without you?" She shook her head. "I remember when your Pops and I first married, and I went to help my sister when she had her first baby. By the time I got back home a few days later, your Pops had burned up half of my pots and had taken to eating with the neighbors for all his meals."

Eight tons of compressed emotional air evacuated Callie's lungs in a single breath. She was home. "Derrick will be fine. He's a grown man. He just...needs to remember that. I'm not so certain I'm going back to LA anyway. I don't think Derrick and I are quite as meant to be as I thought we were a few years ago."

"I'm shocked at that. You used to insist that you were going to get married someday."

"Yeah, I know." *Thank god we didn't,* Callie thought to herself. Not that Derrick had ever gotten around to asking. "He was more of a bad habit than anything else. Someone who was there so I didn't have to be alone, and now...I need a fresh start."

Sympathy broadcast from her nana. She squeezed Callie's hand. "Was he unfaithful? Our church has a reconciliation program for couples who've been hurt by infidelity, so you can forgive and strengthen the relationship."

Callie did not want to forgive, and there was nothing left to strengthen other than her irritation. Besides, what Derrick had done didn't quite qualify as cheating in the normal sense of the word. It was just the stupid icing on the stupid cake of their stupid relationship, but then sticking with things long past the point of any logical reasoning was probably one of her best traits. She fought not to roll her eyes at her own ridiculous mistakes. "I promise I'm fine. Want me to help you fix supper?" She would've agreed to doing most anything to avoid further discussion of Derrick.

"It's a little early for that yet, but if you're hungry, I'll make you a sandwich. Your Pops picked the last of our tomatoes this morning."

She hated to ask her grandmother to fix anything for her, but eating one of Nana's sandwiches was awfully tempting. Soft white bread slathered in mayo with three slices of cheese, two slices of a ripe juicy tomato, a little onion, and a little salt, all grilled in butter on an iron skillet that was four decades older than Callie herself. Yes, please. Maybe two. It never seemed to matter how she fixed them herself, even when she followed her grandmother's methods to the letter, they just were never as good as when Nana made them. "I'd love one of your sandwiches, but I don't want you to go to any trouble."

Pursing her lips at that, Nana whisked to the counter. "Feeding my girl makes my day. You know that. I even got you some of those potato chips you like so much."

After Callie had devoured two of her grandmother's sandwiches and a small bag of Lay's potato chips—because they're a snack not a meal according to Nana she swore more than her belly was full. Her soul was as well.

While the ladies were catching up on Nana's soap opera, Callie's grandfather returned from the bank. Springing off the sofa, she attempted to hug him until she eased the worry lines around his mouth. But when she finally released him, his smile was distant and distracted.

"How's my Calico girl?"

Chuckling at that, Callie rolled her eyes at her real name. Her mother had been born about a decade too late to have been a hippie, but that didn't stop her from trying. "I'm so glad to be home. How are you? What's all that?" She gestured to the stack of file folders Pops had set on the nearby table.

Her grandfather beamed at her. "I see you're still my curious Calico kitten." He chuckled. It was true she'd never been able to resist asking questions about most any topic, even if she was being nosy. "It's nothing much really. Your daddy says we've got to put a new roof on the barn, so

I'm just trying to come up with the money. Same song, second verse for any farmer. I went to the bank to see if I could borrow some against the back few acres. They'll let me know in a week. Ain't looking too good though since I still owe on the loan we took out two years ago."

A vivid memory speared through Callie, and a chill shot up her spine. "Nana, I thought you told me you gave Dad the money to replace the barn roof when I was home last year."

"I told you, Harold," Nana reminded.

"I just don't recall that," Pops shook his head.

"I remember it because the barn roof looked fine to me," Callie insisted.

"Maybe he asked for the money last year, but I didn't have it then either."

"Would you mind if I took a look at those papers?" As far as Callie was concerned, her father was synonymous with distrust.

"Be my guest, sweet pea. Maybe you can make heads or tails of it all. I'm going to fix some coffee. He's going to be irritated when he gets here in a little while. I don't have the money today."

Dread coiled in Callie's stomach. She'd known she wouldn't be able to hide from her father long, not when he still lived on the same farm as her grandparents, but she'd hoped for a day or two at least. "When's he supposed to be here?" scraped from her throat.

"He's been working out at the power station. Usually stops by on his way home around four."

Callie didn't know much about the specifics of power stations, but she highly suspected most workers did not get off work that early.

Checking the clock on the oven, she debated. "Let me take these. I'll go to the library and go through them." A slightly different version of the same desperation to escape that had come over her in California took root in her again.

"You've been gone too long, baby girl." Pops flipped on the coffee maker. "Library's closed on Mondays. The desk you used to do your homework on is still in your room. Why don't you use that? I hate for you to go so soon. I haven't even got to hear about that boy who ain't even worth yesterday's weather report."

"Harold," Nana admonished, but Callie beamed at him.

"I'm getting rid of him," she mouthed so Nana wouldn't hear.

"You always were a smart girl."

Callie scooped up the stack of bank records. "I'd rather not be here when Dad gets here if it's okay with you."

"I know you don't much like your daddy, but that roof hasn't been replaced and it's needing it. If I'd paid to have it done last year, it wouldn't need to be redone now."

Callie told herself to give her father the benefit of the doubt. Not that he deserved it. "I'll figure it all out, and maybe I can help you pay for the new roof somehow."

Her grandfather snuck a few of the remaining chips from her bag. "I'm not taking your money, little one."

As Callie grabbed her bag, she decided what she really needed was a drink, not her father's bullshit slathered on top of Derrick's.

She climbed in her car and drove back to the square. Rusty's Spur, Holder County's own loud, proud honky-tonk was relatively quiet since it was still early. Perfect.

CHAPTER TWO

Ford Holder's eyes refused to leave the blonde seated in the back corner of Rusty's. She was at a table in a honky-tonk surrounded by file folders and some kind of paperwork. He tapped into the guilt he had no real reason to feel anymore to keep him from joining her on the other side of the booth. He desperately, and probably stupidly, wanted to know what she was studying while she munched on the stale peanuts the restaurant kept in metal buckets on the tables, and downed drink after drink.

While most of the patrons scattered the broken shells on the hardwood floor to be swept up at closing, she stacked the broken shells, one half inside of the other, neatly in a small corner of her table, as if she might be able to somehow put them back together at some point. She'd been tucked in that corner for two hours. Every time she looked at her phone her sips of shit whiskey became longer and more determined.

He recognized defeat in her eyes because he'd seen it in his own for the past year and a half, minimum. Worry bubbled in his gut right along with the beer he'd been nursing for the past hour. Could she not afford a meal? If he offered to buy her one, would Meritt even care?

He shook his head at his own ridiculous thought. He'd signed divorce papers in the courthouse at noon to finally bring an end to the entire debacle that was his life. He swore his pride ached worse than his ass that had been on that hard barstool since the blessed event that afternoon. Meritt had been cheating on him for years, so his self-imposed cattleman's code of honor made no sense at all.

"Ford." Cal Rickets took the stool beside Ford and gave him the same sorrowful nod every cowboy in Holder County had offered him as of late. The one he was sick to death of receiving. Ford forced a polite nod, more out of habit than any desire to be polite. He said nothing. God knew Cal never needed any encouragement to start jawing. "Saw you and Meritt coming out of the courthouse 'round lunchtime. I knew she was bad news for years, but you know, what was I gonna say? I hate you're taking it hard though."

Ford contemplated that statement. Was he taking it hard? Shouldn't he be upset? The deeper into his own admittedly wounded pride he dug the only thing that ever seemed to surface was relief. That seemed like a fucked-up thing to say out loud though, so he continued to take slow sips of his beer and to discreetly check the woman in the back corner. Long messy waves of blonde hair teased at the ample swells of her breasts. The long skirt and tank top combo she was wearing made her look like she stepped right out of a '69 war protest, a misplaced flower child caught up in the wrong place at the wrong time.

"How long's he been here, Sally?" The door swung open and Ford heard his brother, Jamie, ask the bartender as he took the other stool beside Ford's. Everyone else in the bar, save Cal, had given him his space. It was a merciful blessing if ever there was one.

"He was here when my shift started." Sally had known the entire Holder family for decades, and it rubbed Ford the wrong way that she was ratting him out. "I'm a touch worried."

"I'm fine," he growled.

"I'll take him home," Jamie explained.

Ford rolled his eyes. "Or you could stop fucking talking about me like I'm not sitting right here." He was no longer able to keep his family away from his vicious mood. All he wanted was to sit in his own miserable relief and drink. Why couldn't the world just give him one afternoon off? Or was it evening already? He glanced out the plate-glass windows of Rusty's. Damn. It was already dark. How the hell long had he been in there?

He stared down at the beer bottle clutched in his hand, half-wishing he was drunk enough to need his brother to give him a ride. But he didn't even have the energy to get shit-faced. Plus, he was too damned old for that nonsense. He'd only had a few beers over the last several hours. By cowboy standards, he was stone-cold sober.

Jamie slapped his shoulder and gave him a consolatory smile, which Ford supposed he should've appreciated. His family had all tried to be supportive through this entire rodeo of pure horse shit, but he swore if he had to endure another round of advice from his daddy or one of his uncles, he was going to lose what was left of his mind.

Besides, he was the one who was supposed to be giving advice. His brothers and cousins had always come to him for that, and now, everyone knew his whole stupid life was a lie. Who'd want advice from a loser who'd swallowed Meritt's bait hook, line, and sinker?

Sally set a cold bottle of Budweiser in front of Jamie. Then she gave Ford another one of her pitying glances. "You know I've long thought that Meritt didn't know how good she had it. Throwing away a man like you," she tsked, "a Holder. And for what? Some crowbait pony with nothing but debt. I'll never understand it."

And suddenly, the entirety of the county that his ancestors had settled, fought, and died for just wasn't big enough. The low hum of bar patrons, scrapes of barstools, and drone of the ancient jukebox, that had managed to drown out a few of his more depressing thoughts, were no longer working. He had to get out of there. Get someplace where no one knew his name, knew his family, or knew about him and Meritt. He couldn't stand the pity and the reminder that he was a failure to everything the Holder name had come to mean.

But the blonde in the corner looked up just then, forced a broken smile that was somehow worse than if she'd been crying, and then went back to her whiskey and her papers. He swore that shattered attempt to keep whatever was worrying her locked behind the lie in her smile kept him rooted to the barstool.

———

Callie blinked several times trying to clear her blurry vision so she could really see the cowboy seated at the bar. She'd been listening to him talk, praying that he'd occasionally give people more than one-word answers when he was spoken to. Finally, that other rancher had come in, and he'd actually talked. His voice was rough and deep, precisely the way she imagined sleeping with him would be. Not that she had any business imagining things like that.

She stared unabashedly at his back as he slid his fingers up and down the beer bottle. Every slight flex of his muscles tested the seams of that button-down shirt he was wearing. She dug her fingers into the almost empty bucket of peanuts and ordered herself to get back to the problems at hand.

Definitely should not have ordered the fifth...whatever it was that she was drinking. She couldn't quite remember. Callie blinked several times, but the numbers on the bank statement continued to back-stroke across the page. The endless texts from Derrick swam across the screen of her phone as well.

Hey, where do we keep the ketchup?

I think we're out.

Pick some up

Mom wants to know if we're doing that thing on Saturday night with them

Where did you put the Chinese take-out menu

The guys are gonna be over tomorrow for a Fortnite livestream. I need you to make the shoot a good one. Toby hooked up with some chick who knows this guy over at Twitch, so we're thinking we can get a feature. This could be it babe. No more having to live under Dad's crap

They went on and on. She'd stopped responding after she tried to explain to him where the lightbulbs were when he informed her that something was broken in the bathroom because the light wouldn't come on.

And then there were the texts from Derrick's mother, Tori.

I've taken the liberty of letting the Mitchfields know that you and Derrick will be at the exhibit Saturday.

Oh and I meant to tell you before you left, we'll need you back home by Wednesday. I told Vivian you'd be happy to photograph Bentley that afternoon. Should I have Camelle book you a flight for Tuesday?

Every ridiculous text resulted in three things—Callie drank more, hated herself more for ever falling for the pretty man-child she thought she could save, and her loathing for Derrick and his family grew exponentially.

She refused to photograph any more of his mother's friends' dogs. Most of the time the animals were more miserable than she was, and that was saying something. Dogs did not want to be in tuxedo ties nor did they want to wear family crests and be posed for photos. Ballet tutus and Ivy League school sweaters were another favorite of the Beverly Hills elite. Good god. Dogs wanted to run free, and bark, and eat, and be loved. For a moment, Callie wouldn't have minded a few of those things as well.

Downing the last of the tumbler, she nodded to the waitress who offered to bring her another. Continuing to numb her own stupidity and confusion over the sheer amount of debt it appeared her grandparents were in was the only thing that made any sense at all. If she were smarter, she would never have fallen for Derrick. If she were smarter, she could figure out where the money had gone. Her father had been right all along—she was just a nosy, useless brat.

Her thumb hovered over the send button. She'd typed out the words - *I'm not coming back ever. Free Bentley!* Or at least she thought she had. She couldn't quite read her own words anymore. They were lost in the swamp of desolate thoughts drowning her brain.

CHAPTER THREE

Jamie downed a sip of beer and thumbed at the label before he spoke again. "I heard Mama use the *other fish in the sea* line on ya this morning. I'm betting that's why you didn't go home after signing them papers."

Lifting his Stetson and dragging his hand through his dirty-blond hair, a shade or two lighter than all of his brothers, Ford grunted his agreement.

"She didn't mean any harm. And I know none of us knows the right thing to say about this shitcreek you're having to paddle, but we know it sucks. 'Course Meritt sucked her way all the way around town so..." he shrugged away whatever else he'd wanted to say.

Ford studied Jamie's features, thankful that at least his brother didn't look at him like he was flat out on his deathbed waiting on the reaper to finish him off. They were the oldest of all the Holder cousins, only a few years apart in age. By god, you could tell they were Holders through and through.

Their Uncle Gentry always said all of the cousins looked like a set of cowboy nesting dolls. Most days Ford didn't mind being one of the set. Lonely wasn't something he'd ever be. Hell, when they were all kids, they had their own school bus. But just then he wanted to be left alone.

He wanted to go back to figuring out what that beautiful girl in the corner was doing studying paperwork in a bar, and maybe more importantly who she was. Everybody in Holder County knew everyone else. He could've sworn he'd seen her before, but he couldn't place her family. He supposed that's what happens when you don't leave the ranch for months at a time because you're trying to salvage a marriage that couldn't be saved. Or maybe it was his reputation he was trying to salvage. The marriage had been doomed from the start.

He formed his features into something akin to a smile, though he was certain his was every bit as broken as the blonde's. He hated that he didn't know her name. He knew everyone, and everyone knew him. The growing curiosity prompted the words from his mouth. "Look, Jamie, I'll be fine. I'm just not in the mood for more of Mama's cooking or for Dad to tell me his stories about the ones that got away before he found the right woman. Okay?"

"That your way of asking me to leave you be?"

"If you don't mind."

"Can I finish this first?" He held up his beer.

"Of course."

"How many of those stories has Dad been telling you?" he asked a moment later.

"Too many. But he met Mama when he was twenty-one, and I'm twice that so none of them apply to me. Doesn't mean he'll shut up about it."

Jamie scowled at him. "Who knew Dad was a player back in the day?" Both of the men chuckled at the thought. "But you aren't too old to find someone else. Plus, you oughta mess around a little. Head into Odell and find you a last-call stranger...or hell, two of 'em. That'd make you feel better."

The words *last-call stranger* had Ford's eyes roving back to the blonde without his permission. Jamie followed his line of sight and gave him a knowing grin. "She's pretty."

Ford grunted to avoid having to agree with his brother outright. "The ink ain't even fresh on those fucking papers I signed this morning. Would you stop trying to get me laid?"

"Now, what kinda brother would I be if I weren't trying to get you laid?" He laughed at his own joke. "Who is that chick anyway? I've never seen her before."

"No idea. She's been in here for a while. Looks upset."

The smirk faded from Jamie's face. "And you want to make her smile. Jaysus, did you not learn your lesson with Meritt? It ain't your job to save select members of womankind just because they're bad off. You can't fix everything, for fucksake."

"Piss off," Ford ordered. "I'll get myself home."

Jamie glanced around the bar and then centered his gaze back on Ford. "Look, I'm not opposed to you busting one with that chick. She's pretty. But you don't want to do this here. Everyone in the whole damn county will be talking by tomorrow morning."

Ford stood, directed his brother to the exit door, and headed towards the blonde's table.

"I'm Ford Holder. You mind?" He gestured to the seat across from hers. A bubble of laughter escaped her mouth. Shit. He should've come over sooner. She was too far gone.

She blinked a few dozen times trying to bring him into focus before she giggled again. "You're...really hot."

He tried not to be flattered. It had been way too long since he'd heard something like that for him not to wonder if she'd still have that assessment come morning when she was sober. "Okay." He settled at her booth. "You have a name, sweetheart?"

"Calico Anna Monroe," hiccup, "the first!" She doubled over laughing.

Ford made a valiant effort to keep from scooping her into his arms, taking her back to the ranch, making sure she had something to eat, and then putting her to bed alone.

"The first, huh?" God, she was a mess, but she was the most beautiful mess he'd ever laid eyes on. Damn him to hell and back if he didn't want to scour the earth of whatever it was that had made her need to drink it away.

"Yeah, but mostly I'm just Callie," she sighed, "but also 'cause there's not another one of me obviously."

"Oh, honey, you are definitely one of a kind. Hey, listen for a minute. You any relation to Abe Monroe?"

She nodded for entirely too long. "But I don't like him," she slurred out.

"That makes two of us, but I think maybe I should call him to take you home. Are you staying out on the farm?" He discreetly slid the tumbler out of her reach and signaled to the waitress.

"She need another?"

"God no. Bring her some water, a Dr. Pepper, and get her a cheeseburger and some fries. Put it on my tab."

"Who are you even? How do I know if you have a tab?"

Shock zinged through Ford's mind. He couldn't recall another time when anyone inside the county lines hadn't practically rolled out the red carpet for him. Before he could assure her that he'd cover the charge, Sally bustled to the table. "Put it on the *Holder* tab, Zoe." She spoke through her teeth. "He just ain't been in, in a while."

"Oh right." Zoe headed towards the kitchen.

"Sorry, Ford," Sally offered.

"Nothing to apologize over. She new out here or something?"

"My niece. Her mama sent her down to live with me when she failed out of ASU."

"Hey, did you know like this whole town thing is Holder, too?" Callie interrupted and seemed to be impressed with her own announcement.

Ford and Sally shared a concerned glance.

"You know, I had heard that," Ford offered with a slight grin. "After we get some food in you, how 'bout you let me take you back to the farm? Let you sleep this off."

Sally shook her head. "You can't take her back to Delphia like that. She'd be devastated, and I'm scared to think what Abe might say to her if you took her over to his house."

"Well, I'm not leaving her here."

"Maybe she'll sober up after she eats."

Ford scolded himself again for not coming to check on her sooner. The damage was too extensive to be fixed with a burger and some water, but at least they would help. "What's going on here anyway?" He spoke under his breath while Zoe delivered the food.

"No idea. I didn't even know she was back in town. Delphia and

Harold used to look after her every summer after her mama left town with her. Last I'd heard, she went off to California when she graduated. Delphia was devastated when she left. Maybe she's in town visiting."

Ford searched the recesses of his mind but couldn't come up with a specific time he'd ever seen her before. He studied her soft features and the pain in her eyes she was trying to bandage with liquor and laughter. She was younger than he'd originally estimated. Some part of her looked out of place there in the preferred sanctuary of cattle ranchers, kind of like the moon when it showed during the day. "Have some food," he encouraged.

She did as she was told and dug in.

"Oh my gosh!" she examined much too loudly, "this is so good...and good."

Pain centered in Ford's chest, and he was oddly thankful for it. He was sick of feeling sorry for himself over the divorce. Helping Callie, with whatever it was she wanted him to do that night, at least gave him some purpose. He couldn't fix his own stupid life, but he could get her home safely.

When she finished the burger and fries, she'd offered him more than a dozen times, she laid her head down on her arms on the table. Her long blonde hair spilled into the empty plate, and all of the pain existing in Ford's chest expanded to close his throat. Poor baby. He would've bet profits on ten thousand head of cattle that whatever had happened her daddy had something to do with it. "Hey, let me take you home." Her grandmother was gonna have to get over it.

"Home?" she repeated as if the word confused her.

Ford stood, determined to help her up, but she tried it on her own. The effort went about as well as he'd assumed it would. He caught her before she fell back into the booth. Panic seized every ranch-earned muscle he possessed when she pulled her keys from her pocket. "Thanks for...burger," she managed.

"You're not driving anywhere," he informed her. "Give me your keys. I'll get you to your grandparents."

"Oh god," Callie suddenly sounded appalled. "Nana will be so sad." Her chin wobbled, and Ford swore his whole world shook.

Sally nodded at him from a few tables over. "She might not know much right now, but she's right about that. If I call Delphia and tell her Callie's staying with a friend, do you think she could stay out in one of your bunkhouses or something?"

If he took her back to the ranch, he sure as hell wasn't leaving her alone in a bunkhouse. Every eye in the bar turned to study him. Half of the county was in Rusty's that night. Most of them were smirking. Fuck him. Jamie had been right. As soon as he got her out to his truck, every tongue in the county would be wagging. It'd probably be in the papers by morning right beside the finalized divorce news. Jesus. He could hear it now—brokenhearted Ford Holder went to drink away his misery and left with a girl who couldn't walk on her own. Great. He'd been a star in this stupid town since birth. He swore he couldn't even be late to church services without people talking. They'd eat this up with a fork and spoon.

"Don't...feel good," Callie whimpered. The devastated look in her massive brown eyes, fogged with confusion, combined with her long blonde hair tipped with ketchup remnants shoved every concern over being fodder for the gossip hens right out of his head.

"Yeah, I know. Let's get out of here, okay?" He sank his teeth into his tongue to keep from assuring her that he'd take care of her. He held her steady on her feet with one hand and scooped up all of the papers she had scattered on the table with the other. Propping them under his arm, he guided her towards the door.

Chet Mathis, who Ford hadn't been able to stand for most of his life due to the fact that the only thing under his hat was hair, laughed as he stepped in front of them. "You dirty dog. That'll show Meritt," he gestured to Callie.

It was good Ford's hands were more than full because if they hadn't been, he swore he would've knocked that smirk off of Chet's face with his fist. "Get the hell out of my way," he demanded.

Chet's hands went up in surrender. "I'm just saying she's a real piece of meat. Grade A prime rib. I wanna hear all about this tomorrow."

Then again Ford was nothing if not resourceful. He managed to turn and cradle Callie closer so she could lean against his shoulder and chest, which freed his right hand. Taking Chet by the collar of his shirt, he snarled, "Believe I told you to haul your ass."

Fear flared in Chet's eyes. "Jesus, Ford, we're friends. What are you so mad for all the time now?"

Just then, Callie nuzzled her face against Ford's chest, and he swore his whole world tipped dangerously. Instinctively, he tucked her head under his chin, like a dumbass. "Move or be moved, fuckwhistle."

The entire bar went silent at that, and everyone moved to give him a wide berth as he managed to guide her out into the warm night.

She didn't protest when he lifted her into his arms to get her in the truck. There'd be hell to pay come morning, but for some unfathomable reason, he just didn't care anymore. He was sick to death of caring so fucking much about what this town thought of him.

Closing his eyes for a split second as he cranked the truck, he cursed under his breath when she laid her head down in his lap. God, it had been so long since anyone had needed him, had curled up on him, and let him soothe them. It had been more than a decade since anyone had their mouth that close to his member. And she just kept nuzzling against him. He wasn't certain if this was heaven or if this was hell, but he knew he was likely headed to the latter from the thoughts currently racing through his mind and the fact that his cock swelled out its approval.

He called himself an asshole for being thankful for the hard-on. It had been getting to him. The worries. The doubt. What if...things didn't work the way they were supposed to anymore? He'd told himself it was the stress and the whole debacle with Meritt, but he'd had his doubts.

But Callie Monroe laid her head in his lap, and he was raring to go again. Relief only added to the swelled effect.

CHAPTER FOUR

He managed to get another glass of water in her before he flung back the covers on his bed and settled her in. She'd roused for a few minutes on the eleven miles of gravel road it took to get to his house from the gates of Holder Ranch. But now he stood back and stared down at her in his bed, this woman he barely knew. Her long blonde hair was splayed across his pillow. Her jaw was slack and the tense lines of frustration she'd worn at the bar were gone. He wondered if the fear that had existed in her eyes was still there. Was it only obscured by her eyelids, or was it gone as well?

Refusing to acknowledge the fact that she looked like she belonged right there, safe, sleepy, and content in his bed, he shook his head. He was ridiculous.

He retrieved a bottle of ibuprofen and made her another glass of water. Leaving both on the bedside table, he retreated to the couch. He really was a lonely sap if he thought this woman looked like she fit into his joke of a life.

It sure as hell wasn't the first time he'd slept on his own couch since he hadn't shared a bed with his wife—ex-wife, he forced himself to remember—in well over a year. As he sank down on the worn leather cushions, he had to admit this was the first time he'd had no resentment over his sleeping arrangements, however.

Exhaustion weighted him, but Callie filled his head with a dozen random thoughts. He'd been in that bar because coming home to an empty house after signing divorce papers was akin to walking through hell again. God knew he'd made several trips. He'd been married for the last twenty-some-odd years. He didn't remember how *not* to be married, and there was another woman in his bed.

How the hell had he even gotten here? He'd gone to Rusty's because he didn't want to be alone. Meritt had moved out three months ago, and he still didn't know what to think of that. Being with her for most of their marriage had been miserable, but it had been a constant. A known when there was so much he was unsure of. He had no idea if he wanted to ever fall in love again, or if he'd ever really been in love before. No. Alone in the dark he saw no reason to lie to himself. It was a joke of a marriage which went right along with him being tricked into it in the first place.

Failure taunted his mind and set up camp in his bones. Everything he'd tried with his ex had gone up in flames.

He'd spent so many days lost in an abyss of failure, not really fully conscious of whether it was day or night even. But that night, with Callie in his bed, he was anxious for daylight. He wanted to talk to her again, make sure she was all right, try to help her through the hangover if she'd give him a chance.

He wanted to erase whatever had caused the fear in her eyes from her existence.

———

Callie wasn't certain why her eyelids were so heavy or what was sitting on her limbs. *Move.* She tried to mentally urge herself upright. That's what she needed to do. She needed to sit up and find coffee and call back and beg that gross editor for that seedy magazine shoot, so she could actually pay Derrick's parents for letting them live in the pool house, even though they insisted payment wasn't necessary. But her body seemed to want to stay right where she was, and her eyes still refused to open.

Her brain was sluggish as well. Had their bed always been so comfortable? She couldn't remember. And Derrick usually kept the pool house so freaking cold. Did he forget to turn the AC down before he went to one of the guys' houses?

She was so warm and something akin to contentment settled through her despite the odd weight in her head and the cotton balls she was certain were growing in her mouth. Managing to turn on her side brought in a rush of sensation that almost convinced her this was some kind of odd dream. The delicious scent of male cologne permeated her lungs. It seemed to be woven into the sheets. A soft sigh escaped her mouth. Some part of her mind, that wasn't mired in the bowling balls in her head, wondered when Derrick had started wearing cologne and if his mother had picked it out. Mostly, Callie just enjoyed breathing in the seductive scent.

But when it was replaced with an even better smell, her eyes flew open wide. Sizzling bacon perfumed the air. Cologne was one thing, but Derrick had never once in their four-year relationship ever cooked anything at all. His parents had chefs for that.

She sat up in the bed and immediately realized that was a grave mistake. Her head fell forward into her hands. Her stomach made violent protest of her rapid movement. Where was she? Her heart thundered against her ribs, doing nothing to ease the nausea.

Terror propelled her to her feet. She prayed the contents of her stomach would remain in place as she stumbled over her sandals on the floor.

Her eyes darted around the bedroom as she tried desperately to place herself. How had she gotten here, wherever here was? Rushing to one of the windows in the room, she stared out at a burnt orange and indigo sunrise sweeping over an endless field. Realization rushed into her mind like a riptide. She was home. No. Not home exactly, but definitely in Oklahoma. Nowhere else had endless skies like Holder County.

Her pulse downgraded from all out panic to a more palatable alarm rate, until she recalled her trip to Rusty's Spur. The acrid flavor of whiskey still burnt her tongue. What had she done? What would she tell her grandmother? Oh god. What would she tell Derrick? They really weren't quite broken up yet because he still hadn't acknowledged that she wanted out of the relationship.

Did that mean she was about to take her very first walk of shame after sleeping with someone she couldn't even remember on top of cheating on whatever Derrick actually was to her at this point? Revulsion and disappointment slammed into her gut like a brick. How could she have had sex and not remember anything?

It was Callie's desperation to get back to Nana, so she wouldn't worry, that gave her the courage to open the bedroom door. Sweat dewed across her back. What did you say to some guy you slept with but didn't remember? Bile ignited the path from her belly to her throat. Whatever she said to him would be easier than what she was going to have to say to Nana, so she tried to take solace in that.

When she stepped out into a wood-paneled living room, she paused. The worn leather sofa had a pillow and a few blankets on it. Someone had slept there. Scanning the rest of the large room, she noted spaces where it seemed furniture had once been. Something heavy had left indentations in the carpet. Since the television was set up on what looked like some kind of bedside table, she assumed an entertainment center had been there recently. A bookshelf sat mostly empty, save for a few rodeo buckles and a stack of Cattleman magazines on two shelves, to her right. Outlines of dust indicated that at one time books had been on the other shelves. It was like half of a life had been erased from the premises. That did nothing to soothe her nerves. She passed by the front door and called herself an idiot for not making a break for it, but she wasn't certain where her car was. She forced her reluctant feet towards the sizzle in the kitchen instead.

Hazy recollections of the night before filtered back through her mind. Money, and bank statements, and whiskey, and—she stepped into the kitchen—that supremely handsome cowboy that had been at the bar. Oh god. What had she done?

CHAPTER FIVE

Turning the bacon over with a fork in one hand, Ford cracked eggs into a bowl with the other. He'd heard Callie stirring in the bedroom, and he'd wanted to have her some breakfast ready.

When he lifted his head to see her timid form swaying in his kitchen, he swore it took him a minute to locate words. A cascade of loose blonde tangles swished over her shoulders. Her eyes were red-rimmed and worried, but it was the nervous way she chewed on her lip that crushed him. Was she scared of him?

Clearing his throat, he set to do whatever needed to be done to get her to trust him, though he had no rational reason for requiring her trust. "I'm not quite sure what you remember from last night, but I'm Ford Holder. You're on Holder Ranch. And...I slept on the couch all night long."

Relief washed over her features which oddly unknotted his shoulders as well. She nodded at him and then cringed and rubbed her head. "I remember meeting you," she whispered. "Just not much after that. I'm really sorry. I don't normally drink much."

Grinning at that, he scooped the bacon out of the skillet and heaped it onto her plate. "Yeah, well, me either. I had a rough day yesterday, and I know the Holder men have a reputation of being way more sinner than saint, but I grew out of the sinner stage a while ago. None of us would ever have done what you're worrying about. You're safe here. Anytime." He half hoped his slight confession might elicit one from her as well, but she just studied him as he scrambled the eggs.

"That smells really good," she admitted almost begrudgingly. "But I really need to get back to the farm. My grandmother has probably already called the sheriff."

"Sally was going to call Delphia last night and tell her you were staying with a friend. At least have something to eat before you go. It'll help with the headache." He refused to admit to himself that he didn't want her to leave yet. He wanted to know more about her. He didn't want to be alone.

If she gnawed those bee-stung lips of hers anymore she was going to draw blood. *Stop looking at her mouth, asshole.* His own mental scolding did nothing to distract his attention from her beautiful face.

"So, uh," she shrugged, "if you were going to sleep on the couch, why did you bring me here? I don't know you."

It was a decent question, and not one he had any kind of logical answer to. "You seemed like you needed a...friend." He finished up the eggs and added them to the plate and then poured her a large mug of coffee.

"And you want to be my friend?"

He hated the skepticism in her tone, and his own issues slithered too close to the surface for him to keep them locked up. "If I've learned anything from all of the shit with my divorce, it's that I don't get to decide whether or not someone else stays in a relationship. But, yeah, I guess. If you need a friend, I'm game. But that's up to you."

When he nodded to one of the barstools he'd shoved up to the counter, since Meritt had taken their kitchen table, Callie reluctantly settled on it. It took Ford a minute to admit to himself that he was jealous of a barstool because it had her ass against it. He blamed his own insanity on the fact that he hadn't had sex in years. Jesus, he was hard up.

He needed to take Callie back to her grandparents' farm. He hadn't been in prison. She wasn't the first attractive woman he'd seen. He had to get his shit together.

But she was so much more than attractive. She was gentle, and her kind eyes seemed to see things others missed. She ignored the food to continue her visual inventory of his face. "I'm sorry about your divorce."

He shook his head. "Don't be."

"Why?" She studied him like she could actually see the man he'd intended to be instead of the one he'd become. "If we're really friends, then I would be sorry that you went through something that made you unhappy."

For some reason, Ford spoke the truth for the first time since he'd filed the papers. "I'm not so sure I'm unhappy. No. Scratch that. I am sure I'm not unhappy. The only part that sucks is the whole damn county talking about me constantly. The fact that she's gone is a relief. I know that sounds fucked-up though."

"I've pretty much figured out that the truth almost always sounds fucked-up. It's easier to lie to yourself. Then we get so used to our own lies that when we're really real we don't recognize it."

Damn. "You a psychologist or something?"

She wrinkled her nose and shook her head. "No, I'm just an expert at lying to myself, so I get it."

This was the most intriguing conversation Ford had taken part of in ages. "What have you been lying to yourself about?"

"Pretty much everything." She broke off a piece of bacon and brought it to her lips and then moved on to the eggs. He shoveled eggs into his mouth to keep from watching the tines of her fork slip between her teeth. He and his hand definitely needed a shower session because this was ridiculous. "This is so good," she moaned and picked up another piece.

That little moan did things to him. Things he was certain were not okay since he barely knew this woman. He called himself an asshole again for good measure. "I'm...glad you like it."

"It's better than Nana's, but never tell her I said that."

That brought a grin to his face. The motion was so foreign he wondered when the last time he'd smiled had been. "I meant to get back here a little earlier and get you some food. I've got six hundred steers on full-feed so I had to get them fed, and then we had a few calves born this morning that I needed to check."

"You've already been to work this morning?" Astonishment lit in her eyes.

He swore every word she spoke strung him tighter. Mildly concerned he was going to snap and do something incredibly inappropriate like pull her in his arms and taste that bacon from her full pink lips, he forced a nod. "Yeah. This time of year we try to get up pretty early. Gets hot on horseback later in the day. Cattle ranchers don't miss a lot of sunrises."

She gave him a timid grin, and a little of the exhausted pain seemed to drain from her features. "You like that."

His brow knitted. "I like what?"

"Sunrises. I could tell when you said that."

"Oh," Ford nodded. People made observances about his life all the time. Oldest Holder grandchild to the oldest brother. Successful cattle rancher. Reliable man. Failure at being married. Expectations seemed to always come with the observations. He'd spent most of his life understanding who he was supposed to be, but he wasn't ever certain he knew who he really was. He couldn't recall anyone ever stating something that was so true it was almost intimate. "Yeah. I guess I do. I know this ranch is in the middle of nowhere but..."

"It's the middle of your whole world?" She took another guess. "That's what I always think about my grandparents' farm. Well...all of Holder County really."

***

Callie had absolutely no idea why she'd just announced that, or why she kept talking between each bite of the first breakfast that didn't involve kale and a Vitamix courtesy of Derrick's mother, who thought Callie needed to lose a little weight. "Have you ever seen a sunset off the California coast? It's beautiful. When the light is just right, for just a few seconds, you can get great pictures. But it's nothing like Oklahoma sunrises. They're the best, I think."

He gave her another grin, and something stirred in her belly that had nothing to do with the food. "Yeah, well, Oklahoma definitely has its perks, I guess."

"The sky goes on and on..."

"Forever," he completed her sentence. "I've never been to California, but I can't imagine anything beats here. Do you like taking pictures?"

"I love it. I'm a photographer. Kind of." Callie wasn't entirely certain what she was. Animal photographer to the wealthy wannabes was not an appealing title. She'd intended to specialize in photography that incorporated everything from landscapes to the beauty of women in their natural form, the way the universe had intended them to be seen. She wanted to do boudoir photography that made women remember how to connect with their own beauty. No photoshop desired or required. That was just the kind of studio she planned to open in New York after her internship. There would be no appointments available for Fido in a toy golf cart with his own clubs.

"If you want some pictures of the sunrises out here, there's no better place to see them than this ranch. Just let me know. I don't mind picking you up early and showing you where you'll get the best shots."

She nodded a little too enthusiastically for the state of her headache. It did nothing to help her decipher why Ford looked like he wished he hadn't made that offer.

Returning to the breakfast, she scooped up another forkful of eggs. She didn't understand why the food made her feel so much better when she'd been worried she was going to vomit a half hour ago, but she decided to question that later.

"Do you live in California now?" he inquired.

Callie considered that. Ford had been honest with her about his divorce and being her friend and even about sunrises, which to her were far more important than either of the other things. "No. Not exactly. I mean...my boyfriend lives there." Disappointment expanded in Ford's icy-blue eyes. She corrected herself both quickly and probably stupidly. "But he's not my boyfriend anymore. It's just...I'm not sure he knows that yet. I've tried to tell him several times. I even finally just sent him an email, but he hasn't even opened it yet. He's not good at listening."

The disappointment that had resided in Ford's gorgeous eyes, that seemed to be a code to his mind, morphed to understanding. "Trust me, if someone's damned and determined not to hear you, they're never going to. On top of that, expecting some kind of closure is like needing their permission to move on. It ain't worth the wait."

"That's what I think too. I'm not going back to LA, so he'll figure it out eventually. I need to be here for a little while but then I'm going to move...somewhere."

"When are you moving?"

"I don't know yet."

"Okay, where are you moving?"

"New York, I think. Maybe. I'm not entirely sure about that either. I sound stupid, right?" She wasn't certain why she cared what Ford Holder thought of her. She used to love living in the moment, but she was concerned that he'd rescued her from a bar the night before and then she was admitting how in flux her entire life was for their first real conversation. Echoes of her father's constant disapproval thundered in her mind.

He shook his head. "You're not stupid. Don't ever say that. There's nothing wrong with taking life as it comes. Seems to me that trying to plan everything out will fuck you over every time."

Callie took another sip of her coffee, but the warmth that was spreading through her veins wasn't coming from the food or from the coffee. "Hey Ford," she tried fruitlessly to keep the next words trapped in her throat, but she recognized that lost desperation she'd been feeling for so long in his eyes as well. She wanted him to know that she appreciated that he was a good guy in a world where she was fairly certain those were an endangered species.

"Yeah?"

"I'm pretty sure I like being friends with you."

And that earned her a full-fledged smile from him. Her heart applauded in her ribcage. "You don't really get to be a Holder without being born into a horde of friends, so I might not be all that good at it.

Family doesn't get to not hang out with you. But I'm a decent listener if you ever want to talk."

She wondered if he'd intended to draw direct distinctions between himself and Derrick. Most of her prayed that he had, but she was sure feeling so close to him was only because of the current state of her life. That and the fact that he did seem like such a good listener even if what he'd said before that was wrong—family did get to decide not to be around. Her mother had decided that a decade ago. She hadn't seen her since. "You're lucky you have a big family." She didn't know much about the Holders, but her grandmother always said that they were the backbone of the entire county. Even just spending the summers there, Callie knew the Holder kids seemed to come by the dozens.

"Sometimes." He chuckled.

"I always wished I had a bunch of sisters and brothers. Most of the time it was just me and," her head fell, and she hated that it still affected her, "my mom. It was a little...lonely."

Suddenly, his substantial hand, roughened with rope-worn calluses, enclosed hers on the table. At his touch, the world that had been spinning so quickly lately seemed to settle. She swore a spark of electricity arced through her palm. "If you want to hang out on the ranch while you're here, I promise you won't be lonely." He gave her a gentle squeeze and then pulled his hand away. The absence stung, and the world picked up pace again. "Can I ask you something else?"

She lifted her head and nodded, still wondering what kind of magic he had in those hands.

"You told me last night you were Abe Monroe's daughter, but I've never seen you around here, and you said it was just you and your mom. I know it's none of my business..." he shrugged away the rest of whatever he was thinking.

Callie eyed the kitchen door and wondered where her car was. She really didn't want to get into her whole life story with Ford. Surely, some guy who had grown up a Holder would have no idea what it was like to grow up the way she did. Supposing she owed him some kind of explanation though, she bought herself another few seconds with another sip of coffee. Swallowing that down, she considered. "Yeah, Abe's my dad, but I grew up in Tulsa with my mom. I spent the summers out here with my grandparents. I love it out here despite Abe."

Ford gave her his last piece of bacon and a consolatory nod. "Forgive me for saying so, but I've never been much a fan of your daddy, but I'm glad he didn't spoil the whole place for you."

CHAPTER SIX

Ford had taken a gamble on asking about her father. The curiosity was getting to him, and being in her presence seemed to erase most of his better sense. If she'd physically constructed a wall around herself, it wouldn't have been any more obvious that she was not willing to discuss her family anymore. He regretted every word of his question.

There was still so much he wanted to know. Harold and Delphia Simpkin had owned that little farm out on County Road 2982 for at least fifty years, and Abe was not their kid. He'd lived there for all of Ford's life as far as he knew. The Simpkins mostly kept to themselves. Ford didn't remember them having a daughter, of course he'd only known the parents of the kids he'd hung out with. He planned to ask his own daddy what he knew about it.

Another wallop of regret centered in his chest when he realized that even if he hadn't always been knee-deep in haying and working cattle every summer, he still wouldn't ever have met Callie. He was too busy banging every girl who looked his way to ever really have paid attention to any of them. Until Meritt had pulled her stunt, his wild side had run several country miles wide. After that, he'd remained faithful. He'd always thought that was how it was supposed to work.

"I really do need to go," Callie's urgency yanked him back from his regretful wonderings. "Nana worries about everything. Even if someone told her I was with a friend, I bet she didn't sleep at all. I feel terrible I did this."

Family obligation was certainly something Ford understood. Plus, he was probably miserable company. "Sure, just let me grab my keys. Don't be too hard on yourself. Everybody deserves a break now and again." He scooped up the stack of paperwork she'd had with her at the bar the night before and handed them her way without comment. He hadn't looked at them, but he recognized the Monroeville Savings and Loan letterhead sticking out of the folders. Was she having financial trouble? Clinging to some need to salvage whatever this was, he kept his mouth shut and grabbed his hat and keys.

She was quiet most of the drive off of Holder Ranch, but just before he turned on the road that would lead them to town, she offered him a sweet smile. "Thanks for taking care of me last night. Your ranch is beautiful. I used to hear people talk about your family and all of your land, but I never really thought I'd ever be out here."

Ford sighed at that. "Don't believe everything you hear, and you're welcome on the ranch anytime."

"I might take you up on those sunrise pictures."

The idea that he'd get to see her again awoke something deep inside of him, something he didn't recognize, something he wasn't certain he was supposed to feel. It yawned and stretched itself back to life. "Uh..." he'd made some utterance of noise before he fully realized what he was doing. What was appropriate at the end of...whatever this had been?

"What?" She stared at him again with those deep brown eyes that he swore felt like they could see through him.

"Nothing."

"What were you going to say?" Her question held no disdain, just curiosity, but since he had no idea how to ask a woman out on a date or even how to ask for her phone number, he chickened out. Besides, why would a woman like her want to have anything to do with him? He was a washed-up divorcé with more land than good sense.

"Just that I hope you enjoy being here for however long you're here."

She grinned at that. "I applied for a photography internship with Nina Morales in New York, which was stupid of me, but I did it. Have you ever heard of her? She's amazing."

He shook his head. "I don't know much about photography, but why is that stupid?"

Her gaze shifted to the endless prairie as it extended its arms before them. "It doesn't even pay anything. I can't afford it. I've just always admired her work so much. She's so..."

"What?" he urged. She gave him a quick shrug and sank her teeth into her bottom lip in some kind of effort to keep the answer from him. Suddenly, all that mattered to him was unearthing this clue to her that she was trying to keep concealed. "Hey, come on. We're friends, right?" He added lame to his lengthy list of things he currently didn't much like about himself.

"Fine," she chuckled, "Nina is so unapologetic, you know? Most of the time I feel like all I do is apologize for everything and do whatever other people want me to do."

He considered that for two beats but went on with the confession locked behind his lips. "I spent a lot of years apologizing for shit that wasn't my fault, so I get that."

"What were you apologizing for?" She sounded offended on his behalf.

He studied her for a few minutes as he made the right on the Main Street square. "If I asked you that, would you tell me?"

"Sorry, I shouldn't have asked that. I'm so bad about doing that." Her beautiful pink lips twisted in consideration, and he caught himself staring at her mouth for too long. Blinking away the foreign desire that played in the periphery of his mind, he pulled into the lot of Rusty's. Finally, she shook her head. "But no, I wouldn't. At least not today."

"Then maybe we can delve into all of that the next time I let you sleep in my bed." He chuckled at his own joke, but a decent portion of him wished he wasn't teasing her. Some strange breath of warmth filled him. Was he flirting with her? God, it had been so long he'd forgotten how or what it felt like when he managed to do it.

Her quiet laughter sent a flood of heat throughout his body. He gripped the steering wheel tighter, trying desperately to get a grip on whatever this girl was doing to him.

"I'm really going to try to never, ever drink so much that I need some stranger to take me home with him ever again. I'm really sorry you had to sleep on your couch, but I appreciate you not taking advantage."

Still lacking any semblance of self-control, he shrugged. "Hey, you don't have to apologize to me about anything." He didn't want to be one of the people in her life that made her feel like everything was her fault.

Surprise lit in those eyes of hers. "Thank you."

"Trust me, it wasn't the first time I've slept on that couch."

He'd never admitted that out loud to anyone. Bracing for the pity he was sure would knot in his throat choking him, she surprised him with a thoughtful smile instead. "I slept on the futon for a while before I left to come out here. I decided that it's better to sleep alone than with someone who'd rather be sleeping with someone else."

Shock reverberated through Ford's worn muscles. "He cheated on you?" His question was perforated with fury. The icy shards of anger fractured some of the numbness he'd existed in for months. He had no idea what kind of idiot would cheat on a girl like Callie, but if he ever met the guy he'd beat his opinion of that into his face.

"Depends on who you ask. Thanks again, for everything."

"She'd been cheating on me for years," spilled from his lips. He wished he could suck the words back into his mouth. Why did he tell her that? God, wasn't it bad enough that the entire county knew what a joke his life was? Why did he have to warn her as well?

But again she didn't flinch or offer him pity, which he loathed. Her face didn't do that thing everyone else's did, where their mouths were speaking apologies while their eyes were strained with thankfulness that it wasn't them. Or worse, the guilt that broadcast from the people who'd known all along and allowed him to go on believing her endless lies.

"It just sucks, doesn't it?" She sighed. "You've been there all this time trying to do the right things and make it work, and you're not even worth the truth."

"Yeah...that's it exactly."

"Whoever she was, I feel sorry for her for not seeing what she had when she had it. I'll see you around." With that, she opened his truck door and slid to the ground. That skirt she was wearing scooted up her long, shapely legs. A hungry grunt lodged in Ford's throat half-terrifying him, half-intriguing him. He tried to cough it away when she spun back to wave at him, making the lengthy skirt fly outwards from her body, like the wings of a butterfly taking flight. "Thanks again."

"Anytime."

CHAPTER SEVEN

It took Callie the entire drive from that bar to her grandparents' farm to remember that she'd left a file folder of their bank statements inside Ford Holder's truck. Her body was now in a permanent state of cringe, and her brain was so obviously sluggish she felt like she'd been drowned in sludge. *God, he must think I'm an idiot.* At the moment, she agreed with the assessment. But a wicked notion, buried deep under the rubble of the woman she'd forced herself to become for Derrick, fought its way to the forefront of her mind. He still had her paperwork, which meant she'd need to see him again soon.

But reality quickly jerked her back to what she'd done. What was she going to tell Nana? She'd be apologizing for this stunt for the next decade at least. The summer she'd turned fifteen she'd met up with some local kids at the street party when the Stockade Rodeo had come to Holder County. On a stupid dare, she'd climbed up the water tower with them and had her first sip of white lightning. It had tasted the way she imagined paint stripper would. One sip had been enough for her that night, but she'd stayed out way past the time her grandmother had told her to be back on the farm. The worry and disappointment in Nana's eyes had been enough to keep her on the straight and narrow for the next three summers.

A spiral of rebellion twisted in Callie's gut. She loved her grandmother more than life itself, but sometimes a girl just wanted to have some fun, do something completely unexpected. Something like getting plastered and spending the night with the most beautiful cowboy she'd ever seen. It sounded a little better than the reality of it had been. If she were going to sleep with Ford Holder—not that he'd offered or would even be remotely interested—she would definitely want to remember it. The night before still existed in hazy shadows.

Nana was already pacing on the front porch. The eggs and bacon Callie had eaten solidified into a block of dread in the pit of her stomach. The sharp edges tore through her. How could she have done this?

Every instinct she possessed wanted to back down the driveway and head anywhere else, but she would never hurt her family like that. She would never be her mother. Swallowing down raw regret, she forced herself from her car. Shame flooded her cheeks, probably turning her normally pale face the shade of a tempestuous apple.

Nana clutched her chest. "Thank heavens you're all right."

"I'm really sorry. I...uh...well I..."

"Spent the night with Ford Holder." Her grandmother's words were laced with heavy threads of disapproval.

"Wait." Callie rubbed her head in an effort to make her brain work again. "How did you know that?"

"When Sally phoned last night to say you'd gone home with a friend, I got worried. I tried to call your phone several times."

Callie fought not to whimper. She'd turned the phone off last night to keep from seeing all of Derrick's endless texts, and she still hadn't turned it back on. "I'm so sorry, Nana. I didn't mean to worry you."

Her grandmother gave her a weary nod. "This morning I tried to call some of your friends that you used to play with in the summers, but most of them have moved away. I finally got ahold of Karen Alexander. Kimberly told her mother that you'd gone home with Ford. She heard it this morning at The Bumpkin." Clearly, Callie had been in LA so long she'd forgotten just how quickly word spread from one boundary line of Holder County to the other. The central life source of gossip in town was The Bumpkin, an admittedly adorable breakfast joint on the square where residents frequently went for coffee, biscuits, and gravy.

Her responses continued to confuse even her. "Kimberly still lives here?"

Nana studied Callie like she might've received some kind of brain trauma. "Yes, she married Tad Bishop three summers ago. Her daddy gave them half of his ranch."

The sudden desire to call Kim and find out a little more about Ford Holder planted itself firmly in her head, but she needed to apologize at least a dozen more times and then figure out how to get those bank statements back without cementing herself as an example of every single offensive blonde joke. "Absolutely nothing is going on between me and Ford. I promise. We're...just..." Shaking off that lack of explanation she asked the question she was sure she didn't actually want the answer to. "Wait, what did Mrs. Alexander tell you happened last night?"

"Well...she only knew what Kimberly told her, which wasn't much. But the Holder boys have quite a reputation, and Ford and Meritt's," she lowered her voice to a whisper before continuing on with the word, "*divorce* just went through yesterday according to Sally. Her sister works for the county clerk's office, so I imagine she'd know."

Trying to wade through all of that information, Callie's responses continued to make no logical sense, and yet the disdain spilled from her mouth anyway. "Ford's wife's name was *Meritt*?" That came before she considered the kind of damage the local bartender being related to the secretary of the county clerk could do to someone's reputation. Ford probably hated that everyone was discussing his divorce. She didn't know him that well, but he seemed like the kind of man who didn't want his private matters discussed publicly. She recalled that he'd scowled at everyone who'd tried to discuss it with him the night before.

The terse pinch of her grandmother's lips did nothing to ease Callie's guilt.

"Yes. Her name is Meritt, and you know I don't like to gossip, but I did hear that she's moved in with the son of that couple who owns the cleaners out in Odell. They're the ones who ruined Virginia Tilson's good bedspread. We've been praying for Meritt at Bible study for years. I always hate to see a family torn apart, but she did seem determined to be unhappy."

That was true. Her grandmother did not like to gossip. She loved it. Callie fought not to roll her eyes. She wondered how gossip had ranked lower than divorce in her grandmother's list of sins.

But it was her grandmother's real hatred of divorce that had led to her father being able to talk his way into staying on land that rightfully belonged to her mother's family, even after she'd left.

"I really am sorry I stayed out all night. It won't happen again. Derrick kept texting me, and I..." she cringed but went on with her full confession, "I had too much to drink. Ford was a perfect gentleman. I'm lucky he was there."

"Devil's water," Nana sighed. "Come inside. I'll...fix you something to eat."

Callie didn't deserve to be fussed over, but she wouldn't deny her grandmother much of anything after worrying her like she had. But as soon as they'd settled at the kitchen table with coffee, Nana probed deeper. "Why was Derrick texting you last night?"

The fact that the entire town was already discussing her and she'd only arrived the day before robbed her of a little of her practiced reserve. Defeat weighted her shoulders. "Because he refuses to grow up."

"Explain that."

"His parents do everything for him. They always have. He expects me to fill that void now that he's grown, I guess. I've tried to explain that I'm not coming back to LA, but he won't listen to me."

"Some men do need someone to look after them," her grandmother reminded her.

"It's not my job to raise him, and I don't want to take care of him for the rest of my life. I shouldn't have given him as many chances as I did. I have to make a clean break. Eventually I have to get through to him." Besides, she was tired of feeling so trapped in his shallow life. She needed to breathe.

Her grandmother reached to gently squeeze Callie's hand. She traced her index finger over her grandmother's fingers. Those hands that had wiped her face and given her baths, cared for her, and fed her thousands of meals drew a confession from the depth of her soul. "I shouldn't have ever gotten involved with Derrick. If I were smart, I would've come back here right after college until I figured out what to do with the rest of my life."

"Honey, you've got a head full of smarts and more creativity in your little finger than most people have in their whole bodies. Getting distracted doesn't have anything to do with your intelligence, but I worry about Derrick not listening to you. I don't ever want you to leave here, but should you go back out there and try to explain things face to face? It seems to me you should try to work it out with him since you've...had relations with him."

An involuntary shudder shook through Callie at that. "We are not discussing that, and I am not going back out there. I'll find some other way to get through to him."

"Okay. Well then, have you figured out what you want for the rest of your life, sweetheart?"

What you and Pops have. She had no idea where that particular thought had emerged from, and she would never speak it out loud. She wasn't even sure what a life like that would look like for her. People didn't fall in love that way anymore. The world was all different now. "I want the internship in New York with Nina Morales...I think. And when I'm ready I want to open my own photography studio."

"What about Ford?"

"What about him? I just met him last night. I told you nothing happened. We're just friends," Callie vowed, perhaps a little too insistently.

Her grandmother gave her a weary nod. "Forgive me for asking."

"It's fine. No big deal."

"Uh huh."

Before Callie could continue to assert that Ford was nothing more than some sweet cowboy, the kitchen door swung open and in walked her father.

CHAPTER EIGHT

Ford was pulling through the gates of the ranch before he noticed the file folder of bank documents wedged between the truck door and the seat. Before he could try to formulate an appropriate response to them, a grin spread the width of his features. He had to return that folder to her, which meant he'd have to see her again. That definitely should not have pleased him as much as it did.

But a man can only exist with self-imposed guilt for so long before he begins to grow weary of his own self-loathing. He had no more business heading into his parents' house at that moment than he had being so pleased, but he was going to do both anyway.

If he'd timed it right, he'd catch his daddy between his meeting with one of their cattle buyers and him heading back out to check the steers.

"Hey, Mama." He grinned as he stepped into the kitchen. That room had been one of his favorite places to be when he was a kid. She was almost always in there. Something was almost always cooking, and they had the perfect view of incoming storms from the window over the sink. As far as he was concerned, there was no better place to be.

"You don't know how good it is to see you smiling," Sara Holder stood on her tiptoes, jerked him down to her barely five-foot height, and kissed his cheek. "Now, sit down and tell me if this sauce needs more salt." She spoon-fed him a bite of some kind of tomato sauce.

He considered. "Yeah, maybe, but I'm a cattle rancher not a cook."

"But you used to like to eat," she countered. That wasn't her first comment about him not eating the way he used to. For the past few months, he just hadn't had much of an appetite for anything.

"It's good," he skirted the comment entirely. "Is Dad still talking to Miles?"

"Miles left an hour ago. He's in there with Dale."

The constant anxiety that had ridden Ford in the last few months bled to terror in an instant. Dale Miller was the lawyer who'd represented Ford against Meritt. His cousin Meridian was the deputy district attorney in Holder County, but Dale handled the civil accounts for the Holders. "What's Dale doing out here? She signed the damned papers yesterday. Jesus, what else does she want?"

And there it was. That sorrow he hated, but that everyone continued to display when they regarded him, formed on his mother's kind features. Everyone but Callie, he reminded himself. "I doubt it's got anything to do with Meritt, honey. It's probably something about us buying that parcel from the Tillmans. I shouldn't have said anything."

"No," Ford sighed, "I shouldn't have jumped to conclusions. I need to get my head out of my ass." It had been an endless battle of Meritt demanding money from the joint Holder Family accounts and the Holder Land and Cattle business accounts, none of which she was owed, nor did Ford have sole access to. He was so tired of arguing over money, he swore if he could work out some kind of barter system for food, equipment, and clothes for the rest of his life, he would. Meritt making demands he had no hopes of meeting had created some kind of knee-jerk reaction for him. He was tired of feeling like a fucking failure.

His mother shook her head at him. "Some people aren't loves, sweetheart. They're lessons. Stop being so hard on yourself."

Yeah, well, if Meritt had been a lesson, it had taken him damned long enough to learn it. He'd obviously been in some kind of remedial course on marriage or something. For a rather large portion of this life, he'd told himself it was love. He'd become an expert on lying to himself the same way Callie said she had. They seemed to have a lot in common.

He didn't know which was worse—to have to acknowledge the truth that he'd never been in love or to realize he'd lived a lifetime mistake. Doubt continued to increase in magnitude until it closed its fists around his throat. Everything he'd once believed in was no more solid than the dusty wind he existed in. He hated that the solid ground he'd once stood on had turned to quicksand under his boots.

The familiar slap of the screen door and murmured talking preceded his brothers spilling into the kitchen.

"Knock the shit off 'a your boots before you come in my kitchen," his mother called without taking her eyes off of the sauce.

Jamie, Dalton, and Wes retreated slightly, toed out of their boots, and then headed Ford's way.

Jamie slapped him on the back, laughing. "You're a dog, man, but damn, I guess you showed Meritt."

"What are you talking about?" Ford demanded. There was nothing like the sensation that you were watching your own life through some kind of old television set without an antenna. Things kept happening around him, to him even, but he seemed to always be the last one to figure shit out.

Wes's smirk was a duplicate of Jamie's. "Are you seriously gonna lie to us about last night? Come on now."

Last night? Ford's mind instantly filled with thoughts of Callie—the sheet marks that had marred her pretty features that said she'd slept well. The soft swish of her long skirt. Her worry over what she might have done with him. The way he wanted to take care of her. None of it made any sense at all, but he was too worn to have much control over his own thoughts. "And I repeat—what the hell are you talking about?"

"Would you three leave him be," his mother demanded. Jesus, that's just what he needed—his mother coming to his defense against his baby brothers.

"We're just proud of him, Mama." Dalton laughed.

"What the hell for?" Ford was growing weary of never knowing what the fuck was going on in his own life.

"Callie Monroe," Jamie spoke through his teeth now, but Sara Holder could hear one of her boys trying to hide something from her four thousand acres away. The distance of the expansive kitchen wasn't going to throw her.

"Callie?" His mother puzzled for a moment. "Are you talking about Abe Monroe's little girl?"

"From what I heard, she ain't so little anymore, Mama," Wes chuckled.

Ford rolled his eyes, but realization wound its way around his chest and made it difficult to breathe. He'd been certain word would get around town that he'd taken Callie home last night, but if all three of his brothers had already heard, the rumor mills were clearly running at full steam. He shook his head. "She had a rough night. I was just helping her out. I barely know her. Nothing happened," he vowed but couldn't quite ignore the hint of regret that tugged at him.

Jamie gestured his head towards their mother in an effort to get the rest of their trio to shut up, as if she was the reason Ford wasn't spilling details on his night. He wondered for a moment where their little sister, Halle, was. She was the only person he knew who could get all of her big brothers to shut the fuck up. If his own brothers didn't believe he and Callie hadn't slept together, he had no hope of convincing the entire town. And some devious part of him couldn't quite help but wonder if it would bother Meritt, if it might hurt her the way she'd hurt him. He shook that off. He did not want to be that guy.

He and Meritt were over, and he didn't want to hurt her, not really. He just wanted to be done with her. He wanted the vicious memories to give him peace. Besides, he didn't want Callie to have anything to do with his ex, even in his own mind.

Before he could futilely attempt to convince his brothers of anything, his daddy and Dale Miller made their way into the kitchen. Since talking to his father was the purpose of his visit, Ford hoped he could get rid of Dale quickly.

"Ford, how are you doing today?" Dale gave him that same polite but doleful smile that made Ford want to drive his fist through a wall.

"I'm fine," Ford insisted and didn't spare his lawyer his glare.

"Good. Good. Takes some time, of course."

"Dad, can I talk to you for a sec?" Ford's tone was more of a demand than a request, but he knew everyone in the room would let him get away with it. At least pity was occasionally useful.

"Sure, son," Barrett Holder nodded. "Can I get some coffee first or is this urgent?" His father, at least, managed to keep his sorrow to himself for the most part. He treated Ford just like he always had.

His mother shook her head. "You go on and talk to Ford. I'll bring your coffee in there in just a minute."

Dale offered the family a wave. "Barrett, I'll check on that lien, but I doubt it will slow up the purchase. They appreciate you buying the parcel off of them. They're anxious to get the papers signed."

His father gave a weary nod. "Well, I'm anxious to get cattle on the grass out there. I've got a shipment of steers heading in next week. Sara gets a little ornery when I have to put them in our yard."

Ford's mother gave them a quick grin. "Not that it's ever stopped you."

Everyone in the kitchen chuckled at that.

"That's because I married well." Barrett cringed at his own state-ment, and Ford fought not to beat his head against his mother's butcher-block countertops. Now even his father was walking on eggshells around him. Great.

"Anyway," Barrett cleared his throat, "having a mutual goal gener-ally makes things easier. Thanks for stopping by."

"Nice to see all of you." Dale headed out the kitchen door.

CHAPTER NINE

Callie stumbled a few steps back. Tension knotted in her neck and throbbed in her head again, though she was fairly certain it had nothing to do with her hangover. "Dad. Uh...hey."

"Nice of you to come see me," he huffed. "I had to hear from Windell that my own daughter was back in town."

Windell was her father's best friend. He annoyed Callie almost as much as her daddy.

"I'm sorry," she winced at her own lie. "It was kind of a last-minute decision to come back here. I'm waiting to hear about an internship in New York, and I...wanted to see you." The saliva in her mouth took on the distinct flavor of battery acid as she continued to spew forth lies in an effort to please her father.

"What kind of internship?"

"Photography." Callie had no idea why she was suddenly, stupidly hopeful that her father might show some kind of interest in her work. He never had before. She'd been telling herself for years that she didn't need his approval. She didn't need him at all. Yet some ridiculous part of her still sought out the praise she knew was never coming.

Abe helped himself to a seat at her nana's kitchen table. "People take their own pictures now. Didn't you hear? Everyone has a camera in their pocket. Even if you'd tried to call to tell me, I probably wouldn't have gotten it. Stupid cell phone company. I swear I don't know where they find their techs. I spent two hours arguing with them last week because they bundled my cable and cell bill. Cable went out and they expected me to wait for some idiot service tech to come out here and get it fixed. When I told them they didn't have brains enough to get out of the rain, and that they could just cancel my cable and I'd go with somebody else they said I couldn't because then my cell would also be turned off. I swear, this is what we get when we let dumbass kids run companies. Like I've got time to deal with stupidity like that. Some of us actually have to work to make a living."

"How long did they want you to wait on the tech?" Callie asked tentatively.

"I don't know. They wanted me to be home between eight and twelve or something. If one of my clients has a problem with my work, then guess what I do. I get off my ass and go out and fix it right then."

Callie's father had tried on several ventures for size throughout her life, none of which ever panned out quite the way he thought they would. According to her father, his businesses always failed due to someone else's stupidity. She wasn't certain whom his clients actually were this time, and she didn't care enough to ask. As far as she could remember, money had always been much shorter than his lengthy list of ideas on how to make it.

"Delphia, how about some eggs?" Abe demanded.

Her grandmother gave him a weary nod and put butter in a skillet. Callie ground her teeth. She needed to get rid of him so she could soothe the rough scrape his presence always left behind. That had been her purpose for as long as she could remember. She would go along behind her father and try to ease the strain he always dumped on the people he interacted with. She tried to make everything better. She also needed him to go so she could get back to thinking about Ford. "So...uh you said something about clients. I thought you were working at the power plant."

"I am, but Windell and I also have our own startup. We were talking one night about funny stuff we say all the time and decided to put a few of them on T-shirts. We haven't quite figured out the inventory system yet, but we're getting there."

"But you already have clients who already have problems with your T-shirts?" Surely, he knew how insane that sounded.

He rolled his eyes. "This is what I get for letting your mother keep you in public school. Where did you even come up with that question? Did you leave the contents of your head out there in LA or something? And what happened to Derrick? He seemed like a nice guy."

Just like every conversation she'd ever had with her father, he left her uncertain which question to answer and what the correct response might be that would prove that she wasn't stupid. "But you just said...the thing about the cable company," she huffed. "And Derrick and I are breaking up."

Her father wasted no time giving her an incredulous look. "God, you are just like your mother."

No one in the kitchen was under any impression that he was being complimentary. Every time Callie had to endure her father she always came away from the experience drained, and yet she never seemed able to place her finger on the exact puncture where he managed to siphon out her peace.

CHAPTER TEN

As Ford's father settled in the worn leather chair behind his desk, he gave his son a consoling grin. "I came by your house last evening. Thought we might go out to Odell and have some supper. Since you weren't home, I'm hoping you weren't sitting in Rusty's trying to drink away Meritt."

The pent-up air in Ford's lungs came out in a huff. "I was at the bar, but I wasn't drinking much. You don't have to keep checking on me. I'll be fine."

"Son, your mother and I are well aware that you're all grown up. That doesn't make watching one of your kids hurt any less awful. You don't have to handle this all on your own. We'd like to help."

"Then stop treating me like I'm on suicide watch." The words leapt from his tongue without his permission. He cringed. "Sorry. I...didn't mean it quite like that."

Barrett chuckled. "I suspect you did. All right, I'll try to stop worrying about you so much. Since you called this meeting, what can I do for you instead of worrying?"

Ford cleared his throat and tried to quickly determine the best way to get the information he needed without having to give too much away. "I was just wondering what you could tell me about Abe Monroe."

His father's face displayed his abject confusion. "Of all the things I thought you might ask, that certainly wasn't one of them." He shook his head. "Are you talking about the guy who's living on his ex-in-law's property out on the county line?"

"Yeah. I heard here and there that he might be in some kind of financial trouble, either him or the Simpkins might be, or something. I met his daughter last night at the bar."

Barrett's confused expression morphed into a grin. "I see. Well, I'm sorry I don't know much about the financial situation of either the Simpkins or the Monroes. I do seem to recall Abe and his wife, Willow, having a falling out more than two decades ago. Willow left with their little girl when she was just a toddler. All the women's circles at church were up in arms over it for a while. I believe your mother took dinner out there a few times. I don't think I ever knew where they moved, but Abe stayed on at the farm. Having a son who just went through a divorce, I honestly can't fathom how Harold and Delphia chose their son-in-law over their own daughter, but that's about all I know. Abe and I don't run in any of the same circles. I don't even remember his daughter's name, honestly."

"Callie," Ford supplied a little too quickly.

His father looked much too pleased. "Maybe you should get to know Callie a little better. Perhaps she could give you some insight into her father's financial troubles."

Still letting his mouth overrun his brain, Ford shrugged. "It's been a long time since I've been on one, but that doesn't seem like the kind of thing to talk about on a date."

His father's smile expanded even further. "When is this date?"

Realizing what he'd just said, he shook his head. "There is no date. Forget I said that. I was just curious if you knew anything."

His father studied him for a beat. "Why is there no date? You're a single man now."

"Dad, I just got divorced yesterday. Let's not put ten carts ahead of the horse."

"The entire town and I are aware of that you're recently divorced. But Meritt has been divorced for much longer than you have. No one can hold a marriage together alone. If Callie interests you, I don't see any reason for you to go on being miserable."

"What makes you think she can keep me from being miserable?" Somehow Ford suspected Callie was capable of making him smile more, but it made no sense. He barely knew her.

"What makes you think she can't?"

"I don't know anything about her other than she had a rough night last night."

"And you think the financial troubles might've led to her bad night?"

"Maybe. She had a file folder of bank statements with her in the bar."

His father nodded. "If you're mixing whiskey with banking, I'd say it's a safe bet that something is wrong. Let me see what I can find out. If the Simpkins are in some kind of trouble, I'd be happy to see what we can do to help them out."

"By help them out, do you mean that the Holders would acquire their property or that we'll give them money?" Somehow Ford doubted Callie or her grandparents would be okay with either of those scenarios.

"Whatever they need. If I can help, I'd like to. I do have a responsibility to my brothers and to all of you kids to make sure that our interests are protected. You know that. I don't take that responsibility lightly. But if I can help out a neighbor, especially one who has my son attempting to smile for the first time in months, I'm happy to do what I can."

"Thanks, Dad. I'll figure out what's going on myself. I don't want you doing my dirty work for me."

"Being worried about Callie doesn't mean what you're doing is necessarily dirty work, but be cautious. Money is a touchy topic for most anyone. People tend to tie up their self-worth with the amount in their bank account. I'd tread lightly if I were you. Maybe work on Callie trusting you enough to tell you what's going on. You never know what might come of that."

Ford restored his hat to his head. "Yeah, maybe I'll do that." If only he had any idea how to go about getting her to trust him, he'd be in business.

CHAPTER ELEVEN

That night Ford was rooted to the same barstool he'd occupied the evening before. This time he hadn't even bothered to order more than a beer. He'd half expected Callie to call him. Everybody knew him. If she'd wanted his phone number, it wouldn't have been hard to come by. But he hadn't heard from her.

He'd debated driving out to the Simpkins' farm, but something told him Callie would be back in Rusty's that night looking for that folder. If she didn't show, he'd go out to the farm the next day and see what he could figure out about her.

When the door swung open again, another ridiculous round of hope had him whipping his head around to see who was coming into the bar. Disappointment was something he should've been accustomed to feeling by now. But this time, it was accompanied by dread. Meritt and that bitch, Belinda Atkins, sauntered in, and Meritt's customary hateful glare was centered right on Ford.

Because life clearly hated him, two seconds after the door had closed behind his ex it opened again and in walked Callie. Right behind her was Chad, Belinda's brother and the man Meritt had been having an affair with for two years. Fuck him.

The jukebox, every scrape of a barstool, and the hard clunks of beer mugs being set on tables were vacuumed from the room. All eyes were on Ford and most every mouth was hanging open. God, how could he have ever felt anything for Meritt? She was such a...but he couldn't call her exactly what she was, even in his own head. He knew precisely why she'd come out that night. Rumors about him and Callie had made it all the way to Odell.

Clinging to the knowledge that he hadn't done anything wrong, he couldn't stand how close Callie was to his ex. God, what if Meritt said something to her? If she let her surly tongue fly, he swore he didn't know what he might do. His ex generally still behaved like a sixteen-year-old brat. The only thing that mattered was rescuing Callie. She was much too close to a viper's den. He of all people knew how vicious Meritt could be when she wasn't getting her way, and he'd never allow her claws anywhere near Callie.

He stood, intent on taking Callie's hand and getting her out of the bar, but Meritt blocked his path. He narrowed his eyes. "What the hell are you doing here?" he seethed.

She speared him with another glare. "It's a free country. I can go wherever the hell I please."

"Oh yeah, well so can I." Whipping around Chad, he closed his hand over Callie's. He had to get them out of there before he did something he'd regret. She glanced down at where his fingers wrapped around her own, then stared up at him and grinned like him holding her hand made her whole day. He swore life itself surged through his veins from their touchpoint.

A few shocked gasps drew their gazes from each other to the dance floor where Meritt had pulled Chad. She was now wrapping her arms around his neck and grinding against him just to piss off Ford.

He rolled his eyes. Why the fuck did that still gall him? That morning he'd sworn he was happy she was no longer his brat to try to manage. And in that realization, he had his answer. She wasn't his brat to manage, but the fact that she was doing this in front of half the town shredded what was left of his pride. Maybe he should've been trying to get rid of the pride that had kept him in the hellish marriage for so long. It kept rearing its ugly head.

Callie was surveying the heads turning back and forth from

Meritt's display on the dance floor to Ford. Her mouth hung open for a split second just like everyone else's. "Wait. Is that Meritt?" she whispered.

Squeezing his eyes shut in an effort to erase his ex's existence from the earth itself, he prayed for patience. "I've got that folder in my truck," Ford pled. "Can we just go get it? Please."

When his eyes flashed open, Callie's teeth sank gently into her bottom lip. Ford had no idea why that was suddenly one of the most seductive things he'd ever seen, but he stared at her flushed bottom lip for far too long. A mischievous smirk formed on her features when she lifted her eyes to his. He watched the neon lights shimmer in their dark brown depths. "Would you like to dance?" That smirk turned into a full-fledged grin, so wide her eyes almost disappeared behind her cheeks. God, he'd never seen anything so honest, so real. So beautiful.

Summoning determined strength from somewhere in his body, he shook his head. "I don't want you anywhere near her." Where the hell had that come from? He'd just admitted how badly he wanted to protect her. He was just too raw, too wounded, to keep anything from her.

"I'll be fine," she insisted. "I survived middle school with a terrible perm and headgear. I've dealt with my fair share of bullies. Come on."

She led him towards the dance floor. His legs wobbled oddly for a moment as he tried to remember the last time he'd danced with anyone. His wedding reception maybe.

He watched the sway of Callie's long blonde hair that danced to the beat of her hips as she guided him on. His heart thundered out its adamant approval. She'd replaced that long skirt with a pair of ripped blue jeans, and honest to god he wasn't sure which he preferred her in. In that moment, he would've followed her anywhere.

Spinning back to face him, she sank into his arms. The few moments he'd held her the night before rushed back to him. His memory of it hadn't done the warm curves of her body justice. Stunned at the effect she had on him, he moved far too mechanically, trying to remember to sway her to the beat he couldn't really hear, and ordering himself not to inhale the honeysuckle and watermelon scent of her hair. Instinctively, he guided her closer, wrapped his arms tighter around her, seeking to keep her safe. He longed to absorb her healing warmth and the tenderness that exuded from her.

When she nestled her head on his substantial shoulder, fitting herself into the crook of his neck, he swore his existence tilted and whirled out of his control. He lost the rhythm he'd only barely been able to keep, and the apex of her thighs brushed against his cock. A grunt wrenched loose from his chest, freeing more of the restraint he'd been trying to cling to.

Like a runaway train on a downward track, his hand slipped down the arch of her spine and found purchase against the curve of her ass. The sweetest sound in the entire world reached his ears—a soft moan of satisfaction. She clung tighter to him. Suddenly, the bar, every eye trained on them, and most importantly his ex-wife were all erased from his vision. Everything evaporated until there was nothing left but her and him and warm neon lights that spun around them.

Twenty minutes before, he would've sworn to anyone that he hated to dance. The awkward movements and constant self-doubt it elicited in him weren't worth it. And yet, there he was spinning her around the dance floor wishing the song would never end.

Callie was equal parts reckless and desperate. She wasn't certain how she'd even gotten herself back into Ford Holder's arms or what to do now that she was here, but she owed everything she had to whatever force in the universe that had arranged this.

It hadn't taken a genius to figure out what was going on when she'd seen the raw pain and fury in his eyes when that awful woman with burnt-auburn hair had approached him. All Callie had wanted to do was to replace his anger with some peace, but this dance had gone way beyond her helping him get back at his ex.

Her heart and her stomach seemed to have switched mailing addresses as she breathed in the scent of saddle leather that clung to him. With another inhalation, she caught the underlying flavor of soap and of man.

Proving what a witch she really was, Meritt and the guy she was practically dry humping edged closer to Callie and Ford. When he tensed under her gentle grasp, she lifted her head.

His seeking gaze pierced hers like she was the only woman in the world who could save him. The hand that had previously been cradling her back tenderly stroked her face. It scrambled her thoughts and any semblance of good sense.

With her gaze still held safely in his own, she licked her lips thirsty for him. Her chest rose and fell against his making her nipples frantic for his caress. All thoughts of Derrick drowned in the solid cage of muscle surrounding her. There had never been a time when Derrick had held her like this, where she felt safe enough to exist without apology.

He dipped his head lower. His hand still cradled her face.

"Are you going to kiss me?" squeaked from her.

His Adam's apple contracted with a harsh swallow. His gaze dropped readily to her lips. "I don't think I can," came out in a gruff whisper laced with regret.

"Why not?" She ordered herself to stop talking, certain she sounded like a fool.

"Because, sweetheart, you barely know me. And...lord almighty, if I start, I don't think I'll be able to stop."

Heady with the knowledge that he wanted her even half as much as she wanted him, she gave him a timid grin. "What if I didn't want you to stop?"

A pained grunt met her lips when he plastered his mouth to hers. She devoured it. He tasted like dark beer and raw hunger. The flavors ignited in her mouth as she consumed. Every rough scrape of his light beard on her chin only served to amplify the need arcing between them. His lips were the perfect combination of tender exploration and brutal possession. He feasted on her like she was the only thing he'd ever need to survive, and from the depths of her soul she wished that were true. But it couldn't possibly be. As he'd just pointed out—they barely knew each other.

His tongue seemed to want to rectify that situation. It took careful inventory of her mouth, dancing with her own in an almost erotic tug-of-war she happily let him win.

He kissed her like breath wasn't actually necessary for survival. In that moment, she was pretty sure it wasn't. All of the boys she'd ever kissed, including Derrick, held nothing on being kissed by this man, by this cowboy, in the honky-tonk in her grandparents' hometown.

Somehow his touches both soothed and enlivened her. Just when she was certain she was going to die of sheer pleasure, applause and wolf whistles broke out in the bar. It took her far too long to understand that they were applauding them.

Ford wrenched his lips away and seemed almost as dizzy as Callie felt. Before she could protest, he cleared his throat. "Want to get out of here? Please."

Too dazed to really consider what he was asking her, she managed a nod.

CHAPTER TWELVE

Frantic in his haste to get Callie away from their audience, Ford half dragged her out to his truck.

"Ford." Her voice was frantic. "I'm sorry. I didn't mean to upset you."

That halted him in his tracks in the middle of the gravel parking lot. He spun back. "You have nothing to apologize for. I'm the one who's sorry about all of that." Defeat deflated him. "I didn't mean to...take advantage." God, why'd she have to taste like hot summer nights and ripe watermelon? Like something he'd been craving his entire life but hadn't known where to find it.

Longing to cage her between the cool metal of his truck door and the warmth of his body took stronghold of his better judgment. She'd been doing him a favor, trying to save a little of his sanity from Meritt's claws. Callie surely wasn't looking to be manhandled, but he swore the craving to have her back in his hands consumed him.

When people began spilling out of the bar hoping to see more of the show, he took her hand again. "Let's get out of here. I never meant to put you on display."

He stopped short of buckling her in himself, desperate to keep her safe. Gravel spit in the air from his tires as he floored the truck. She was quiet as he pulled onto the main drag through town. He wondered what she was thinking—this woman who'd tried to save him. Before he could ask, she spoke up, "You didn't."

"I didn't what?"

"Put me on display. You didn't take advantage either. It was my idea to dance."

"That's not how our first kiss should've gone." His own words sent another shockwave through his head. When had his mouth taken to overrunning his brain? Hadn't he learned after being married to the wicked witch of the Midwest to keep his thoughts to himself? Callie made no response, leaving him to drown in his own stupidity so he continued talking. "By tomorrow morning, the whole damn county will be talking about...that." Her eyes seemed to be searching the moonlit horizon until a quick gasp had him turning towards her to make certain she was all right. "What's wrong?"

"Oh nothing. I was just thinking. I mean, it's probably stupid but—"

"It's not stupid. Just say it. Whatever it is." He was certain she was about to demand to be taken back to her grandparents' farm.

"Have you ever climbed the water tower?"

The girl sure as hell did keep him guessing. His brow furrowed. "Yeah. Not in two decades or more, but everybody's climbed it, haven't they?"

Another eye-crinkling grin expanded the width of her cheeks and rendered him breathless. "I've only done it once, because I didn't grow up here, but you said you wanted to get away, and it's kind of perfect for that."

"Let's do it." He shrugged.

If she wanted to climb the Holder Water Works tower, he was game. Besides, he was sick of always doing exactly what was expected of him. No one would ever look for him there. It was perfect, just like she'd said.

When he was in his teens, he used to go up there to figure shit out, to find some quiet away from his family, away from the whole damn town. Maybe it would still work that way in his forties.

"Really? You want to do it?"

What he wanted was to take her back to his house, to take her to his bed, to figure out some way to make her moan out his name between his sheets. But Meritt's constant derision about his demanding preferences had him doubting himself, and he wasn't certain he could withstand being told he wasn't good at yet another thing. So, the water tower was a much safer option, not to mention they were a long way from jumping between the sheets, and he wasn't certain if he should even want to get there with her. "Yeah. You just keep coming to my rescue. That isn't the way it's supposed to work either."

This time she called him on the lack of filter between his brain and his tongue. With a broad, knowing grin she asked, "How's it supposed to work?"

Ford had never considered himself any kind of chauvinist but sitting there wishing he could explain that he really needed to be the hero, right then and maybe always, he began to doubt his original assessment of himself. Before he could apologize for a statement he hadn't yet made, another symptom of living with Meritt for years, Callie saved him once again. "Last night you rescued me from a really awful night, let me stay at your house, and took care of me. You even slept on the sofa and gave me your bed. I don't know anyone else who would've done that. Dancing with you definitely isn't a hardship. So, as far as hero territory goes, you're still way ahead of me."

Something in her lengthy list of praises made him worry. He didn't like the idea that she didn't know anyone else who would've taken care of her when she was having a bad night. It didn't sound to him like she knew people worth knowing. Suddenly, he was determined to let her know him, for however long whatever this was lasted. He wanted her to know there were guys out in the world who weren't only after one thing. He wanted to be someone she was proud to have known when this all came to an end. Because it inevitably would. Everything did. Besides, no one would really want to hang around to watch him try to put himself back together.

That uncomfortable realization churned in his stomach. He had an ugly gaping hole to try to climb out of. She shouldn't want to have anything to do with him right then, should she?

———

Callie would've given any willing deity all of her worldly possessions to have known what Ford Holder was thinking just then. Determination had set in his rugged features. That look in his crystal-blue eyes did things to her. Crazy, spinning, twirling things in her belly. The very same feeling she always experienced at the top of the Ferris wheel, when the wild Oklahoma winds whipped through her hair and the whole world was within her view. Potential, raw and delicious, existed somewhere between them. She wondered if he felt it, too. She wished she could take his picture right then, so she could memorize the way that expression made her feel, but she was sure he would think her even more weird if she pulled out her phone.

He threw the truck into park and was standing at her door before she processed that they were parked under the old water tower. She couldn't recall anyone in her entire life ever being on board with her mostly random, occasionally illogical ideas. Her grandmother constantly willed her to be more practical. Being practical had gotten her a life with Derrick. That thought propelled her out of the pickup truck and had her clutching Ford's offered hand.

He guided her to the metal service ladder and gestured for her to go first. "Be careful now," he cautioned sweetly.

Most of the time when people told her to be cautious or not to do something, she found it highly annoying. But Ford's concern was so thoroughly genuine, she grinned. Some small place deep in her chest warmed and the sensation spread outward to her limbs. "I will."

When she was four rungs up the ladder, he climbed behind her. A dozen flirty comments about him effectively staring up at her ass flitted through her mind, but he seemed so concerned over the kiss she managed to keep them locked behind her lips. It was no small feat.

She was two rungs away from the top when the heel of her boot caught, and she slipped. A quick gasp burst from her lungs. Before her other foot could slip backwards off the ladder, leaving her hanging by her hands, Ford had her. His solid right arm locked around her waist and cemented her back against his firm chest. She was surrounded in his warmth. He was holding them both to the ladder with one hand, but he never faltered. "I've got you."

She managed a quick nod. "I'm sorry," squeaked from her.

"You've got to stop being sorry for things that aren't your fault. I'll never let you fall. Can you put your right foot back on the rung?"

Until that moment she hadn't realized that she still didn't hadn't righted her feet on the rung. Everything around her felt solid. Her heart, which was attempting to slither back down out of her throat to its rightful location, pounded out an appreciative beat. She hung there in his arms for much too long given that their goal was to get to the top, but he didn't seem to mind just holding her there halfway between the ground and the sky.

They eventually resumed their climb, and she made it to the top without further incident. She let him help her to a seated position, and then paused long enough to appreciate the endless starlit view as he settled beside her.

"I haven't been up here in ages," he admitted like that was some kind of flaw on his part. "But, uh, if you look out that way," he pointed to their left, "you can see the Maxwell Stadium. Team's pretty good this year. Your grandparents' farm is out that way, just beyond the Baptist church steeple." He pointed the other way.

She turned her gaze back to those silver-blue eyes. They were even prettier than the stars. "I'm guessing since you haven't been up here in ages, that means you don't follow clumsy girls on their crazy ideas too often."

With a soft chuckle he shook his head. "It doesn't look crazy from where I'm sitting."

Callie had no idea if he was referring to her or to the view of the tiny town and endless pastures surrounding them. "Where's your ranch?" she whispered. There seemed to be some kind of broken compass in her chest. It continued to spin like it couldn't quite find North until she knew where Holder Ranch was.

His smile slowed the spinning dial. "It's behind us. We can walk around to the other side of the tower if you want." He helped her up and guided her to the other side where they took seats with much the same view, but her shoulders eased.

Her pulse still danced much too quickly, though, and her shallow breaths were uneven. All of those sensations combined with the delicious scent of him that was filling her lungs. It made her a little dizzy. That wasn't really ideal given their current location, but somehow she knew if she slipped again he'd be right there to catch her before she fell. It was such an odd sensation. She couldn't remember the last time she'd had someone to rely on. "My grandmother put me on restriction for two weeks the last time I did this. I only got to be here for the summer so that sucked." She tried and failed to explain what this meant to her.

He chuckled. She had no idea how something so simple could be so impossibly sexy. "My daddy didn't believe much in restriction. He'd just work you to death." Ford shook his head at the memories. "I never much minded working, so I'm not sure that concept went the way he planned."

"Were you the kind of kid who was always getting in trouble?" She leaned closer to him instinctively, wishing she could remember if she'd ever seen Ford during one of her summers in Holder County.

"I ran fast and hot for a while. Too long, really. But I was also always too busy trying to keep my brothers and cousins out of trouble."

Unable to wrestle her own thoughts into submission, they became words without her explicit permission. "I feel like I was always in trouble with my parents, but I never really understood why. I guess I was just always in the way even though I never meant to be." She shook her head and wished she could erase that admittance from the universe. "That's stupid though. I mean, I wouldn't have gotten in trouble if I hadn't done something wrong. Forget I said that."

"No," Ford's tone fell to a soothing whisper. "Meritt was always mad at me. I swear from the day we got married I had always done something wrong, even if none of it made any sense to me. She used to scream at me because she said I didn't help out around the house more. So, I started doing the laundry and fixing supper. But I never did it the way she wanted it done even when I tried to do exactly what she said. I just never made her happy, no matter how hard I tried. I was always standing in *her* way. A year or so ago, it finally occurred to me that I was never going to be able to please someone who was determined for me to fail. That's when I finally filed for divorce."

CHAPTER THIRTEEN

Ford kept his eyes locked on Callie, wondering what she'd make of his story. Jesus, he really was a sad sap. Poor girl would probably rather be up on that water tower with anyone else. Kids made the climb to do a lot of things, but one of them sure as hell was not so they could sit up there and whine.

Her long eyelashes made a slow blink before she stared up at him with what he finally recognized as need. His ego had been damaged so badly it took far too long to fully understand that what she required he could provide. That just couldn't possibly be true. Could it?

A harsh swallow drew his eyes to her delicate neck. They roved quickly to the plump swells of feminine flesh just below there and then back to those bee-stung lips of hers that he found so utterly intriguing. "Hey Ford?"

"Yeah?" His voice took on the consistency of gravel. He ordered himself to stop staring at her, but he would've had an easier time throwing himself off of the damned tower.

"How should our first kiss have gone?"

A thousand ugly doubts gripped him by the throat. With an invite like that, he needed this to be good, needed to know what he was doing. He needed to not fuck this up like he had the last one. Kissing her like he'd just been paroled from a life sentence wasn't happening, but Jesus, that's how he felt. Gentleness and self-restraint and everything else he knew he should've been able to summon seemed too far below them for him to reach.

Desperate to make this good for her, he cradled her cheek in his hand and angled her face to his own. Her nervous tongue slipped over her bottom lip and he had her close enough that it caressed his as well. A rumbled grunt tore from his chest before he could swallow it back. Her chest rose and fell against his in rapid pants.

"It shoulda gone something like this," he managed. Threading his fingers through those soft blonde waves, he cradled her head and ordered himself to relish every moment of this because at some point she was going to realize he was a mistake.

But when he caught the flavors on her lips as they melded with his own, some part of the man he'd been before Meritt was restored. She pulled him from the drowning doubts and endless distrust not only in himself but in the world itself.

More. He needed more. Her hands wound around his neck as she pulled him closer. The knowledge that she needed more as well bolstered his ego like nothing ever had. Their tongues met and danced in her mouth, and his own hands took on a mind of their own. Sliding from her back to her thigh, he gripped the skin hidden behind worn denim. His thumb encountered one of the rips in her jeans, and he began to stroke her exposed flesh. He longed to shred the jeans to expose her all for himself.

A quick shiver shook through her. He'd done that. Her body readily reacted to his touch. Her hands skated closer to the firm bulge behind his zipper, hesitantly, deliciously, perfectly.

When Callie's head fell back and she gasped for breath, he took the extended invitation and moved his half-starved kisses to her neck. He inhaled the sweet scent he found in the hollow of her throat and spun his tongue there. That watermelon-candy flavor of her drove his body from desperate restraint to devour in a second flat.

Feeling distinctly sixteen years old again, he let his fingers graze the side of her breast. Her back arched making him yet another undeniable invitation. This time her tender tremble was accompanied by a soft moan. It drove him wild. Those moans, her gasps, he'd done that. They belonged to him.

Refusing to allow the cool air surrounding them to have any part of her sweet sexy sounds, he returned his lips to hers and consumed. Her next groan of pleasure made it no further than his tongue. She traced the outline of his cock with her thumb and index finger, refusing him her touch.

He longed to demand that she grab him, that she ease the suffering she was responsible for, but demands would've required him to stop kissing her. He was just as unable to do that as he was to deny himself the feel of her skin. He shoved his hand back into that rip at the top of her jeans that made him insane with need and squeezed with more force than he'd intended. His throat tightened. He eased his grip. She probably didn't like that. Meritt hated it.

And with his mind's acknowledgment of his ex-wife's name and her preferences, he pulled back and set to apologize.

Callie was panting deliciously. She stared him down with heavy-lidded eyes and kiss-swollen lips. "Ford, please." Her eyes closed, and her body rocked beside his. "I'm so wet," she admitted in a half-choked whisper. "I need..." her plea drowned into a frustrated whimper.

Holy fuck. Shock fractured the pieces of his past that still clung to his current reality. Like she'd torn his doubts apart at the seams, and he emerged in full form. He drew her head to his shoulder, kissing and tending her cheek as he let his hand explore all of those beautiful curves. "I've got everything you need, baby," he assured her in a rasping growl. "I'm gonna take good care of you."

But when he heard those words, as they left his lips, the reality of what the hell he was offering her settled on his chest and robbed him of breath. He'd tried to take care of...fuck...no. He had to stop thinking about Meritt.

Something in his pause shattered a little of the craving between them. She lifted her head and stared him down. "What's wrong?"

"Nothing," he answered much too quickly. He shut his eyes and ordered himself to be the man he wanted to be for her. "Callie, honey, what are we doing here?"

He blinked his eyes open in time to catch her timid grin. "I thought you were going to take me back to your house, but now that I think about that, I need to not do that tonight. But that doesn't mean that I don't want to do that ever," she added quickly.

Ford threaded their fingers together. "Listen, the ink is barely dry on my divorce papers, so I need to not go there tonight as well. But even more important than that, I need to do right by you. It's important to me."

"What does that mean exactly?"

"It means that I don't want to do the one-night stand thing. Honest to god, I think I've forgotten how. I'm old," he admitted.

She laughed at that, and he fought the desire to lean and drink the echo of her laughter with another drugging kiss. "You're not old. Maybe you're just old-fashioned. I really like that."

"I'm pretty sure I'm both, but I need to call and ask you out on dates and take you places. I want to bring you flowers and kiss you good night on your front porch. I need to impress your grandparents, really let you get to know me before I take you to bed. I need to take this slowly. That's what you deserve."

He needed to do everything differently with her than he'd done it with Meritt.

CHAPTER FOURTEEN

Callie swore she fell just a little bit in love with Ford Holder at that moment.

Derrick. She fought not to scowl at the thought of his name. Still, she needed some kind of confirmation from him that they were over. Didn't she? Wasn't there some rule that said that before she could let Ford bring her flowers and kiss her on the porch and impress her grandparents and all the things he'd said he wanted to do she had to...? To what? Have Derrick's approval? Fuck that. But there was still a part of her that was sure she could make him listen somehow.

New York. She knew she had no business getting involved with anyone right then. But Nina Morales wasn't due to announce her next protégé for weeks yet so maybe there was nothing wrong with her and Ford getting to know each other, especially if they were going to take it slowly.

"Is that okay with you?" Fear scraped through his question.

"Yes," she assured him. "As long as you promise to really call me and do all those other things."

Concern tensed in his brow. "What made you say that?"

"Say what?"

"Why don't you think I'd do what I said?"

Her cheeks flushed like he'd just turned a hot spotlight on her face. She tried to shrug off a little of the attention. "I don't know. Most guys don't...do what they say."

With that, he leaned, scooped his arms under her legs, and set her in his lap. Her breath tangled in her throat. For a quick moment, she'd felt like she was free falling. But then his strength surrounded her again, and the only time she'd ever felt so thoroughly safe was when she stepped inside her grandparents' home.

"Listen to me," he soothed. "I just got out of a relationship that was way more lies than it ever was the truth. I see no point in lying about anything. If I tell you I'm going to do something, I'm sure as hell going to do it. I am not most men."

No, he definitely wasn't. "Good," she whispered.

"Let me take you back to your car. But first, put your number in my phone," he handed her his cell. "I'm taking you out tomorrow night."

At one time in her life, Derrick's laid-back, dispassionate approach to life had been somehow appealing. But Ford's commanding presence and his determination stirred something awake inside of her. She wanted absolutely nothing to do with calm, cool, or collected ever again. Beaming up at him, she nodded. "Yes, sir."

Another one of those eager grunts lodged in his throat. She swore the noise had already taken up residence in the marrow of her bones. She wanted to spend the next few weeks doing and saying things that made him make noises like that.

He shook his head at her with an adoring grin. "You're not going to make this *taking things slowly* thing easy on me, are you?"

Not quite certain what had elicited that remark, she giggled. "Challenge accepted."

An hour later, Callie paced in her bedroom with her phone to her ear. On the eighth ring of her fourth call she finally accepted that Derrick wasn't going to answer. *He's probably out trying to find ketchup at the grocery store.* She rolled her eyes. She needed to get this over with so she could fill her mind with thoughts of Ford and feel no guilt. Not that Derrick had ever felt any guilt when he was jacking off to all of those women in those chatrooms he frequented. She gagged. God, how had she stayed with him for so long? Disgust crawled over her skin. Deciding she needed a shower, she checked the time. It was two hours earlier in California. She'd try Derrick later.

When she emerged from a long, hot shower there was a message on her phone but not from a number she recognized. Grinning at that, she flopped on her bed. The damp towel she'd wrapped around herself fell open leaving her completely naked. She didn't care. She wanted to listen to the message.

"Callie, it's Ford. I know it's only been a couple of hours since we were together, but I couldn't stop thinking about you. Guess I wanted to prove that I really am going to call you. I had fun tonight. More fun than I've had in," his pause spoke volumes, "well I don't even know how long. Sleep well, sweet baby. I'm picking you up at five tomorrow night. But I'm probably going to call you again before that. Night."

Torn between bouncing out her glee by jumping on her bed and immediately calling him back, she chose the latter. Besides, jumping on her bed naked would definitely horrify Nana. Ford had just gotten divorced from an awful woman who'd been cheating on him. Callie didn't want him worrying about why she hadn't answered her phone.

He answered on the first ring. "Hey there." A note of sleepiness hung in his tone.

She cringed. "Were you asleep? I didn't mean to wake you."

His chuckles were just as addictive as his grunts. "Nah, I wasn't asleep. I'm in bed though."

"Me too. Well, kind of. I was in the shower when you called."

Another one of those grunts. So far, she liked talking on the phone to him almost as much as she liked being in his arms.

"Did you get dressed before you called me back?" rumbled from him.

Her breaths came much too quickly all of a sudden. "No."

"Damn, baby." His mattress gave an audible squeak. The rustle of his sheets reached her ears. "My bed still smells like you."

For as long as Callie could remember, she'd worn watermelon-scented lotion. She loved the smell. It reminded her of Holder County summers. Bringing her arm to her nose, she inhaled and grinned. She'd just put some on after her shower. "Do you like that?"

"Way more than I should." More rustling and another breath-laced grunt.

"Ford, what are you doing?" She finally gathered the courage to ask.

"Trying to figure out how to sleep when I'm harder than concrete and twice as heavy."

Another dose of sticky wet heat gathered between her thighs. Her nipples tightened. She ran her free hand over them, thinking of Ford, taking her own breath away. "If I were there," fell from her lips.

"If you were here, we sure as hell wouldn't be taking things slow, and I told you I'm a man of my word. I'm gonna do right by you. I'll take care of this."

Oh my god. They were miles apart, and she swore the only other time she'd ever been this aroused was when he gripped her thigh, rough and ready up on that water tower and kissed her like he was signing a deed to her body. "You're making me wet again." It was somewhat easier to say things like that to him when she wasn't in his physical presence.

"Damn, baby, when you say things like that," he rasped. "What are you doing to me?" Now his tone threaded towards desperate, almost starved. It hurt her that he was in need, and she couldn't be there to ease it. The sounds of the sheets and squeak of the mattress turned rhythmic.

"Are you...?" Her question dissolved as she fully understood what he was indeed doing, and he was doing it to thoughts of her, to her scent. A heady sense of feminine power filled her. "I want to get on my knees for you." She let her eyes close and the fantasy form fully in her mind. "I want to know what you taste like."

"Christ," ground from his mouth, but she wasn't certain if he meant it as a curse or a prayer. She was good with either. "Keep going," he demanded.

"I want to lick your slit until I know the flavor of you. Oh god, I want you to make me take you deep." Her breaths staggered from the thought. "I want to suck you, to feel you get even bigger in my mouth. I want it to be all because of me."

"It's all you, baby. All fucking you," came from him in an agonized groan. Finally the sound of flesh on flesh reached her. "Wanna make you suck me. Wanna hear you moan over me." That was followed by another desperate grunt.

Her own hand drifted down to the need gathering between her thighs. "It makes me even wetter when I suck you." She had no idea how she knew precisely what he needed to hear, but she was too far gone to consider her words. She teased at the apex of her slit drawing a soft gasp from her own lungs.

"You keep your hands on me. I make sure of that. If you touch yourself, I'll bind them behind your back. I take care of that wet pussy. Only me," he ordered as he lost the ability to maintain his self-control.

"Yes," she whimpered both from his command and his loss of restraint. "I want you to make me drink you," she begged in a tone she barely recognized as her own.

"I will," he assured her before his harsh male shudders became apparent via the noises she could make out. "Make you take it all down your throat, sweet baby. I'll make you tell me how good it tastes." Another groan. "Fuck. I'm coming."

She'd done that. She'd turned him on so much he'd done this over the phone with her. This rough, rugged cowboy who thought he could be an old-fashioned gentleman for her. She'd worn him down just a little. It had been all her.

For a few seconds, only the sounds of his heavy breathing filled the phone. Then she heard several rough scrapes in succession and finally determined he was pulling tissues from a box. "That was incredible." She wanted to make certain he felt no shame over what they'd just shared.

"Yeah, but it was only incredible for one of us. I don't like that. I know I came off a little rough, but I'll never be a selfish lover, honey. I can be gentle if you want. I don't have to be like that. It's just...it's been a long time. I didn't know what I was saying."

She grinned at that. "Trust me, you have no idea what you just did for me, and I like your rough side. I can't wait to experience in person."

"Yeah well, I'm not sure what just happened qualifies as taking things slow." Disappointment rang his sleepy tone now.

"Maybe not, but it was perfect. Are you still picking me up tomorrow at five?"

"Isn't that what I said?"

"Yeah." She hoped he could hear her grin over the phone.

"Then that's exactly what I'm going to do."

It wasn't until Callie was drifting slowly off to sleep with thoughts of Ford taking up almost all available space in her brain that she realized two things—she still hadn't gotten her grandfather's folder back and she still hadn't talked to Derrick. Damn.

CHAPTER FIFTEEN

Checking his watch for the fourth time, Ford grinned and fished his phone out of his pocket. He'd been circling the mustangs housed on Holder Ranch, checking the wild horses to make sure they were all good, before he headed back to the barn to clean out his feed truck.

The sun was slowly crawling across the endless pasture painting the indigo skies in deep shades of auburn. It was his favorite time of day, and he hadn't been able to think about anything but Callie all night anyway.

The uneasiness wasn't letting up. Why the fuck did he jack off with her on the phone? He'd never even done that when someone was present in the room with him, much less over the phone. Being vulnerable with her like that was idiotic. Hadn't he learned that after being married to someone like Meritt?

She answered with a whimpered hello on the fourth ring.

He couldn't help but chuckle despite the awkwardness twisting in his gut. God, she was adorable. "You still asleep, sweet baby?"

That got him a huff. "It's...only seven in the morning."

"I know. I waited until late to call. I've been up for three hours."

"Dear god, why?"

"Got a ranch to run, remember? Besides, I miss you." Dammit.

What the hell was he doing? He knew he sounded completely insane, but for some reason he struggled to keep his shields up with her. She was the first thing in years that made any part of his life good, and he didn't know how to stop from holding on with both hands for as long as he could. Ford just needed to make sure he hadn't blown this all to hell. He wanted to make sure he hadn't frightened her.

Her sleepy tone took on that sweetness he was growing addicted to. "I miss you, too, but you know you're not supposed to tell me things like that. You're supposed to be all aloof and make me wonder if you really like me and make me doubt myself."

Oh, he liked these early morning conversations. She was even less guarded. He liked how she seemed to exist on the edge of an impulse constantly, but she was usually a little afraid to make the leap. Maybe if he taught her that he'd catch her when she wanted to fly, she wouldn't be so afraid. "That's what I'm supposed to do, huh? Men are dumbasses," he informed her.

She laughed, and again he wanted to devour it. "You're a man."

"No, honey. I'm a cowboy. I'll let you go back to sleep."

"No, I'm getting up. I've got to get something done this morning. Just need a pot or two of coffee."

Ford took another sip of his own coffee. "Now, that I can get behind. I still have your file folder. Do you need me to bring it out to the farm before I come get you tonight?"

He could hear the smile in her sleepy tone. "Are you trying to come up with an excuse to see me earlier?"

"Maybe, but I thought I was supposed to be aloof."

"I take that back."

"Good. Because I'm a lot of things, but that ain't one of them." He had no idea where his newfound confidence had come from, but he was thrilled it was attempting to make a return. Something about being on the ranch, on his turf, bolstered him.

"Good, but I don't need the folder before tonight really, unless you just want to come out here. Let me make sure my dad isn't going to be around."

"Why can't I talk to your daddy?"

"Why would you want to?"

Ford didn't have an argument for that. Abe Monroe wasn't good for much as far as he was concerned, but it bothered him that Callie held the same opinion about her blood. If he ever found out that Abe had done anything to her, he'd have plenty to say about it.

He reminded himself that he'd always had a tendency to get ahead of himself. He wanted to ride before he took time to saddle the horse. Plus, he'd promised her they'd take this slowly. That's what he needed to do. Whatever her relationship with her father was, it wasn't really any of his business. "If you're sure you don't need it before tonight, I'll be there at five. I need to round up the mustangs and get them moved to another pasture. That's an all-day job."

"Do you mean like wild mustangs? Do you have those on your ranch? How does that work? I thought you all raised cattle."

"We do, but the government pays us to let the mustangs live on a few of the pastures we're not using for cattle. As long as they're here they stay safe, but they can still run wild. We look after them, and we have the land to support them. They're beautiful but ornery to move. I'll bring you out here and let you see them sometime."

"Can I take pictures of them?"

"Of course."

"You're kinda awesome."

"Gonna have to figure out how to get you to remove the kinda out of that statement, sugar. I'll see you tonight."

———

Callie wriggled free of her sheets still beaming from her phone call. "A girl could definitely get used to that," she informed her old butterfly stuffed animal as it tumbled from her closet when she opened the doors. "And this girl needs to not get used to it because she is going to be Nina Morales's new intern." Callie firmly believed that if you told the universe what you wanted, it would help you get it, even if she saw absolutely no possible way that Ms. Morales would ever choose her. Half of her submitted portfolio had been of pissed off pets.

Despite her spoken words, she wondered if working with Nina was what she really wanted anyway. She shook that off. If she could get some amazing shots of wild mustangs out on Holder Ranch, that would be fantastic for her portfolio, and her portfolio was all she needed to be focusing on. She was just going to help Ford get over his awful ex-wife. He needed her, and that was such a nice feeling. Maybe he'd even be able to help her move past her mistakes with Derrick.

Resolute in her decision, she dressed and headed to the kitchen for coffee. As soon as she was caffeinated, she had to call Derrick and make him listen to her. Callie eased down the hallway listening for any voices in the kitchen. If her dad had dropped by for breakfast, she'd find something to do in her room until he left. He never failed to ruin a good mood, and she had no intention of dealing with two men who refused to listen to her all in one day. Derrick would be more than enough.

Pleased that she didn't hear anyone, she slipped into the empty kitchen and poured a mug of steaming coffee. Nana made the best coffee. There wasn't a coffeehouse anywhere in California that could out brew her grandmother. When the warm liquid brought that sense of peace she'd been searching for, Callie was so thankful to be home. This pit stop was the best idea she'd ever had.

When she was staring at the bottom of her second empty mug, she knew she had to get on with this. Tucking herself back in her room, she listened to the phone ring and then Derrick's stupid voicemail message play. "Hey, you're talking to the D-Man aka Noob_Slayer69, your go-to gamer guru. I don't phone so hit me up on a DM."

Grinding her teeth, Callie considered doing just that. Maybe if she messaged him, he'd actually read what it said. But breaking off a four-year relationship via direct message was an awful thing to do even if you really couldn't stand the guy anymore. On the other hand, she had exhausted all other available resources.

She ended the call and then immediately phoned him again. Eventually he'd answer. It was barely six in the morning in LA Surely, he'd want to stop the noise if nothing else. But seventeen rings later, she wasn't so confident. Fine. She opened Twitter. Since he was one of the only people she followed, she accessed his page quickly and scanned through his latest tweets where he'd complained about the lack of ketchup. He'd then asked his followers to keep watching Twitch to see him on there soon. His followers, most of them women who loved to flirt with him, responded with offers to bring him ketchup. A few others had called him a dumbass.

At least someone saw through his bullshit. Another eye roll made Callie's head ache. When she got to a message box, she paused. Breaking up with him this way was something her mother would do, and she just couldn't go there. She quickly typed a message telling him that she needed to talk to him immediately and shut down the app. She repeated the same message and sent that via text. There, now he had to see it somewhere.

Boredom swept in quickly. It almost always did. She didn't like sitting still for too long. An idea sprang to her mind pushing the boredom away. Grabbing her Canon, she headed for her car. She knew precisely what she wanted to shoot that morning.

CHAPTER SIXTEEN

Ford checked his watch again. He'd texted with Callie a dozen times that day, and still couldn't make sense of why it felt perfectly natural. He knew he had to be coming on too strong. He was fucking this up, but damn if he could stop himself. It was soothing that every time he texted her she responded. She seemed happy to hear from him. It was so different from his experiences with Meritt. He'd inhaled every response like a drug that would soothe the last twenty years of his life.

She'd sent him a few photos she'd taken of the old water tower. He didn't know anything at all about photography, but the girl made rust patches look like works of art. She seemed to somehow capture the rebellion that was housed with the water in that tower. That breathless moment that occurred when you took a seat up there high above to stare out at whatever version of the world you were able to understand.

People took pictures all the time. It wasn't special anymore. But what Callie did was on a whole other level. She'd even sent him an image of the fading spray paint that had said many things in the last few decades. It generally sported the Maxwell High graduating class's year. She'd shot the overlapping numbers in a way that he was able to see the stories play out in the chipping paint. She made idiotic teenage pranks tell the story of the kids trying to leave their mark on the world.

Ford wondered if she noticed the FH and MK initials he'd carved in with his pocket knife. He'd tried to create a past for their relationship that had really only existed as a quick hookup in the back of his truck after the rodeo.

The initials were somewhat obscured by the sheer number of class years that had been spray-painted over his carving. If she'd seen them, he wondered if Callie knew that was him. If only he could've seen the future from way up there on that tower the day he made the marks. Would he have done anything differently? He'd been an idiot from the beginning. Meritt had never been anything but a lesson in the fact that people don't change. You can't save someone who's determined to drown. Carving their initials into steel didn't keep them from eroding. They couldn't stand the test of time.

At three fifteen, he told himself it didn't make him a complete pussy if he started getting ready for their date. He didn't want to be late. He'd been pacing for the last fifteen minutes, so it was a relief just to let himself do what he'd wanted to do for the last several hours.

But when he stepped out of the shower and slung a towel around his waist, he heard voices he recognized in his house. Grinding his teeth, he stomped into the living room. "What the hell are you doing here?"

Jamie and Maddox, one of his many cousins, were seated on his sofa with cold bottles of beer they'd taken from his fridge. They stared up at him like the answer to his question was obvious.

"We're here to talk you out of this date," Maddox informed him.

"Get out," Ford demanded.

"Man, just listen to him," Jamie pled. "He knows what he's talking about."

Ford loved his cousin, but as far as he was concerned Maddox was an idiot who didn't recognize something good when it had been handed to him on a silver platter. Ford sure as hell wasn't taking advice from him.

Maddox however was going to give it, it seemed. "You got tricked by Meritt, but you were all in. You wouldn't listen to any of us when we tried to tell you that she was a grade A bitch and wasn't ever gonna change. Now, you're going to go throw yourself all the way in with Abe Monroe's daughter and get your gnads stomped to pieces again. I'll give her that Abe's an ass, but her mama left him without so much as a word. She's got leaving in her blood. You can't overcome that. I don't want to watch you walk around here looking like death's great-grandma for another two years."

"Get out of my house. Now." Ford pointed to the door they'd let themselves in.

Maddox huffed, "You don't even know *how* to date now. It's different than it used to be. You need some cushions and a few tumble-fucks before you go falling for somebody else. Leave the possibility of breadcrumbing her in case you need to."

Narrowing his eyes, Ford glared at his cousin. "Do you think you're speaking English, or have you had some kind of stroke we should all know about?"

The idiots still seated on his couch both rolled their eyes. Maddox shook his head. "He doesn't even know the lingo."

Jamie's expression turned grave. "You're going to get your heart broken again like Mad-dog said. She's got leaving in her blood."

"I thought he was worried about my nuts, not my heart," Ford huffed. "Neither of which are in any danger. So, for the third time, get out."

Maddox, at least, stood. Ford took this as a good sign since it was one step closer to getting them out the door. "You don't need to be dating anyone. You need to get laid. One doesn't have anything to do with the other anymore. You need some cushions, like I said. A few side chicks that you can get some tail from if this whole thing with what's-her-name goes south."

"Callie," Ford ground out. "Her name is Callie, and I do not want side chicks, cushions—whatever the hell those are—or tail. I want you to leave. I'm not going to do anything stupid."

"Are you going to buy her flowers before you pick her up?" Maddox quizzed.

"Is there some kind of problem with that?"

"Yeah, because that's doing something stupid. You're going to scare her off if nothing else. She's probably dated in this decade at least. You have to play by the new rules. And you need cushions so you have something to fall back on. See how that works."

Though it was true that Ford hadn't dated in the last two decades, he had no interest in learning anything about whatever all of those words Maddox had just spouted off meant. Except maybe one. "Okay, what the hell is a tumblefuck?" He instantly hated himself for asking. The smirk on Maddox's face only made Ford double down on the self-loathing. "You know what, never mind. Forget I asked."

"It's kind of like a fuckbuddy but one who doesn't mind getting filthy with you. They get turned on when you get rough. That'd let you work out some of that frustration you've been living with for the last twenty years."

Keeping the towel clasped tight in one hand, Ford marched to his front door and swung it open. "Out. Now."

Jamie stood. "Just simmer down for a minute. Have you even stalked her feeds yet? Do you even know how? Before you let this girl get in your head, you need to know what you're getting into."

Ford had absolutely no idea what that meant, but he wasn't asking any more questions. And he didn't have to. Before his very eyes, Jamie pulled up Callie's Instagram account and started scrolling through images. "Damn, she's gorgeous."

"Give me that," Ford almost dropped the towel in an effort to get his hands on his little brother's phone.

"Careful. Don't double tap anything, or she'll think I'm stalking her on your behalf."

Her feed was an odd combo, half filled with animals in ridiculous costumes. The other half, however, was filled with an endless number of California sunsets and a series of manhole covers that she'd somehow made look interesting. They told a story the same way the old water tower had given her its secrets.

Ford came to an image of Callie herself blowing the wispy fluff from a dandelion. Those lush curves that made him harder than concrete were clad in a barely-existent bikini, and Ford swore it was all he could do to lock his hungry moan behind his teeth. Her lips were drawn in a perfect pucker. He skipped right over imagining kissing her and went straight to how those bee-stung lips would look wrapped around his shaft. His cock twitched at the image, and that towel wasn't going to cover jack shit if he didn't get things under control. He shoved the phone back to Jamie. "Turn that off, and don't let me catch you looking at it again. She ain't yours to look at."

"See that. That right there. That's what I was worried about. You're already talking like she's yours to protect. Promise me you're not going to fall head over boots for this chick. It's all over town that you were licking her spit last night at Rusty's." Of course it was. Because he couldn't do anything in that godforsaken county without everyone knowing about it. "Where'd you disappear to after that, by the way?"

Thanking the Lord for small favors, since it seemed no one knew where they'd gone when they'd left the bar, Ford grunted out his annoyance instead of answering. He'd be busting up frozen ponds in hell before he'd tell anyone where he'd taken Callie. Besides, his family would surely think he'd lost his mind if they knew they'd gone up the water tower.

"I'm not holding this door open for my health," Ford reminded them.

They needed to go, so he could get on with dealing with all of the doubts this ridiculous conversation had brought on, stacked right on top of all of the rest of the doubts he'd been carrying around all day. What if he didn't know how to take things slowly? What if he didn't do right by her? What if he was too old for her? What if she wanted someone who knew what the hell breadcrumbing was? Was that something he should know? God, how the hell was he this old when there was still so much he hadn't figured out?

This wasn't at all how he'd envisioned life in his forties. God, when he was that dumbass kid up on the water tower with a pocket knife, he couldn't even see the single lie that was right in front of him. That lie had robbed him of twenty fucking years of his life.

Maddox shook his head. "Fine. We're out, but do three things for me. One, fuck her but don't fall for her. Two, do not talk about Meritt to this chick. Three, don't shave."

Giving his cousin a complimentary eye roll to go with his huff, Ford stared him down. "Why the hell not?"

"Women like a little scruff. A little beard burn south of the equator reminds them who was spending time in their lap of luxury."

"Out," Ford seethed. He gritted his teeth until his molars protested, but no amount of willpower kept his mind from envisioning the images Maddox had painted. His heart pounded out its approval at the idea of tasting her, of marking her, of letting her soak down his chin with her juices. He wanted to know her flavors, and that was sure as hell not what he needed to be thinking of before going to pick her up for their first official date.

Before he could slam the door behind them, Maddox handed over a box of condoms Ford hadn't noticed he was carrying. "Let's not make the same mistake twice."

"Get the fuck out of my house." Ford shoved them to the porch and sealed his door shut. He threw the condoms in his bedside-table drawer and ordered himself not to put one in his wallet. Surely, he wasn't that guy anymore.

He returned to his bathroom. Lifting his razor from the counter, he stared in the mirror and wondered what Callie saw when she looked at him. An old cowboy incapable of taking care of what was his? She'd told him he was hot the first time she'd seen him, but she was also drunk off her pretty little ass. That wasn't exactly a steady foundation from which to figure things out.

———

At four forty-five, Callie smeared light peach gloss on her lips and stepped back to inspect the dress she'd selected. It was her favorite. A dark lavender sundress that swept the toes of her boots when she walked. The spaghetti-strap top showed off her boobs rather nicely in her opinion. Not too much. Not too little. It was the perfect first-date dress. It was kind of odd, considering what they'd shared the night before, that this was their first date, but she wasn't going to get hung up on it.

Her grin expanded further when a knock on the front door sounded ten minutes before five. She wondered if he'd been counting the minutes all afternoon the way she had. Racing to the door, she cursed under her breath when her father beat her there. When had he shown up? And why did he have to have such terrible timing? Her stomach clenched, and dread slithered over her. "It's for me. I've got it." She tried to whisk past him without actually coming into contact with him.

Abe gave her that all-too-familiar look of disdain as he turned the knob. Ford barely spared her father a glance before his eyes landed on her. "Hey there." He winked at her, and her knees turned to the consistency of overcooked spaghetti.

"Hey," she drew the single word out into far too many overly breathy syllables. She was locked in his hungry gaze for much longer than was customary for a first-date greeting, but she didn't care. The fire in those icy-blue eyes warmed places in her she'd forgotten existed. He was carrying what looked like a hand-picked bouquet of sunflowers. They were her favorite. How had he known? She took them from him and lovingly touched each flower.

"Aren't you one of the Holder boys?" Her father's question both punctured the moment and dripped with contempt.

Ford cleared his throat. "Uh, yes sir." He offered Abe his hand. "I'm Ford. I'm one of Barrett's sons. You and I have run into each other a time or two, but I know I look like all of my brothers."

After twenty-eight years of life, Callie still hadn't figured out how her father managed to make his nods come off with disapproval.

Abe narrowed his eyes. "Well, that tells me who you are but not why you're here."

"Dad," Callie huffed, feeling a little more brave than she normally did in Abe's presence, a side effect of Ford being so close, she suspected. "He's here to pick me up."

"Pick you up for what?"

Ford edged his way in the door, forcing Abe to step back. "We're going out to dinner, but I'll have her back at a decent hour...sir." The final word rang with a note of irritation that Callie rather liked. Maybe he already had her daddy figured out.

"I'm way too old for a curfew," she informed both men. "Let's just go." She needed to get him out of there before her father managed to do or say anything else.

That twitch of recognition in Abe's eyes was never a good sign. She scooted closer to Ford, placing herself between her father and her date, and braced for impact. Her father looked much too pleased with himself.

He went in for the kill. "Don't you have some kind of bad blood with that guy Chad Atkins? Is he the local rep for PETA or something? I thought I heard about a fight between the two of you recently."

Callie had absolutely no idea who Chad was, but Ford must've despised the guy. For a split second utter hatred clouded his eyes. He cocked his jaw to the side and huffed, "I wouldn't say we were on friendly terms, but you heard wrong. He ain't worth me letting my fists fly. You ready to go, Callie?"

The universe must've had wretched PMS that night. Before she could take Ford's offered arm, her cell phone rang in her hand. She'd been waiting on Derrick to return her numerous calls and messages all freaking day. He'd waited until that very moment to do it.

"Aren't you going to answer that?" her father demanded.

He'd seen the name on the screen. She mentally cursed Chad, Derrick, her father, and technology in general. "Uh, no. I'll talk to him later." She forced a smile for Ford. "Let's go."

"Let me get this straight," Abe continued. Callie swore she could hear the audible tearing of flesh as her father continued to spin the knife. "You're refusing calls from your fiancé," then turned to Ford, "and I'm pretty sure you're married. Callie, you are the epitome of your mother."

"He's not my boyfriend anymore," Callie vowed.

"I *was* married. Heavy emphasis on the was," Ford corrected right on top of her statement.

"Sure." Abe shook his head.

CHAPTER SEVENTEEN

Ford offered Callie his hand to help her up into his truck.

"I'm so sorry he's like that," she started in as soon as he was settled.

"Hey, what have I told you about apologizing for things you have no control over?"

"But he's just so awful. He does things like that just to be an ass. He loves making people uncomfortable." She eyed Ford cautiously for a split second. "I don't even know who that Chad guy is, or how my father knows him."

"He's the idiot I caught in my bed with Meritt. He's friends with your old man, so I have no doubt Abe knows he's not a PETA rep. And don't worry, I'd gotten a new mattress before I let you sleep there."

Callie hid her face in his hands. "I am so, so sorry."

Since he hadn't yet put the truck in drive, he ran his fingertips under her chin, reveling in that silky soft skin, and tipped her head back up to look at him. "You have nothing to be sorry for. You didn't have anything to do with any of it."

He fought the desperate urge to demand to know about Derrick. He'd seen the name on her phone screen. The asswipe still hadn't gotten it through his head that they were over. The idea that Derrick might be trying to get her back flooded Ford with possessive ire. But she wasn't his to claim. Yet.

"My father isn't all I have to apologize over. I know you saw who was calling me. I swear to you I have tried everything I can think of to get Derrick to understand that I'm not coming back to California. And even if I was, I don't ever want to see him again. He just won't listen to me. I've called over and over again. I'm shocked he called me back. I even wrote him this long email spelling everything out in short readable sentences. I thought surely if he saw it in black and white, he'd get it through his thick head. But I don't think he's even opened the email."

Keeping her face cradled in his hand, he tried to sort through the endless complications now associated with this date. "If you need to talk to him, sweetness, I understand."

A tender smile played at the corners of her mouth, and she shook her head. "I've been talking to him for years. Nothing I say is going to make him listen. All I want right now is to get out of here and not think about Derrick."

"You look so damn beautiful I have no idea how I'm supposed to keep my hands off of you tonight," spilled from his lips without his permission.

And there it was—that eye-crinkling, beaming grin that undid him every time he saw it. "Do you really think so?" She lifted her head from his hands and stared down at the dress Ford longed to see in a lacey puddle on his bedroom floor.

"I don't say things I don't mean," he reminded her. "You're fucking gorgeous. I'm trying to be a gentleman, but damn baby—you're not making it easy."

He watched the words resonate in her head. She couldn't seem to stop grinning. "Nana thought it showed off too much cleavage," she admitted with an adorable giggle.

Ford laughed. "As long as you're out with me and I'm the one getting to see them, Nana and I will have to agree to disagree."

"Thank you for the sunflowers and for saying that. It's been a long, long time since anyone thought I was pretty."

"Was the boy blind along with being deaf, honey? My god."

That brought on a quick laugh that held far too much sadness in its depths. "I guess I could ask you the same thing about Meritt."

Since this Derrick asshole wouldn't listen to her, Ford wanted her to know that he would. "My cousin told me not to talk about Meritt on this date, and I don't want to, but I also want you to be able to say whatever you need to say. I want to hear it, whatever it is."

"Wow," she breathed the word. "I don't think anyone's ever said that to me either."

Oddly pleased at that, he cranked the truck. "Anytime you want to talk, I'm here for it."

"I always ask the wrong questions," leapt from her mouth before she bit her lips together.

His brow furrowed. "Explain that."

"People tell me that all the time. I mean...I was just gonna...ask something stupid. I was trying to stop myself. Forget it."

"Questions aren't stupid, baby. They're how we figure things out. Maybe you've already got more figured out than you think, so the questions most people ask you already know the answer to. So, ask me whatever it was." He sounded more demanding than he'd intended, but he wasn't going to redact his order.

"You're sure?"

So hesitant. He wondered if there was ever anything she did that she didn't question first, and he wondered if that was a product of Derrick the way his rampant doubts were a direct result of Meritt. "I'm sure."

"Well, it's just when you said that Chad is who you caught in your bed with your ex, you said for me not to worry because you'd gotten a new mattress before I slept there. I guess I sort of wondered why you were worried about me being there instead of yourself."

She didn't ask the wrong questions, Ford determined. She asked the hard ones, the ones people didn't have ready answers to, so they told her she was the one that was mistaken. He refused to be a person who didn't answer her questions, even if his answer was *I just don't know*. "I think," he paused and really considered, "I just don't want you to have anything to do with her. I don't want whatever it is we're doing here to be associated with Meritt and me. I don't ever want you to think I'm on the rebound or whatever. Does it make me an asshole to say I don't want you tainted with her?"

"Not at all. I don't really want to have anything to do with anyone who hurt you like that. And if I do ever end up back in your bed, I want it to be with you and I don't want her to have ever been there."

Oh, she was going to end up in his bed over and over again if he had any say, but he was still determined to do right by her. It wasn't going to be that night. "You are aware you're killing me, right?"

"Sorry." She wrinkled her nose.

He shook his head at her. "I'm debating if I'm going to let you apologize for that one. I want you in my bed, baby. More than I should. But I have to do this the right way. You deserve the right way."

"How'd you know sunflowers are my favorite?" There was another one of those questions that spiraled out of her mouth seemingly without her permission.

And again he wasn't entirely certain how to answer her. She just seemed like a sunflower kind of girl. Beautiful. Wild. Strong. Those big brown eyes that were just a little bit too big for her face and lips that drew naturally into a smile, genuine and full. "I've never given it too much thought, but I think they're my favorite, too, and you just seem like a sunflower kind of girl."

"What kind of girl was Meritt?" she asked and then cringed. "See, I always ask the wrong things. You don't have to answer that."

"If you ask me a question, I'm going to answer it. Stop thinking you've done something wrong. I don't think she was any kind of flower. She refused to be nurtured anywhere long enough to bloom."

Callie considered that for a beat too long before she nodded. "You can ask me stuff, too, you know. I don't mind."

"What's in that file folder?" He gestured to the folder still shoved in the door of his truck.

CHAPTER EIGHTEEN

Callie had been certain he would ask something about Derrick. She was surprised he wanted to know about the folder. Grinning to herself, she realized how much she liked that she hadn't quite guessed him correctly. Maybe he asked the wrong kinds of questions, too.

"It's my grandparents' bank statements. My dad's being weird and told my granddaddy that we need a new roof on the barn. But I swear they've already given Dad the money for that. I remember it. I just can't really tell when the roof was last replaced. It looks okay to me, but it's definitely not new. I have no proof that my dad is up to something. I just don't trust him as far as I could throw him."

"You okay with me asking you a tough question?"

"Sure."

"What's going on there with your daddy still living with the Simpkins even though he's not their kid?"

Callie half wished he hadn't asked that, but he hadn't shied away from any of her crazy questions so she'd muddle her way through this. "That's kind of a long answer."

"You don't have to tell me, but we got a decent drive ahead of us. I'm taking you to a steakhouse out in Odell."

Childhood memories resurrected themselves in her mind. Her mouth watered. "Are we going to McCoy's?"

He nodded. "Yeah, but I was kinda hoping you hadn't been there before."

"Nana and Pops used to take me the first day I arrived every summer. It was tradition. I love it there. It was always this place where I knew good things were about to happen." Something in Callie's belly did that flipping, twirling thing again. She had no business hoping that McCoy's was going to mean that an exhilarating relationship with Ford was about to happen. She was going to New York. On her own. She emphasized every word in her head and hated the way they sounded. "The steaks are delicious," she added quickly.

"We've got a table on the grill-it-yourself side. I'm hoping you'll think my steaks are even better than the chef's. I cook a mean steak if I do say so. Honest to god, I'm fighting with myself not to just take you back to my place. I can cook for you there, but I'm having enough trouble keeping my hands off'a you in my truck. If I take you home, all bets are off."

Unable to help herself, Callie grabbed the hand that was positioned on Ford's muscular thigh and laid it on her own. "Don't try too hard, but I always wanted to try out the grill-it-yourself side. Pops isn't a great cook, and they couldn't afford to go out very often so he didn't want Nana to have to do anything when he did get to take her out. But it always looked like people were having so much fun over there."

Ford squeezed her leg, and Callie suddenly wished she'd worn a much shorter dress. She wanted those calloused hands on her skin again, the way they'd been the night before. "Harold is a good man. I've always admired your grandparents."

It took her far too long to register his statement. She was too busy wishing away the clothes between them, which was stupid because they were supposed to be taking this slowly. "Me too. I love that they have that kind of love story that you just know isn't ever going to end even when everything else always does."

"I know I'm probably a dumbass for still thinking this, but I refuse to believe everything does. But you still haven't told me about how your daddy is still living with your grandparents. Do they need help kicking him off their land? All they have to do is ask."

Callie wished Nana and Pops would take Ford up on his offer, but she knew they never would. "Nana doesn't believe in divorce," she offered sheepishly. It was uncomfortable saying that to someone who had just gotten divorced. "I mean, she knows they happen but she uh..."

"Doesn't approve," he filled in the obvious blank on her behalf.

"Yeah."

"I'm not offended. Keep going."

Relieved at that, Callie shrugged. "My grandparents are just very old-fashioned. They're very religious. Nana tells people that we're related to Noah all the time. It's embarrassing."

Ford's chuckle was easy this time, like he genuinely enjoyed the story. "I s'pose we all are, aren't we?" He winked at her.

She tried to cover her embarrassment with a quick laugh. Her grandmother was awfully judgmental when it came right down to it, but Callie didn't like speaking negatively about Nana. "I'm pretty sure Nana doesn't think that, but yes, we are."

"I have a great-aunt on my mama's side who's convinced we're all related to Garth Brooks on *her* mama's side. She tells me I look like him all the time. 'Course her vision's about as good as a one-eyed bat, but she's still ornery that Garth and Trisha didn't have the wedding in Holder County."

This time Callie's laughter was genuine. She couldn't remember the last time she liked talking to anyone as much as she loved talking to Ford. "You're way better looking than Garth," she informed him.

He cocked his eyebrow at her. "You think?"

"I don't have to think. My vision is much better than a one-eyed bat. I can see you."

"Yeah, well, the point is sometimes you just gotta let people think whatever it is they're going to think. You're not going to change their mind. It's not worth your time trying. So, your grandmother doesn't hold with divorce. More power to her. But keep going with the story about your daddy and your mama."

"When my mom left, my grandparents took my dad's side, even

though they don't really like him either. He stayed on the farm, and he helps them take care of it along with his other jobs. I've always sort of thought of him like having a splinter."

Before she could explain that ridiculous statement, Ford laced their fingers together and once again seemed to read her mind. "He was the annoyance that kept you from fully enjoying your time with your grandparents, and you couldn't get rid of him."

"Exactly."

"If you want, I can come take a look at the barn. I can give you a pretty good idea of when the roof was replaced. I have a fair amount of experience with that kind of thing. And I can go through those papers with you, too. I know all of the local contractors, so I'd recognize a payment to one of them."

"You'd really do that for me? It's not a very sexy newly dating kind of thing. Plus, I feel really bad suspecting my dad of something when I have no proof."

"This is the first date I've been on in something like twenty years, so bear with me while I fuck it up because I'm surely going to. I have no clue exactly what's supposed to come in what order, but if I can help you do something, I want to. It'd make me feel useful if nothing else." Callie started to assure him that he wasn't fucking anything up, but he kept going. "And don't feel bad about suspecting somebody's up to something they shouldn't be, even if it's supposed to be someone you trust. I had doubts about Meritt for years, but I refused to listen to my gut. I would've saved myself a lot of misery if I'd just trusted myself."

"Do you think that's really true though? I mean you would still have been in a relationship with someone like her, and that comes with misery I think. It does for me, anyway." Once again, Callie spoke without thought. She clamped her mouth closed and sealed it with her teeth. With every birthday, she wished that she'd outgrow that particular tendency, but it hadn't yet happened. "Sorry. Again. Forget I said that, too."

Ford gave her that low, rumbled chuckle that she swore sent the butterflies in her stomach into rapid flight. "I don't want to forget you said that. You're right. The only way out was through. I need to remember that. So, again, you don't have a single thing to apologize for."

"Sometimes I wish I could just keep my mouth shut." A distinctly naughty smirk formed on Ford's features, and Callie's stomach did a somersault as she giggled. "Go ahead and say it. I know you're thinking it."

"I'm trying to be a gentleman," he insisted.

"Yeah, I know, but I don't want to be the only one who keeps saying things she shouldn't."

"Fine. I'm gonna say it, but I don't mean it quite as dirty as it's going to sound. I really like your mouth wide open, baby."

Her giggle morphed into full-blown laughter. "How could that possibly not sound dirty?"

He gave her hand a gentle squeeze. "It means I really like talking to you along with all of the other ways that statement could be taken."

"I really like talking to you, too. But I don't get why you're so certain you're doing something wrong on this date."

Ford eyed her, and she didn't care for the caution in his gaze. "Can I be completely honest with you?"

Disappointment threatened to implode in her belly. "I really don't have any interest in being in any kind of relationship with anyone who isn't completely honest with me. I've done that. It sucks."

"I get that. Believe me. And I'd never lie to you. I guess I was just asking if you were sure you wanted to know what's going on in my head."

"I'm sure."

"My brother looked up your Instagram account. I told him to shut it down, but I feel kinda bad about it. And I know I keep telling you that I don't know how to date, but you may not understand how inept I am at all of this. I have no idea what breadcrumbing, or cushions, or tumblefucks are or anything like that. It's kinda like I've been living in a vacuum for the last twenty years. The world went on without me. I don't feel like I'll ever catch up."

The humble honesty he extended erected some kind of solid foundation Callie hadn't even been aware she needed. She gave him a grin that she hoped would fill in the gaps her words were inevitably going to leave. "Breadcrumbing is a horrible thing to do to people. It's just leading someone on but leaving your options open in case someone better comes along. Cushions are something to fall back on." She rolled her eyes. "I'm glad you don't know what they are. And I don't know what a tumblefuck is either, but that one sounds like way more fun."

Ford's chuckle didn't come from his soul. It was too shallow, held too much contempt. "My idiot cousin probably made that one up."

"It's okay that you saw my Instagram account. Lots of people look at it. That's kind of the point of having the account, I guess. I'm supposed to upload my photos to it more often. A lot of photographers get clients from there. But sometimes I want to do something without needing photographic evidence of it. That's probably a dumb thing for a photographer to say."

"It doesn't sound dumb to me at all. Sounds like you want to live your life sometimes instead of just recording it, which I swear is all people do nowadays." He threw the truck into park in the lot and was standing at her door a half second later.

CHAPTER NINETEEN

Despite what he'd told her, the more Ford watched her in that dress the more he swore it was going to be his undoing. Damn thing was frustratingly opaque. Half of him wanted to cover what was exposed. Those plump tits she was showing off were for his eyes only. The other half of him wanted to tear it from her body. He wanted to devour her, to stake a claim that couldn't be undone. He may have been out of practice with dating and women in general, but he was fairly certain she was sending a message with that dress. She was showing off for him. He couldn't wait to assure her that the message had been received loud and clear.

Offering her his arm, he reminded himself of the many complications. She was planning on moving to New York. He sure as hell couldn't follow her up there, and he had no business even thinking that way. He was tied to the land that was tied to the county that his family founded. Those were ties that couldn't be undone. Not for her or anyone else. The ones on her dress however, those sure as hell could be.

He swallowed down another dose of rampant desire as they approached the hostess stand. "Holder, reservation for two on the grill side," he spoke the words out into the ether. He couldn't take his eyes off Callie long enough to address anyone in particular.

"Give us five minutes to scrub down your grill, sir. You can wait at the bar." The hostess gestured to the large high-top bar directly behind her.

Truthfully, he could use a drink. Anything that would dial down the conflicting emotions at war in his body would be a merciful blessing. But given that they'd begun this friendship or dating relationship or whatever the hell this was with her being drunk off her ass, he wasn't certain drinking was a great idea. Guiding her towards the rainbow display of liquor bottles and beer taps, he cleared his throat, "you want something to drink?"

"I promise never to get drunk again. I swear. I don't normally drink like that. It was just all too much."

"I don't mind you drinking, baby, as long as you don't push it to extremes. I just don't want you doing it unless I'm there. I'm aware that makes me sound like a possessive asshole."

She grinned at him and shook her head. "Then I must really like possessive assholes."

The bartender gave her a somewhat concerned smile. "What can I get you two?"

Ford cleared his throat. "Uh yeah. I'll take a Jack and Coke, and the lady will have...?" He turned to her. Keeping her gaze locked on him, her teeth sunk into that full bottom lip again. Ford swore his hard-on was now choking him.

"You know," she turned to the bartender, "what I really want is an Old Fashioned."

Ford wasn't certain where the rumbled noise of pure hunger had come from exactly, but suddenly, he knew that he had what she needed and maybe more importantly, what she wanted. He decided that was all he really needed to know.

His hand caressed the bare skin of her back as he guided her towards their grill. He swore the slight friction could set the whole restaurant ablaze. Those huge brown eyes of hers met his hungry gaze. Her body tensed and a delicious breath of air escaped her lungs. The way she responded to him was a hundred-proof shot right to his chest.

There was power in the arc between them. Was he just imagining that? He somehow still doubted himself. But Jesus Christ, if he could make her needy touching the dip of her back, what might happen if he got his hands other more exotic locales. No. Dammit. Slowly. He was supposed to be taking this slowly. She wanted an old-fashioned romance. That's what she was going to get.

———

Callie's heart continued to dance in her throat. She swore when Ford touched her back she felt it places much deeper inside of her, places she really shouldn't beg him to touch even though that's exactly what she wanted to do. Chill bumps skittered across her bare shoulders despite the heat emanating from her. A moment of guilt tugged at her when she recalled that Derrick had never had that effect on her even by half. But she brushed that moment away and focused on the way the stubble on Ford's jaw sharpened its already impressive angles, and the assuredness in his hands when he pulled out her chair for her and let his fingers graze her shoulders like perhaps he didn't want to let go.

If Ford would ever allow her the honor of photographing him, she'd want shots of those hands, strong and capable, of his shoulders substantial and strong, and of his ass caught up in those Wranglers that she swore she'd learn to sculpt if she could somehow recreate that.

"Sit tight, baby doll. I'll be right back." His announcement yanked her out of the visual inventory she'd been taking of his body.

"What? Where are you going?"

"You're cold," he gestured to the chill bumps still residing on her shoulders. "I'm getting you my jacket." He shot what looked like a warning glare to every man in their general vicinity and then returned in record time from his truck. He draped a deliciously soft leather jacket on her shoulders. Suddenly, she was surrounded by the scent of leather and of Ford. Unable to help herself, she dipped her head to the coat and drew a deep breath. For the first time in her life instead of feeling small, despite the size of the jacket on her petite frame, she felt protected.

For a girl who hadn't been cared for in so long she wasn't certain how to react, she melted. "Thank you."

"You never have to thank me for doing my job, but I should probably thank you."

"Why?" Intrigue expanded in her mind. There were still so many questions she wanted answers to. They constantly bubbled up from her throat.

"For letting me be a gentleman." He shook his head. "For not being a bitch. There I said it. Meritt used to yell at me if I opened a door for her. She said it was insulting. Of course, when I stopped doing it she'd yell at me then, too."

Callie considered for a scant half second. "You know what I think?"

"What's that?" She swore that grin of his should be qualified as a Class A addictive substance.

"I think sometimes it's hard to remember that you deserve better. It's not just this one big, bad decision that you made one time. It's a thousand small, insignificant things that we chose not to see. The lens was out of focus, and we never corrected it."

He grunted what sounded like an agreement then lowered his head. "You're right. You're so damn smart, too. I had nothing over a blind man if I was choosing not to see. But I'm correcting that lens now. I'm sorry I brought her up. I don't mean to do that."

Before Callie could insist that she really wasn't very smart and that she didn't mind him bringing up Meritt, a waiter approached. "What are we grilling tonight, Mr. Holder?"

"Oh, do you two know each other?" Callie grinned. It would be fun to meet some of Ford's friends.

Both Ford and the waiter paused uncomfortably. "Uh," Ford cleared his throat, "I'm sure we've met out here a few times."

"Everybody knows the Holders," the waiter insisted like Callie clearly wasn't very bright.

"Oh. Right." Somebody really needed to invent some kind of word vacuum that would allow her to suck all of the wrong words she continued to say back into her brain.

"Bring us two tri-tips, some potatoes, some corn on the cob, I'll shuck it, and," he turned his attention to Callie, "do you want a salad?"

He seemed pained to ask. She wasn't sure if cowboys didn't agree with having a salad with a steak, or if Meritt had some kind of issue with him offering her a salad as well.

"What kind of salad?"

He shrugged. "The only kind I know how to make is pretty much just lettuce with cheese and those hard bread things with ranch dressing."

Dear lord, she was quite certain that the entire state of California did not know that ranch dressing existed. At least no one in Los Angeles County did. The salad Ford had just described, including the croutons, sounded as heavenly as she was certain the steaks were going to taste. "That sounds perfect," she assured him.

"Good. But if you want something different, I'll figure it out."

"I don't want anything but you. Uh," she cleared her throat and fought not to visibly cringe, "I mean the salad just like you said."

A flash of a cocky smirk appeared on his features, and Callie decided maybe she wouldn't have vacuumed that admittance away just to see him grin like that.

Since the restaurant really only provided raw ingredients to the people manning the grills, the food came out quickly. Ford expertly tore the husk away from the corn and lined up a few spices for the steaks. Callie sat entranced with the assuredness in the way he moved, the flex and bunch of his biceps and roll of his shoulders as he turned the meat. Appreciation tumbled through her mind. There'd been no debate or discussion on what they were ordering. No apathy about trying to select from a dozen tasteless choices. Ford knew what he wanted, and he went after it. She couldn't recall Derrick ever making plans for them. If they went somewhere, it was because his parents made him go and bring a date. They made all the plans. Never him.

If Ford taught her nothing else, she knew beyond any shadow of a doubt that laid-back California cool was not something she ever wanted again.

CHAPTER TWENTY

"How do you want your steak, sweet thang?" Ford grinned at his date. He was actually on a date and having a damn good time. It still felt like he was living somebody else's life.

"Medium well," she leaned closer to the grill, closer to him.

He shook his head. City girls. "You want me to burn it?" he teased just to hear her giggle. "If I cook this past medium-rare, it'd be a crime. They'll throw me out of the Cattleman's."

"Well, I wouldn't want to cause you to lose your membership. I just prefer it not to still be mooing."

For some ridiculous reason that he had no hope of figuring out, Ford made a low bellowed noise, precisely like cattle, when he turned the steaks on the grill. He did make certain only she could hear him. He hoped. When she doubled over laughing and clutching at her chest, he decided being an idiot was worth it if he could keep her laughing like that. Honest to god, he couldn't recall the last time he'd just been stupid with someone. He loved the intimacy of it. If he'd done something like that with his ex, she would've called him a dumbass and told him to stop embarrassing her. But Callie's hearty laughter surged life's blood through his veins. She laughed hard enough to draw laughter from him as well.

"You have a great laugh," he informed her.

Her eyes all but disappeared again as she gave him a megawatt grin. "You have a great moo."

He'd laughed more in the last five minutes than he had in the last five years. "I do have a fair amount of experience listening to it."

"I'm really excited about taking pictures on the ranch if you're still okay with that. I'd like to add them to my portfolio before I..." she clamped her mouth shut.

"Before you what, baby?"

"Nothing."

Ford didn't care for that at all. He'd lived too many lies, kept too many things locked tight behind his jaw. "I thought we were going to be honest with each other."

A bolt of pain flashed in those eyes of hers. "Sorry. I was going to say before I send the second installation to Nina Morales. But...something about that felt weird to say."

Did that mean she was rethinking New York? He couldn't possibly allow her to do that. Christ, not because of him. And that one lie he was still living resurfaced in his head. The one that had kept him sane for the past few days. *They barely knew each other.* But that really wasn't true. How the hell did he feel so close to her? "Uh," he forced a nod, "I can help you get some good shots. Tell you where to stand and all of that. I want to help you, like I said."

"That would be great."

"Do you want to get started tomorrow morning?"

"I'd love to, but I can't stay with you tonight. Nana would...well you probably know what she'd say and how she'd worry."

"We're taking this slowly, remember? Let me at least get Nana to like me a little before I go and blow it by keeping you tied to my bed." Once again, he lamented his choice of words. Where did things like that keep coming from? His lips parted on an apology, but the intrigue in her eyes kept him from verbalizing it.

"That sounds very interesting," she whispered before she took another slow sip of her Old Fashioned and glanced away from him. Heat climbed from between her lush breasts to her cheeks in seductive swirls. Whether it was the alcohol or embarrassment at what she'd just said, he wasn't certain, but he intended to find out.

He cleared his throat and began plating their food. "I can come pick you up in the morning."

"What time?"

"I need to be on horseback by five thirty."

"You mean like five thirty in the morning? But...I'm not even sure my coffee maker works that early. The sun isn't even up then."

His grin expanded further. "The sun not being out is what makes it great. It's cooler out, and like I said there's not a prettier sunrise anywhere than on horseback on Holder Ranch."

"Oh, I have no idea how to ride a horse. I'd just slow you down." Fear perforated her excuses.

He set her plate in front of her and then took the seat beside her. He lifted her chin with his hand until she had nowhere to look but in his eyes. "I'm about to do that thing where I say something that could be considered kind of crude."

Her cheeks slipped along the calluses of his fingertips as she smiled. "Say it anyway."

"I'll teach you how to ride, baby. Whenever you're ready. And I won't let you fall."

She managed to nod against his palm. He slowly returned his hand to his own lap as she asked, "Is it okay if it's not tomorrow? Learning to ride a horse while taking pictures seems like a lot to manage."

"Of course. I'd never force you to do anything you don't want to do. I'll get my brothers to pick up my slack, and I'll take you out in the truck."

"I don't want your brothers not to like me," slipped from her mouth as she speared a piece of steak with her fork.

"They'll be fine. Don't worry about it." He'd catch hell for loading them with more work, but she was worth it. The absence of her skin from his hand stung. Without thought he returned his touch to her thigh under the lace of that dress. Her breath gave a slight hitch. Her reactions to his every touch continued to shred his resolve to take this slowly. He was clinging to a cliff with one hand.

A waitress carrying a water pitcher interrupted their moment. "Can I get you something else from the bar or refill your waters?"

Ford turned and offered Tammy Decker a nod. Her family lived on the outskirts of Holder County. He wondered how long she'd been working out here. "I'll just take some more water." He lifted his eyebrows to Callie in question.

"Me too. Just some water please."

Tammy refilled their glasses and then set the water pitcher down. "You know, Ford, I just have to tell you I think it's great that you've moved on from Meritt so fast...even if she is awfully young."

Before he could come up with any kind of appropriate response to that, not that there was one, Tammy whisked away to refill more glasses.

CHAPTER TWENTY-ONE

"I'm not that young," Callie immediately insisted, but the waitress was no longer nearby.

"I'm sorry about...that and...her," Ford stumbled over an apology.

"I'm not that young," Callie repeated. It was as if saying it over and over again would somehow make it true. But she didn't feel that young. She'd lived a lot of life. That should matter more than the years. Ford worked his jaw visibly. She wondered if it was the comment about moving on that had thrown him or the one about her age. "I'm twenty-eight." She beat him to the inevitable punch. He was trying to figure out how to ask her that very question. She wanted to make it easier on him. That got two slow nods. "How old are you?"

"Forty-two," he coughed over the numbers and downed half of the water the waitress had provided. "I told you last night I was old."

"I don't think you're old, but is this going to be a problem for you because I don't really think age has anything to do with anything. I've known people who were young in their nineties and people who were just existing in their twenties. It's just a number. It's not a sunrise." She squeezed her eyes shut and again wished for that word vacuum.

"What does that mean, honey?" Ford's hand gently soothed her thigh.

She shrugged. "Sunrises matter. How you spend a day matters. Minutes matter. Sometimes even whole hours matter. What you've been through matters. Years don't. I mean, do you remember every single thing you did in a whole year?"

Suddenly, he was nuzzling his face in her hair and brushing kisses on her cheek. "So damn smart. I spent a lot of years just existing so I get what you're saying. It's not a problem for me, but we're likely to get a lot of comments like that." He gestured towards the waitress. "And if you decide I'm too old to mess around with..."

"I'm not going to decide that. You're a sunrise."

"You think?"

"I know," she assured.

"I'm starting to think you're the whole damn day, baby. I still feel like I need to take ten steps back. I don't want to tie you down."

She did consider for at least a full second before the comeback that was poised on her tongue sprang free. "But tying me down sounded like fun."

The rumbled groan that he planted in her ear was worth it. "Be careful what you wish for. It's been a long damn time for me."

"I thought it was just last night," she couldn't help but remind him.

"I'm still not okay with that, and that isn't what I meant."

"I wish you were okay with it because it meant a lot to me."

Ford tossed his napkin down on the table. His steak was gone but the salad and potato were still only half-eaten. "Do you want to get out of here?"

Callie still had a few bites of steak left. It had been the most delicious thing she'd ever had in her mouth, but suddenly that just wasn't what she wanted to taste. "Please."

After several long moments of silence as they drove, Ford finally admitted, "I don't trust myself enough to take you back to my place. Honest to god you look so fucking beautiful I couldn't keep my hands off of you in a restaurant."

Callie loved that she did this to him, that she made him lose control, loosen the tight reins of self-restraint he kept on himself. They drove past a dirt road turnoff that she recognized in the unincorporated land between the Holder city limits and Odell. "Do kids still park up at Cliffhart Ridge?"

"If they do, they'd likely kick me out for being too old." So the age thing was getting to him. Disappointment twisted Callie's stomach. She'd just have to show him that it didn't matter.

"I love the story of that place. It's really romantic." The way Callie had heard it, the daughter from one feuding family out in Burns fell secretly in love with the son of the other family. When they'd turned eighteen they'd run up to the ridge and built a house. They'd had a little farm up there. From the highest vantage point nearby, they could see people coming in case their families tried to come after them, but the trees were thick enough around their cabin that they couldn't be seen. Those same thick trees had provided cover for lust-driven teens for the past eight decades. Callie had never been up there, and she'd always wanted to go.

"Is that your way of saying you want me to take you up there?" He didn't sound like he minded the idea so much, just that he was trying to figure out what she wanted him to do.

"I always wanted to go, but Nana would never have let me when I was here during the summer. Plus, no boys were ever interested."

"I don't believe that for a minute. You weren't the problem. Haying was."

"Haying?"

"Cattle ranchers hay all summer. We almost never leave the ranches. Nobody took you up there because no one was around to see you. I haven't been up there since I was sixteen, but if you want to go, sugar, say the word."

"I want to go."

Ford spun the truck around in the middle of the empty road. Callie beamed at him. Freedom, pure and wild, burst through her.

CHAPTER TWENTY-TWO

The truck bounced and lurched as the dirt road up to the ridge grew more narrow. Ford knew the terrain should've been familiar. He'd brought girls up there dozens of times when he was a teenager, and yet it all felt strangely new and untainted.

Callie was almost buzzing in the seat beside him, and he loved getting to show off the outskirts of Holder County for someone who still appreciated all of its eccentricities. Low tree branches painted the windshield of his truck as he pushed them deeper into the woods.

"I'm so excited," she squealed. "This is perfect."

And it was. Since it was a Tuesday night, there were no kids up there. They were entirely alone to watch the sunset over the ridge. He couldn't have planned anything more perfect if he'd tried.

Her mind fascinated him just as much as those sinful curves of hers. The way she'd take off on an idea without any careful planning, without wondering what people would think if she asked for what she wanted. It was so refreshing he swore she was baptizing him anew.

Two yellowtail hawks circled over the ridge as the sky tinged pink silhouetting the surrounding trees.

He put the truck in park and tried to remember if he'd ever had any moves worth using. Probably not. Never dating as an adult put him at a distinct disadvantage. But when she turned to him with that come-get-me grin and those killer eyes, he knew he never would've been able to use moves on her anyway. She was just too real, too authentic in a world that wasn't.

"I haven't just not been up here. I've never been parking anywhere." She scooted a little closer, and he swore his breath disintegrated in his lungs. "But I think this is the part where we kiss."

"Come here to me," he summoned on a low growl. "But I'm going to give you the same warning I gave you last night at the bar. Once I start, I might never be able to quit."

"Good. I don't want you to quit."

"Back to me being a possessive asshole, but it's a fucking turn-on that I'm your first for this."

"I told you I must like possessive assholes."

"So fucking beautiful," were the last intelligible words he made before he dipped his head to hers and drank in her kisses like good whiskey on a cold day.

———

When Ford's fingertips tracked down over her breasts almost cautiously, Callie arched into his hesitant caress. She swore her boobs had swollen to the point of being painful trapped in the dress. She prayed he'd take the offer. Her body knew he could bring her relief. And he did. Jerking the cups of the dress down on a low growl, he revealed her. Her nipples throbbed out their appreciation.

"This dress," he groaned before he swirled his tongue around one nipple and then the other. "Damn thing has been driving me to distraction all night." On his next pass he suctioned his mouth to her and sucked with fervor. Releasing her, he panted out, "Is that what you wanted, doll baby? Did you intend to drive me wild?"

"What if I did?" she challenged on a half breath.

"If you did, then I'd be of a mind to brand your tits with my mark, so you wouldn't be showing them off for other men."

"Oh god." She shuddered. "Do it."

He straddled her over his lap. The long skirt portion of the dress rucked up her legs, granting her pussy access to the promise of the steel-hard ridge centered at his zipper line. For most of her life, she'd believed that you couldn't ever do things for the first time again. But something about that cowboy who was visibly struggling to figure out what he was allowed to touch in his truck that night changed the things she'd been so certain of. She swore she was sixteen again. The interior of that truck in the middle of that sunset ridge became her whole world, the past and the present.

A harsh shudder tore through her as he began to punish and then forgive the skin of her breasts with his wicked tongue. Those massive hands of his gripped her ass holding her at his mercy. God, she loved the aggression just as much as she loved that she was the one who made him lose control like this. That aggression became a requirement, a necessity. Screw water and air. Those hands, his mouth, his still-trapped erection behind his Wranglers—that's what she needed to survive.

Unable to remain still, she ground against him desperate for pressure and relief. When he finally released her breast from his mouth, his head fell back against the seat. He gasped for breath and stared at her, like he wasn't quite certain what to do next.

"Ford, please," she urged.

"You make me so fucking hard. Christ, do you have any idea how long it's been since I've been like this? I was...worried."

The devastation in his voice drowned a little of her fervency. She cradled his face in her hands and gave herself the length of one breath to revel in the scrape of his stubble on her palms. "There's nothing wrong with you," she soothed. He'd been grieving a marriage that ended long before it was officially over, but she didn't want to point that out just then. Her reproductive organs wanted much less talking and much more fingering. "Do you have any idea how long it's been since anyone made me feel this way?" She gestured to her own crotch under the messy folds of satin and lace.

He locked those steel-blue eyes on hers, and with delicate precision let both of his hands ascend slowly under the dress. He never dropped his eyes. He only watched her as his roughened fingertips explored her thighs. Gradually. A scant inch at a time.

A shiver quaked through her. She'd had two other boyfriends in college before she'd gotten caught up in Derrick's world. But never had anyone ever actually taken their time with her. Half of her was appreciative. The other half was frantic for him to move faster, to press his fingers where she was swollen and soaked, to ease the empty ache that seemed to have carved a path all the way through her soul.

With that same hesitancy, his thumbs circled the wet patch of lace between her thighs. She shook with a need she didn't recognize, the kind that gripped her with such force she wasn't certain she would ever recover.

"Baby, you're drenched," he pointed out the obvious. Her breaths stuttered as they attempted to escape her lungs. "Is that all for me?" Disbelief tore the ragged edges of his tone. She heard the echoes of her own question to him from the night before. Her hatred for Meritt increased tenfold.

"It's all you," she readily assured him. "Please, I need...I need to come with you inside of me."

CHAPTER TWENTY-THREE

With her desperate little plea, Ford swore the tether that held him together snapped so loudly it was audible. The man he'd been so certain he was met the boy he'd been and both sought to bring her the kind of tortured satisfaction he longed to give. "Is that what you need, baby?" rasped from his throat, strung tight with pure need.

"Please," she continued to whimper.

"I think what you *need* is to see what happens when you set out to make a man hurt with wanting you."

Her responding question came accompanied with a naughty smirk that set him on fire. "What happens, cowboy?"

As far as he was able to determine she'd been dating some big-city shitlicker who surely had more money than balls.

Cowboy. Fuck yeah. That's precisely who he was, and he'd show her what happened when she was sloppy-wet and begging for a real man.

The internal blaze deep in his groin seemed to ignite the one in her eyes as well. He dipped his fingers under the crotch of those deliciously innocent panties. Disbelief continued to taunt the desperate drive to own her. God, how was she real? How was he sitting in his truck with someone who wasn't Meritt? How had his life gone from supreme suckage with an extra helping of bullshit to this?

Maybe the shame had done him in. Maybe she was some kind of heavenly angel sent to bring him on to the other side. If she was there, he decided he wouldn't mind going on, as long as heaven had prairies and horses it'd be pretty good.

He slipped two fingers between her folds. She shook. All for him. His body bucked under hers in response, driving his fingers deep in a fluid demand. Her mouth fell open and a delicious gasp left those kiss-swollen lips. "Yes," hissed from her as she gripped his shoulders and began to ride.

"It drives me fucking crazy," he rasped, "that the last man's cock who was between these lips wasn't mine. Makes me want to fill this tight, wet, little pussy so full of me I fucking ruin you."

Her moans bled to breathy pleas of both his and her maker's name. "You call my name when I have you like this. This belongs to me. I'll make you beg for God later." She was so damn tight he swore he almost came in his jeans just thinking about spilling himself so deep inside of her she'd never be rid of his seed, of his claim. He drove his fingers in fast without reprieve. "Let me feel how wet you get for me. You have to learn to follow my rules if I'm gonna own that pussy."

"Oh god," she gasped.

She began to ride his hand in earnest. The fleshy mounds of her tits rubbed his jaw. Hungry pulses from her pussy assured him he had indeed died and gone to heaven. Fuck the prairies and horses. If heaven had her like this, he'd sell his saddle now. "No, baby." He wrapped his free arm around her and pinned her against his chest allowing her no movement at all. "Take it. You take what I give you. That's the rule. You come because of me. You understand that? Only me." She felt like sin and redemption all tied up in a hot Oklahoma wind. He held her tighter, refusing to let her blow away.

Ragged hunger clawed under his skin. He was so desperate to own her that every ounce of restraint disintegrated in the thick air fogging the windows of his truck.

"Mine. Say it. You tell me who you belong to when I let you come."

With that, she collapsed against him. Her body spasmed around his fingers, drawing them deeper. Her heavy breaths feathered over the sweat gathered on his neck just before the sweetest word in the world made its way to his ears. "Yours."

———

Her breath was snatched from her lungs. Ford seemed to have mastered her entire body. For most of her life Callie had been certain she was at the will of the wind. The few anchors she'd ever tried to cling to were always ripped from her grasp. But there was something about Ford—the firm set of his jaw, the primitive need in his steel-blue eyes, his substantial embrace as he held her tight. He'd never allow her to fly away again, and that felt like the answer to every prayer she'd never known how to speak.

The mix of hard-line authority over her body along with his tender care spoke directly to her wayward soul.

She buried her face in his neck and attempted to catch her breath as he cradled her gently now. Her tongue swept over the skin pressed to her lips, so hungry to absorb his flavors. Another one of those carnal grunts tensed from his chest. The eager promise of his swollen cock was still pressed to her other set of lips. She skated her hand between them needing to wrap her fingers around him to bring him the same relief he'd just given her.

But he caught her wrist and lifted her head so she was staring at him as he cradled her face. "No, honey." The hunger in his eyes was unmistakable. It was desperate and greedy, and heaven help her she wanted more of that.

"Why?" she whimpered.

"The first time I come with you it ain't gonna be in your hand. It's gonna be down your throat, and then I'm gonna fuck you so hard you can't even stand up outta my bed. I'm gonna watch my seed drip down your thighs. But none of that's happening tonight in the cab of my truck. I had no business letting it get as far as it did but Christ Almighty, woman, you blow my restraint to hell."

Her swollen lips pulled into a coy grin. "Is it bad that I really like that I do that?"

He shook his head at her and matched her grin. "Guess we'll have to figure that out, won't we, sugar?"

Her brow furrowed but she didn't have the strength to ask him what that meant exactly. Good grief, the man had robbed her of the ability to ask questions. He'd given her so much peace she was okay with not knowing for a while. But he seemed able to read her mind anyway.

"The first time I take you to bed I've got no hope of being gentle with you. God, I'll try, but I make you no promises. We'll have to see if you really do like my rough nature."

If that's what he was worried about, she'd prove him otherwise. Cuddling against his chest, she reveled in the way he cradled her tenderly to him. "Do you really think you're going to scare me?" The question joined the caw of a hunting hawk and the low bass of a few nearby bullfrogs.

"Little bit," he admitted.

"Well don't be. I've spent most of my life afraid of things. Afraid of my father, of something happening to my grandparents, of leaving Derrick, of everything. I'm terrified of storms, but I am not afraid of you. I never will be. You're a sunrise, remember. Night time is for fears, don't you think? Sunrises are never scary."

"Life can be damn terrifying on occasion, but so help me Jesus I will not let you be scared as long as you're mine. I'll keep you safe from everything you just listed off and anything else that ever has intentions of doing you harm." Callie lifted her head again. She needed to see the fervency in his eyes of his spoken vows, but he shook his head again and guided her back into his arms. "Let me hold you, baby. Let me prove myself to you."

CHAPTER TWENTY-FOUR

The only possible way this night could've been better was if Callie had managed to talk Ford into taking her home, taking her to his bed, and doing all of the things he'd described. But he'd proven his stubborn side, or perhaps his gentlemanly side, and had driven them back to her grandparents' home instead.

It was probably all for the better. Nana would've been worried and then disappointed in her if she'd stayed over at his house. But as his tongue took another slow inventory of her mouth, she wished she'd quit worrying about what might upset her grandmother.

He pinned her between the clapboards of her grandparents' front porch and the solid wall of his chest. She was caged in muscle and heat, and for the first time in her life she never wanted to escape. Whiskey lingered on his tongue, but nothing was as intoxicating as the flavors of his hunger.

Nothing about him was reserved or cautious. He was in full form, and she was careening headfirst into dangerous territory. A girl could become completely addicted to being the object of his adamant attention. How would she ever leave this? How would she ever leave him when this was all over?

When he moved his kisses to her neck to allow her breath, he cautioned, "If you keep grinding against me like that, you're gonna come again. I know now, don't I, sugar? I know how sweet and easy you come for me."

Lost in a lusty haze, she hadn't been fully aware that she was indeed thrusting against him constantly. A shallow gasp of breath was her only answer. She made no effort to stop her needy movements against his cock.

She could just make out the glint of warning that flared in his eyes from the moonlight. One of his capable hands gripped the curve of her ass and pulled her tight against him. He slowed her grind, intensifying every move. "If you're gonna do it, doll baby, do it right."

He drew her right leg up his thigh and centered his denim-trapped cock right where she needed him. A harsh shiver coursed through her, and he caught her gasped groan with his lips, taking it all for himself. He met her thrust for desperate thrust, until her head fell back against the rough wood. Her eyes closed, and she let him take over. "Let's have it. You're so damn needy for it. Take it."

Callie's breaths dissolved into wispy threads that failed to fill her lungs. All of her thoughts centered on the building pressure between her legs.

Her body shook against his. "Ford," whimpered from her as she fought the riptide threatening to pull her under. She couldn't do this on her nana's front porch. Surely. And yet, that same pressure she'd felt in his truck was moving up her spine. She wanted nothing between them, wanted to run her hands over every rough plane of his body. Wanted him so deep inside of her she had no hope of knowing where he stopped and she began. She tensed and clawed against his shirt wishing she could tear it from his body.

"There it is," he growled. "You can't stop it now can you, baby? Let it go for me. I've got you."

Lost in his voice, in the firm grip he had on her ass, in the heat surrounding her, her body spasmed as a choked sob flew from her mouth. She trembled and collapsed against him once again. True to his word, he wrapped his arms around her now and cradled her tenderly. "Feel better now, sugar bee?"

If she wasn't mistaken, there was a hefty dose of pride in his question. Pleased at that, she nuzzled her head deeper into his neck and gave an awkward nod.

"I will never get tired of watching you come apart for me. Does a helluva lot of good for my ego. I'm going to need to see it a lot more often." He brushed kisses on her cheek and in her hair.

"You mean more than twice in like two hours?" She cringed but then laughed at herself.

Suddenly, the harsh glow of the porch light split their moment in half. Panic burst from her chest as she tried to wiggle out of Ford's arms, but he held tight. "Going somewhere?" he teased.

"You know Nana's probably about to come out here."

"Been a long damn time since I got caught by a porch light. Did you have some kind of curfew you failed to tell me about?"

Another round of laughter shook her form against his. "I'm sorry. I think they keep forgetting that I'm not sixteen."

"What if I just start kissing all of those unnecessary apologies away? Would that work?"

Her kiss-swollen lips turned into a smirk. "Maybe."

"Worth a try." He sank his lips to hers again, and she was whisked away in the rough glide of his whiskers against her chin. Ford strengthened his hold of her and they lost themselves in each other as their tongues danced in her mouth.

The obnoxious beam of yellow light that had so rudely interrupted disappeared. Callie groaned out her approval as Ford's right hand tracked to her breast. But almost as quickly as it had left them in the darkness they longed for, the light returned. Off. On. Off. On.

"Oh, for fucksake," Callie fumed. "What the hell is she doing?"

Ford shook his head and then let it fall back with laughter. Callie was momentarily taken with how much she loved hearing him laugh, almost as much as she loved hearing him moan. "Careful now. Your country girl is coming out," he teased. "I figured it was in there somewhere." He brushed another quick kiss on her forehead as her grandmother continued on with the strobe light effect. "I better go. I'll pick you up right at five. Sleep well, baby."

Callie stared unabashedly at his gorgeous ass in those well-worn Wranglers until he climbed in his truck, blew her another kiss, and drove down the long gravel drive. When he was gone, she spun into the house. "Nana, that was completely unnecessary." She tried to quell a little of her irritation but was sure she sounded disrespectful.

"The Holder boys are known for one thing and one thing only, Callie."

"Actually, they're known for several things. The first being that they are the best and the biggest cattle ranchers in all of Oklahoma. Second, that they do a lot for this community and the surrounding towns. You've said that my whole life. You're the one who used to tell me stories about how the Holders would pay off other people's land, who were down on their luck, and let them pay the money back without any interest no matter how long it took. Now, why are you so worried about me and Ford dating while I'm back here?"

"Ford Holder is barely divorced and not the kind of man you need to associate with."

"Oh, so that's it. I should've known. You know, sometimes marriages just don't work out. His ex-wife is a horrible person. She cheated on him, and you should've seen her the other night at the bar. She's awful."

"I will not have you ending up just like Willow."

Everyone's favorite words to throw in Callie's face hit her square in the jaw. But this time she shook her head. Something about Ford's fledgling confidence mixed with the bravado that came so naturally when he forgot all about Meritt gave her a little of her own. "I am not my mother, and I will see Ford whenever I want to. I would like it if you were okay with that." With that, she flew to her bedroom still feeling distinctly like a scolded child.

———

Surreal disbelief rose around Ford like the gravel dust swamping his truck as he drove back to the main drag through town. What the hell was he doing? He had no business wanting to spend every waking moment with a woman who was more than a decade younger than him. Fuck, she even still talked like a kid half the time, going on about sunrises and being frightened of storms.

But he swore every compelling word that left those lips ensnared him. It took every ounce of stubborn he had to keep from turning the truck around, driving back to the Simpkins', and asking her to run away with him. He half thought she would in a heartbeat. That seemed to be her style. And for a man who'd been the stable foundation for his family, his animals, and the wife who'd never wanted anything he had to offer, the magic Callie Monroe held in those big doe eyes wasn't something he could turn down. Jesus, it just felt too good to be with her.

He lifted his phone to his ear and touched her number. He wanted to talk to her again before she fell asleep.

"Hey." Thrill lit through her single-word greeting. "I miss you."

"Yeah, well, same goes, sugar." How was he supposed to keep from falling in love with a woman like her? She was everything Meritt had never been and a million things Ford never even realized he wanted. He made the two turns around the square and headed down County Road 5290, the road that would lead him home. A smirk formed on his features as he drove past the old water tower. All of the places he'd always associated with Meritt seemed to be getting a facelift in his mind. "Are you getting ready for bed or is my city girl gonna stay up late tonight even though I'm going to be right back in her driveway early tomorrow?"

"I'm not a city girl, remember. I spent every summer right here. But I kind of like being your girl."

"This *taking things slowly* thing isn't working, is it?"

"Not really."

"Want me to try harder?"

"Not even a little bit."

"Good."

"I wish you'd come back right now." There was a distinct edge of defiance in her tone now. Ford wondered if Mrs. Simpkin had commented on their front porch session.

"Let's not make your grandparents hate me just yet. I'm still hoping I'm going to be able to help them get rid of Abe."

"Oh my gosh! Ford, I forgot those papers again."

He couldn't remember the last time he'd laughed this many times in one night. It had to have been years, but another chuckle filled the cab of the truck. "I'm not going to lie to you, knowing I keep you that distracted pleases me more than it should."

Another one of those sweet giggles reached his ear, and he swore if he could bottle that sound and keep it in a flask, he'd never go sober. "I do like pleasing you, so maybe it's okay that you make me forget everything."

His suffering cock perked right back up at that declaration. He'd been hard up for hours now, but he didn't mind. The reassurance that it was all of the shit he'd endured that had quelled that reaction made it more than worth it. "I had a really good time tonight," he vowed.

"Me too. I haven't had that much fun in years. I love talking to you...and all of the other stuff."

"Same goes," he repeated his signature phrase. "I'm gonna want more of all of the other stuff as soon as you get your sunrise pictures taken tomorrow."

"And the mustangs," she reminded him.

"Those too. Go on to bed, sugar. I'll be back in just a few hours."

"I can't wait."

A pair of headlights washed over his truck as he tossed the phone in the seat. His family had paid for streetlights to be installed throughout most of the town but they hadn't run them all the way out to the ranches. Ford tapped his brakes wondering who was coming towards him. His family owned every square inch of land down this road and the next three. It had to be one of his cousins. But when the jet-black Nissan Frontier—that she'd pitched a fit for and he'd purchased—passed him by much too slowly, a hot knife of betrayal stabbed through his chest.

What the hell was she doing out there? This was his land. It was his fucking county. She had his grandmother's ring, his dignity, his pride, hell she even still had his state championship letterman jacket. Couldn't he have his hometown? She'd always hated it there anyway.

Ford had always been a man who took the high road. His daddy had drilled that into him and all of his brothers. "Never take on a fool and never corner anything meaner than you," was one of Barrett Holder's many expressions. Meritt was mean as a striped snake. She always had been if he was being honest. It was his father's advice that kept him from phoning the sheriff and explaining that there was a trespasser out on Holder Ranch.

He pulled under the ancient metal sign declaring the land to have belonged to his family since 1889 and put the truck in park. If she thought she was getting on his ranch, he'd love to see her try. He mentally dared her to turn around, but she sped up and disappeared from view.

CHAPTER TWENTY-FIVE

Thunder rumbled across the ranch. His own house shuddered under Mother Nature's incoming wrath. Ford hadn't been sleeping anyway. His own demon mistakes had intruded on sexual thoughts of Callie's gorgeous body. My god she was perfect. Saliva flooded his mouth again from the memory of her flavors. He longed to sink his cock between both sets of her lips repeatedly. The thick curves of her ass and thighs meant he could nip and spank and have no worry of hurting her, only of making her beg for more.

Easing to his other side, he reminded himself that she might not like his rougher preferences. Then again, she might. Meritt hated them. He drove his fist into his pillow and shook his head. Meritt hated him, he mentally corrected.

Burying his face in the crater he'd created in his pillow, he caught the faint scent of Callie's watermelon lotion again and gave up on ever getting any sleep at all.

When lightning split the pitch-black sky, severing the endless moments of loneliness, he rushed from the bed, scrubbed his hands over his face, and tried to talk himself out of grabbing his phone. But it was useless. When it came to Callie, he couldn't seem to talk himself out of much of anything. If Holder Ranch was hearing the approaching storm, that meant it was sitting right on top of her grandparents' home. It was nearing two in the morning, but that didn't matter.

He texted her a quick: You okay?

She responded instantly: Not really.

He answered: I'm on my way.

With that, he yanked on the dirty jeans he'd been wearing and sank a Cinch ball cap on his head. He shrugged into a worn flannel shirt, grabbed a coat for her, and sprinted to his truck. The thought that she was frightened tore through him as he flew towards the gates of the ranch.

———

Callie had hated storms since she was seven. Furious thunder had shaken her awake from her pallet on the floor in their old one-bedroom apartment. She'd searched through the rest of their home for her mother, but she was still out on her date with one of the many men she cycled through after leaving Abe. Callie was entirely alone. The howling winds and soul-shattering cracks of lightning had muffled her sobs of fear.

No matter how old she was now or where she was when a storm blew in, she seemed to revert back to that little girl huddled in the closet praying for the storm to go away and her mother to come home. The shame and terror tore her apart. Her father always made fun of her for sticking close to her grandmother during summer storms. Derrick had teased her for being frightened as well. She should've told Ford not to come get her. She was certain nothing frightened Ford Holder. He seemed perfectly willing to stare down most anything without so much as flinching.

But the fear kept her from insisting that she was fine. As it was, she needed to figure out how to get out of her grandparents' house without waking them. Leaving to go with Ford in the middle of the night would only upset Nana more. She'd already told her grandmother that she was going to photograph Holder Ranch early the next morning. Thinking quickly, she scribbled a note that Ford had arrived earlier than she'd thought to pick her up and stuck it on the fridge.

That was when she noticed the motion detector beside the front door from the security system. It was probably the only home in Holder County with one, but Callie's mother had spent most of her teen years coming up with creative ways to sneak out. The security system had been installed to keep her safely at home. Callie wasn't going to be able to open any of the doors to get out without setting off the alarm. She was going to have to go out her window.

I am not my mother became her internal mantra. Several minutes later, the lights of Ford's massive truck illuminated her escape route, but they flipped off. She assumed he was taking precaution not to alert anyone to his arrival. Callie eased the window up, prayed that her grandmother would never find out about this, lowered her camera bag to the ground by the strap, and squeezed the top half of her body out the small opening. That was when her ass got stuck. Her heart pounded out a prayer that Ford would not see her half hanging out of her grandparents' home in a storm. She wiggled back and forth. The window frame scraped an angry mark on her thigh, but at least she was going to get out. It was then that she realized she hadn't fully thought this through. The porch rails were too far away for her to reach. She had nothing to brace herself on, and she was going to fall face first onto the porch.

Before she could either attempt to wiggle back in or wake up the entire house as she crashed to the concrete flooring, Ford caught her. In her effort to get out, she hadn't seen him coming for her. A quick yelp escaped her mouth before she sealed her lips shut. "I've got you, baby. Here." He eased her out of the window and set her on her feet. She clung to his wet form. The juxtaposition of heat from his open shirt and the cold winds left her lightheaded.

"Sorry, I didn't really think that through." She wondered for a moment if that was another unnecessary apology and decided it wasn't. He'd had to get out of his truck in a freaking flood to rescue her.

Another rumble of thunder almost robbed his response from the air but she just made it out, "Before you leave for New York, I'm going to convince you that asking me for help when you need me isn't something you have to apologize for." He tucked her close. "Let's get."

He raced her out to the still-running truck, flung her door open, and lifted her inside. When he slung himself in the driver's seat, her breath tangled in her lungs as his form so thoroughly dominated the cab of the truck. He paused before slamming his own door to stare her down.

The soaking wet white Lakers T-shirt clung to her curves. Her nipples were drawn tight from the cold. Every bump was on vast display. A shiver worked through her, not from the chill but from his low grunt of approval. But he shook his head. "Take that off. You're going to freeze in it." He produced a Sherpa-lined Carhartt jacket, and kept his keen eyes trained on her as she followed his orders.

She peeled the T-shirt off and dropped it to the floorboard.

"Damn baby," came out in another low grunt as he helped her into the coat. Once again she was absorbed in his masculine scent and his protection and in his obvious desire. And once again she asked herself how she was ever supposed to leave him.

"Thank you for coming to get me. You didn't have to."

"I wasn't sleeping anyway. You said you didn't like storms and..." he shrugged as he backed away from her grandparents' home.

"I know it's a stupid thing to be afraid of. It's not like you can avoid storms. It's just when I was a little girl..."

He shook his head. "It's not stupid. No one who's ever survived an Oklahoma storm would think that. Mother Nature's wrath deserves respect. People get off on thinking they're powerful, but she'll prove them wrong every damn time. It'll give me peace knowing you're safe with me, either in my bed or in my storm cellar. Maybe we can both get some rest."

"Are you going to be in the bed with me this time?" She was tired of weighing her words and regretting her questions, so she asked.

"You just peeled a soaking wet T-shirt off in my truck. You've got the most gorgeous set of tits I've ever seen, not to mention everything else we did earlier. Christ, baby, you come like the best freaking wet dream I've ever had. If you really think I'm capable of letting you sleep alone in my house, you overestimate my abilities. The one night almost killed me, and I didn't know you then like I know you now."

All traces of her earlier fear dissolved in his declaration. "I think you're capable of most anything, but I'm hoping you won't try to let me sleep alone."

"Trust me, I've got no intention of making any real effort." He cleared his throat as if that might dislodge the electricity constantly coursing between them "I'm, uh, scared of snakes. I can't avoid them either, but that don't mean I want to make friends with 'em. Everybody's scared of something. There's nothing stupid about them. Fears are part of life. They have to be dealt with like everything else."

"Thank you for not making fun of me." Callie tried to tuck herself further inside his jacket as she wondered how he'd respond to that.

Despite the rain pummeling the truck as he slowly made his way down the long gravel drive, he turned to stare her down. She could see the confusion and anger in their own storm in his eyes. "I would never make fun of you for anything ever," he vowed. "And if anyone ever makes fun of you, not just for being afraid of something but for anything at all, you let me know. I'll put a stop to it."

The one man who'd made fun of her all her life, the one who made her feel so stupid for most everything she'd ever done, lodged in the periphery of her mind. To acknowledge her father there meant she had to admit to herself that he frightened her more than any storm, and she didn't want to tell Ford that. Not yet anyway. So, she sat quietly and pretended the flashes of lightning dancing around the truck were just the flash on Mother Nature's camera, and that she was getting some killer shots of Ford's chiseled jawline as he fought their way through the storm.

CHAPTER TWENTY-SIX

By the time Ford was pulling under his carport, Callie was curled up inside his jacket sound asleep. He watched the lightning shimmer across her alabaster complexion. The thunder didn't seem to concern her at all now. As much as he would've loved to have laid her out in his bed and pounded into her hard and fast until she forgot everything but him, he swore it was twice as satisfying to know that she felt that safe with him. He got off on being a hero. He always had. It was all he'd ever wanted in this world.

He climbed quietly out of the truck and eased his door shut. She never stirred. As he made his way to her side and cradled her in his arms, he had to admit to himself that his brother was right. He'd set out to save Meritt from herself. He'd been tricked into marrying her, sure, but that hadn't really mattered to him. His hero complex had fucked him over time and time again with his ex. How the hell was he supposed to keep from making the same mistakes with the beautiful girl in his arms? It would be like trying to figure how to pull flesh from bone. He was too old to try to be anything but what he was. And all he wanted right then was to be Callie's hero for the second half of his life.

He kept her safely in his arms while he opened his door and hung up his soaking-wet ball cap. But she tensed when he was lowering her into his bed. Raw need hammered through his veins. He tried to soothe her but was certain he was doing a shit job. His own hunger for her was too strong.

Half-asleep she slipped out of his jacket and dropped it to the floor. Then she unsnapped those sinfully short cutoffs and managed to wiggle them down her legs. She kicked them off and then turned over to reveal her gorgeous ass caught up in nothing but a lacy thong.

Jesus Christ. He couldn't recall ever doing anything he'd qualify as categorically wrong in his life. He'd always tried to exceed the code of cattle rancher, but he sure as fuck was being punished. Or maybe this was temptation incarnate. A few days in the desert with Satan didn't seem so bad compared to the pinup-worthy woman who'd somehow taken control of his shitty existence despite the fact that his cock was a weeping, whiny asshole about not getting what he wanted. How was Ford supposed to resist this? He wasn't a fucking saint.

Besides, they couldn't find twelve men in a thousand-mile radius who'd convict him for what he wanted to do to her. Not if they knew the heavenly temptation laid out in his bed with her ass on ripe display and her swollen pussy lips tucked there between her warm thighs.

He'd been harder than a steel fencepost off and on for hours now. Most of him didn't mind. It was almost as reassuring as it was painful. But damn he wanted to wake her up and order her to tend the case of blue balls she'd brought on. The only problem with that plan was that he could fuck her all night long and into the next morning and knew he still wouldn't be satisfied. He'd still hurt for her. He knew.

Clenching his jaw, his hand slipped down his chest and pressed instinctively against the agony as if that would bring him relief. He jerked himself once, twice. Unless he got to unload all over that ass he needed to sacrifice some kind of offering to, his cock wanted nothing else to do with his hand.

Ford shed the rest of his clothes and climbed into bed around her form. When she gave him a contented sigh and cuddled up beside him, nuzzling her head on his chest, he knew he was set for heartbreak all over again. The months he'd spent hidden away in his house to avoid facing the endless pain Meritt had brought on had been just as point-less as they felt.

He was going to have to live with the emotional pain that was so potent it was physical all over again. A man couldn't be something he wasn't. He wrapped his arms around Callie and prayed to a God he'd refused to speak to for years that somehow he'd be able to do something to get to play her hero for the next several decades. That was all he really wanted.

He brushed a kiss on her forehead and let himself enjoy the whisper of her even breaths over his chest hair. How fucked-up was it that they were both naked in a bed that they hadn't made love in yet? He'd worry about that in the morning. For now, he was going to cradle his sweet baby for as long as she'd let him. He'd already been through hell once. Maybe it wouldn't hurt so badly the second time.

Another crack of thunder split the sky wide open. Ford's house shook from the force. Callie jerked awake and tried to determine what to do. The storm cellar or maybe under the bed would work. What did cows do in a storm? What if they were hurt? Panic unraveled her until two solid brick arms cradled her gently and drew her back to the firm planes of chest where she'd been resting. "I've got you, baby. I'd never let anything hurt you. Take a deep breath for me." Unable to resist his commands, she filled her lungs with the heady masculine scent of him. "Good girl," he soothed, but it had the opposite effect he was going for. Her body enlivened with his praise. She wasn't soothed. She wanted to do things that would make him call her that again. "There's nothing to worry over."

Tucking herself tighter into the sanctuary of his chest, she tried to reason through his promise. "How do you know that? What does me taking a deep breath have to do with the storm?"

He eased slightly to his side so she could hide entirely in his strength. A quick graveled cough said he'd been sleeping well before she'd startled. "Twisters have a scent to 'em. I can smell 'em long before they tear across this ranch. This is just a storm. I promise I've got my girl."

"I like it when you say that," she mumbled into his chest.

"Good. 'Cause I'm gonna keep saying it."

When the deep breaths rolling through his broad chest started to rhythmically sway her back to sleep, Callie understood that it wasn't ever the storm she feared. It was that no one ever had her back, no one was ever there looking out for her. Her parents had failed epically in that part of parenting. Other than her summers in Holder County, she had existed in a hollow loneliness, searching for something she instinctively knew she wanted but had no power to demand.

Wasn't her fear of being alone what had driven her directly into Derrick's bizarre Enquirer-level surreal life? Wasn't that terror why she'd stuck around so much longer than she ever should've? And wasn't it why she stuck with things way past any point of logical reason?

Defeat swiped through her belly leaving an entirely different fear in its path. Was it that fear that had driven her into Ford Holder's arms? Was that why she was so hesitant to send new photographs to Nina Morales? My god, what was she doing there? Was this going to be just like Derrick, where she stuck around because the fear of the unknown was far greater in her mind than the fear of taking a chance on herself? She swallowed down raw regret.

"What's wrong, sugar?" rumbled from the most gorgeous cowboy she'd ever seen, the one she'd been throwing herself at because she couldn't handle being alone for even one day. Because she was weak and what if she ended up hurting him, too? Bile backstroked through her stomach. She should get up and leave now so she didn't make his life even worse. He'd been through enough.

"Nothing," she whispered out her lie.

His eyes opened and he shifted so that he could hold her chin in his hand. "It ain't nothing. Please don't lie to me."

"I just...don't know how I got here."

Concern shimmered in those blue-grey eyes. "I came to get you at your grandparents', honey. You okay?"

"No, I mean I know how I got here," she gestured to him and then to his bed. "I just don't...want to hurt you. And what happens if we fall in...attachment?" There. That kind of worked.

Despite the abject horror drowning her, he gave her a gentle chuckle and settled her nerves. "Attachment, huh?"

"Yes. What happens then? But I'm doing it again, aren't I? Asking the wrong questions. The ones I'm not supposed to ask."

"Hey," he released her chin and laid her back on his chest, "remember what I said. You ask me anything you want to ask anytime you want to ask it. I'm not going to let us fall into *attachment*." He spoke the word like a curse. "I know you don't think it matters, but you have your whole life ahead of you. I'm just an old cattle rancher. I've got no intention of ever letting you give up anything for me. I have a plan."

Anxiety twisted up her spine. What if his plan was to end this now? Or tomorrow? Or right after they slept together? That didn't sound like the Ford Holder she knew but...."What's your plan? And shouldn't I have some say if this plan involves me?" she demanded.

"Simmer down now, baby girl. If you don't like the plan, I'm willing to compromise. I just like being with you. I like spending time with you. There. That's it. So, I figure if you like spending time with me, too, we could just spend as much time as we can with each other. When it's time for you to go on and live your life, I'd never do anything to try and stop you."

What if I want you to stop me? The plea in her head went from a whisper to a roar in a split second. *What if the thing I really want is for you to want me to be here forever?* She cleared her throat wishing she could also clear her mind. "I love spending time with you. I just don't want to hurt you just because...I don't want to..." she couldn't tell him that she didn't want to be alone because what an awful thing to say to someone she cared about so much, "hurt you," came out again.

But again, he saw right through her lies. "I was in a marriage that made me feel entirely alone for years. Trust me, I don't mind being alone, but I like being with you a whole lot better. Let's just enjoy it while it lasts. No pressure. Okay?"

"You're sure?"

"Never been more certain of anything."

Callie nodded against the Holder brand tattoo on his arm, letting it settle her. "Okay," she gave the only real answer that would suffice because for the first time in this relationship Ford Holder was lying. She could feel it. She just didn't know if he was aware of it yet.

"Let's get some sleep, okay?" he spoke softly.

"Do you have to get up so early since it's storming?"

"We're not riding in this and the mud'll be a bitch when we finally do get out in it, but for right now I'm gonna hold my girl and see if I can't get her back to sleep."

"Are you sure you want to sleep?" Her hand skated down his chest, wrapped around his cock, and teased until he rose mightily to the occasion.

"Fuck, baby." He half growled. "You getting needy again?"

"What if I am?" If he wanted to lie to himself and to her about whatever this relationship was going to inevitably be, then she refused to be anything but honest over what she wanted. "I want all of you. I want to watch you enjoy me. I want to see this rough side you keep warning me about. I want...this." He wanted to enjoy their time together. Fine. She wanted him to make her forget New York, and Nina, and Derrick, and everything else but him. She wanted his claim so strong inside of her she never doubted being right where she was. If he filled her pussy to overflowing, maybe it wouldn't leave room in her mind for anything else.

CHAPTER TWENTY-SEVEN

Guilt layered like bricks in Ford's gut. She didn't want to hurt him. Christ, she was still trying to save him. That wasn't her job. He wasn't going to allow her to spare him the pain. They couldn't stop this thing any more than they could hold back a freight train. It wasn't even worth it to try. They'd already fallen into *attachment*. He almost laughed out loud at her word choice. Nothing hurt like love. He'd already learned that. He just needed to keep her from having to live it.

He just couldn't let her know that any more than he could stand to think that she'd given up anything for him. If she wanted to go off to New York and be some kind of kickass photographer then he would never stand in her way. He wanted that for her. Wanted her to have every good thing her life could possibly offer her. There was no way he was one of those things. He'd fucked up the only life he had when he was twenty-two years old. There were no redos. No one got a second chance to do it all over again. That just wasn't how life worked. She still had a life left to live. He wouldn't keep her from it.

But he also wouldn't ever deny her anything she wanted, and right then she wanted him. He rolled her under his body, sank his lips to hers to capture that sweet little gasp she always gave him, and let his cock languish between the lace-trapped folds of her pussy. She was so soft against his solid strength.

Every protective instinct he possessed sizzled through his musculature. His mouth took her tongue hostage, and he slipped his cock back and forth tempting her clit with the lace. A needy little moan spilled into his mouth before he finally let her have breath. "That what you're wanting, honey? You needing me to enjoy what's mine for however long this lasts?"

"Please." She clawed at his back now unaware of her own hunger. Sexiest fucking thing in the world.

He sat up on his knees and slipped that thong down her legs. "Oh honey, I'm going to enjoy it. I'm going to make you hurt with how much I enjoy you." He knew precisely what she wanted to hear.

"Oh god, yes," she whimpered.

Her sweet little body tensed under his. Fading tan lines highlighted precisely where he wanted his mouth, but he laid back over her letting his cock revel in her swollen need. Wet heat coated him just from his own brand of filthy talking. "I know, don't I, honey? I know what you want to hear." My god, they were going to set his sheets on fire. Hell, not just his sheets, his bed, his house, his yard, his whole fucking life. It took him a half second to understand that if what was left of his life all went up in flames, she'd be more than worth it. She rolled her cock-tease body against his, so anxious for it she drove him wild. "You're getting ahead of yourself, aren't you?"

That got him a frustrated whimper as she attempted to lure his cock right where she wanted it—deep inside of her. He throbbed against her. If he had to give her up at some point, then he was going to give himself enough memories of her to get him through the endless lonely nights that taunted their horizon.

She continued to thrust against him. Impatient little thing. So fucking needy for him. Nothing was as intoxicating as that. "I'm gonna make it feel better, but you need to remember the rule."

Her eyes closed, and she all but purred out, "I take what you give me. I need it."

"I know, baby. But I want a taste of that sweet cream you make so good for me first. Been craving it for hours. You're gonna take my tongue before you take my cock."

He let her feel every rough scrape of his body as he moved down hers, let the friction push her closer to the brink. God, he'd missed this. The sky had lightened just enough to allow him to see her pouty slit. The ripe musk of her arousal filled his lungs—thick, warm, and spiked with wild abandon.

Impatience churned through his veins. He'd always loved the flavor of woman, and he knew Callie's nectar would be sweeter, better, more than any he'd known before. As he descended her body, he noticed something he'd missed in his truck. A naughty little chain of wild-flowers she'd had inked from the tender spot where her leg met her pussy all the way around her hip. "Bet that hurt didn't it, sugar?" He spun his tongue along the chain, reveling in the sweet and salty flavors of her skin.

She shuddered and bucked in his face. "Do you like it?" she murmured, half question, half flirtation.

"It's a fucking temptation I'll never be able to resist just like the rest of you. Makes me wish I'd been there to kiss it better for you." He slid his open-mouthed kisses to the thick curve of her ass and nipped. "Makes me crazy that someone else did that, took what's mine." He pinned her thighs wide open and let his tongue bathe the slippery wet heat coating her.

The only portion of his brain that hadn't taken up residence in his lower head wondered if it made him an asshole that he loved that she was almost bare. She'd waxed recently. He hoped to Christ himself she hadn't done it for her ex. Pale, tender hairs barely covered her, and he indulged the silky folds until she whimpered for more. A harsh tremble shook through her as she half gasped and half groaned out an exhala-tion of pleasure. Oh, fuck yeah. "Hold yourself open for me. Show me where you want my tongue."

With another low moan, she complied. The lips of her pussy were so wet they slipped through her fingers. He bit back another order to hold them wider and gave her a minute to be able to separate them enough to reveal that sweet little pearl. He sank his tongue to her timid clit and coaxed it into his mouth. She thrashed against his face.

———

Ford gave her things she craved but refused to admit even to herself. His fingers dug into her hips, rough and primal in his claim. He pinned her to the mattress as he indulged her clit with rapid lashes of his hungry tongue. She couldn't move. She never wanted to. She prayed he would fuck her with that same rough, primal intensity and that there'd be marks of his ownership imprinted on her skin. She needed something concrete to prove to herself that he was real, that this was real. It was all too close to the dark fantasies she allowed herself when she had a moment to be entirely alone. The fantasies were often how she kept the lonesome at bay. She'd imagine some rough, rugged man who was only ever satisfied by her surrender.

"You taste so fucking good," rasped from Ford. "So sweet all for me."

Callie was incapable of anything but soft, reedy moans. Every pulse point in her body timed itself to the ministrations of his tongue, the juxtaposition of his rough stubble against her soft thighs and pussy, and the obvious pleasure he found in her.

Pressure built constantly between her legs. God. She had to move or scream or...something. It was going to tear her apart. It was too much, too good. She clawed at his sheets, seeking purchase but finding only his strong grip on her thighs keeping her safe. He swirled his tongue and backed off ripping the orgasm from her grasp.

"Ford," she choked out his name.

"No, baby. Not yet. Not 'til I say. Not 'til you beg."

"Please." She trembled in his arms. Other pleading words tried to leave her lips but were mired in the ecstasy that pulsed through her.

"We're gonna find your edge, sugar. This ain't it. But when I find it, it's gonna be all mine. You're gonna learn to take more for me."

All Callie wanted was to take anything Ford Holder offered her and then to beg for more. He released her clit again and rasped his beard against her right thigh spreading her legs further. Then he punished the thin skin with suckled kisses that grew in intensity until she understood the point. He was marking his territory, branding her.

With that, he shattered any propriety she'd been trying to cling to.

"More, give me more," she gasped in a breathless plea. A very loud, very male roar of ownership vibrated against her skin as he granted her request.

When she bore his marks of ownership, he released her, allowing her restless hips to beg for him. "Let me hear how good I make it feel when I let you come," he ordered.

He speared two fingers deep in her channel, tracked to her G-spot like he had a map, and worked her over. To add to that overwhelming sensation, he kept his tongue and suckles soft on her clit. The push and pull, the tender and the demanding, the beast and the man all consumed her. It was all Ford and all her and all entirely too perfect.

"Ohhh...yes." She walked a fraying tightrope of unadulterated bliss. Half of her wanted to fling herself off, certain he would catch her. The other half knew to wait until he gave her permission to fly.

"That's it," he groaned. "Right there. You ready to come for me, sweet baby? Beg me."

"Please, please," were again the only words her brain seemed to understand.

"You know what I want to hear. Say it."

His name sang readily from her before she fully understood what he wanted. Oh, the man could tell her stories about being able to let her go when it was time, but the beast he housed in his soul knew no such lies. He was much too real. No practiced patience or reserve, no polite manners or breeding. Just honest to god truth, and so she fed the beast he held captive deep inside of himself and hoped she'd figure out some way to free it.

She opened her eyes, stared into the blue horizon in his own, and spoke the truth, "Yours."

CHAPTER TWENTY-EIGHT

"Damn right you're mine. Now come for me," Ford ordered. He stared down at her gorgeous curves as she shattered in his hands. Her head shook back and forth on his pillow. His name sang from her lips like a hymn, like only he could absolve her.

As he rose to his knees above her, precum seeped from his cock and dripped to her swollen mound. He gripped himself and milked more from his slit bathing her body with his seed.

Her eyes held dark fire in their depths. Her body rolled so anxious for him. Her tits swayed in a mesmerizing dance. Her nipples strained, needy for his mouth.

He dragged two rough fingers through the fluid on her mound. "Taste," he commanded as he brought his fingers to her mouth.

A breathy moan escaped her lungs before she swirled her tongue over his fingers and then began to suck with fervor. He longed to replace his fingers with his cock, to feel the heat of her velvet mouth as she took him deep. Christ, he wanted to feel her throat contract around his head, wanted to make her swallow him down. She shuddered against him. Her eyes closed as she suckled so fucking perfectly he swore he was going to come long before he was buried balls deep inside her. Pulling his fingers from her mouth, he replaced them with his own lips. "Now, taste us together, baby. Your sweet pussy juices all over my mouth. So fucking good."

Ford's kiss was demanding and possessive, all the things he felt but knew he shouldn't. He was too far gone to care. He had to make her his. Had to figure out some way to give her the life she wanted and still be able to have her all for himself. Longing to tie her to his bed and nurture and care for her endlessly rooted in his soul.

When he allowed her breath, he swept his tongue along the lower curve of her breast and then kissed a trail of heat to her nipple. He teased and tempted until, "Suck me. Please. I need..." spilled from her, but her plea drowned in an all-consuming moan as he nipped at her and then soothed the pain.

She scaled her hand between their bodies and wrapped her fingers around his cock. Jesus Christ. He throbbed in her hand. But then she pressed his shaft to her slit and slid him back and forth against her clit.

He roared both from the sight and the sensation. "Take what you want, baby, 'cause I'm sure as hell about to take mine."

She released him and panted out her need. "Take me," she urged. "Now. Please. I can't wait anymore."

The pool of precum gathered at the apex of her slit sent a shockwave of panic through him. He made quick work of locating the condoms Maddox had supplied him. But as he used his mouth to tear one open, she grabbed his hand. "I'm on the pill. You don't have to use that. I don't want anything between us."

Her body continued to wriggle urging him to do as she'd asked. But the shockwave of panic bled quickly to a deluge, drowning him. Thundered echoes of his past wrapped its fingers, cold and tight, around his throat and cut off his air supply. He'd heard those very words before. He'd believed them. Hell, he hadn't only believed them—he'd been thrilled by them. He'd devoured the lies but hadn't been able to taste their poison until six months after the wedding, when there was no baby but there was constant turmoil.

Nonsensical words tried to form on his tongue but all he managed to do was shake his head.

"Ford," Callie soothed. She slid upwards until she was seated in his bed. "Hey." She gently ran her hands over his cheeks. The motion slowly grounded him in the present. "What's wrong?"

"She..." He couldn't look her in the eye. He was terrified his vision would blur his past and present the way his hearing had. He squeezed his eyes shut and tried to explain. "She told me...and I...I believed her. I was a dumbass kid." He was well aware that he made no sense.

Yet somehow, she understood. "Oh my god. She told you she was pregnant." He forced his eyes to open. Realization and understanding struck like lightning in her own. She took the condom wrapper still dangling from his fingertips. Keeping his gaze locked in her own, displaying her fervency, she positioned the Trojan at his head and did the work for him.

"Callie, I'm...sorry," he choked. He was still a dumbass, trusting a piece of latex more than this woman who'd pulled him from the crashing waves that were overtaking him. She'd brought breath and a semblance of peace back to his life. He hadn't had either in so long he barely recognized them at first.

"My mom got pregnant with me when she was nineteen. I know that's not the same thing, but I get how confusing this must feel. Don't apologize. Just make love to me."

But he remained motionless, still lost in an abyss of confusion, caught somewhere between his past and his present. Callie's sweet grin yanked him back from the depths. And he did the only thing that made any sense at all. He brought her lips to his, and tried with everything he was to believe that he was tasting his future. That kiss sank through him, soothing his rough edges, healing the jagged wounds Meritt had knifed into his soul. Every insult, every threat, every insinuation that he would never be enough met its conquering angel, the one who said he was her everything.

She turned over and rose up on all fours. Then she shot him a look that he swore swelled his cock back to full form in a split second. "Come on, cowboy. Show me what you're made of." With that she shook that gorgeous ass back and forth, a temptation he had no hopes of denying himself.

Cowboy thundered in his blood. She wasn't Meritt, for Christ's sake. She was his. Meritt had never been his. He drove home that point by centering himself behind Callie's lush ass and impaling her pussy on his cock as she cried out from his force.

———

She'd longed for Ford to fill her so full it would rob her of every doubt that anxiously picked her apart. He did that and so much more. He filled her to overflowing, leaving no room for uncertainties. Her body wept for friction that he denied, keeping himself so deep she could feel his sack rub against her sensitive pussy.

"Please," she urged again.

She turned to look back at him. The lust-fueled awe in his eyes quieted her need for him to move faster. He shuddered against her. "God, it's so good. It's not supposed to feel so damn good." His confusion was apparent in the grunted words.

The satisfaction of making him look like that, of making him *sound* like that, sated her thoroughly. He withdrew by mere inches and then sank balls deep once again. "Fucking love seeing your juices all over me. Fucking love this."

Another withdrawal and slow return made her tremble. "I'm making you mine, honey." And then she understood. He'd waited until her body gave way, until he'd fit her to his girth. "I'm gonna make you understand what it's like to be fucked by a man on fire for you. Tell me you're ready."

"So ready," she whimpered.

And then her cowboy rode. He ravaged her with brutal force, snatching the air from her lungs. The powerful grip of his hands on her hips, the heat of his body, the rough scrape of his leg hair against her thighs, the raw masculine scent of him filled what parts of her his cock wasn't occupying. Her entire world became Ford Holder. For the first time in her life, she had no doubts as to where she belonged. He was the answer to every question she'd ever wanted to ask.

Nothing about his dedicated thrusts felt like an invasion. No, they were a fulfillment.

Her pussy wrapped tight around him, begging on her behalf for him never to leave. If he wasn't there, the questions would return, and she never wanted to think about them again. She pressed back against him with every thrust, trying desperately to deepen their connection even further.

"Spread your legs further, baby. Put your head down. Take a hold of that headboard. Let me enjoy this."

Callie immediately obeyed. She had no doubts in this man. This was what she wanted—to see his restraint vanish, to see Ford finally wild. "Good girl," he spoke the words that had her writhing and trembling. And then, as if what he was already doing to her wasn't pure bliss on its own, he traced a rough finger to her clit and began to stroke. He freed something so deep inside of her she wasn't certain she knew how to survive without it. Something primal, instinctive. Something wild.

She clung to the rails of the headboard, but it was no use. She was going to shatter. She was going to fly. She seemed to exist in some kind of alternate state, neither here nor there. Only him. Desperate to understand how anyone could possibly make her feel like this, she slipped one hand from the slat and traced herself back to the place where his hand was working her clit. He roared.

She had to find some way to anchor herself in him. He was the only thing strong enough to hold her. "Please," she managed in a breathless whisper. "Please let me feel you."

This time he complied. His rough grip returned to her hip, and she managed to get two fingers to his latex wrapped cock as it slid wildly in and out of her. "Oh god," she groaned. She was soaked with pleasure. Another roar drowned out the storm.

"It's mine," he demanded. "Feel me own you, honey." His thumb began to tease between the cheeks of her ass, and she dropped her hand to claw at the sheets. Every pulse point of her body throbbed out her pleasure. "That feels good doesn't it. Feels so good right there. I know."

Her breaths disintegrated. Her thoughts both scrambled and then centered on the pure, uninhibited carnality he'd unleashed. The pressure overwhelmed her. She couldn't contain it.

His grip eased. He leaned forward over her allowing her to be fully absorbed by him. "Let yourself come, baby. I'll catch you," he soothed. "Then I'll take mine."

His vow to catch her shattered the locks she'd thought kept her safe. She flew. Her pussy spasmed and then milked his cock relentlessly. She trembled as he brought her to the mattress and held her tight. "You're so damn beautiful when you come for me," whispered in her ear. "So fucking perfect."

CHAPTER TWENTY-NINE

Ford's body was at war with itself. Nothing should ever have felt that good. Nothing should ever make him feel so certain. It was dangerous. But the absolution and the restoration he'd felt deep inside of Callie tore away the warnings chanting in his mind. He needed more. Desperate to heave himself upon the pyre in sacrifice, he knew precisely what he wanted and what he needed to do.

He gently eased his cock from her. He was so hard he could've driven fenceposts with his greed, but there was something he had to do before he gave himself to her. Turning her in his arms so she was facing him. "I know you're sore, baby. I'll be gentle this time."

She trembled in his arms and nuzzled her face against his chest, scattering kisses over his sweat-covered pecs. When she spun her tongue over his collarbone, tasting him, he groaned and tried to cling fast to some kind of control. She was far too good at making him lose his grip on anything but her.

Sliding away from her just a few inches, he removed the condom. Nothing would block any part of the liquid redemption buried so deep within her only he could access it.

Shock danced in her eyes lit by the cloud-covered sunlight trying to filter into the room. "Are you sure?"

"Never been more sure of anything in my life." With that, he laid her back underneath him, and gently baptized himself deep in his saving grace.

Another tremble coursed through her and pushed him closer to the edge. Her warmth, her tenderness, her smarts, all of those questions she asked that she thought no one had answers to, he vowed to himself to be those answers. He needed to be her everything. It was the only thing in his life that had ever made sense.

Prior to that moment, he'd allowed life to happen to him. Not anymore. He was going after the life he'd always wanted and that was nothing more than to be able to hold her tight in his arms every night and to be the man she needed every day.

He sank to his hilt letting her healing tides wash through him with nothing between them. "Gonna fill you full, sweet baby. So fucking full of me." It was a groaned warning.

"Yes," she whimpered. Her eyes closed in ecstasy.

"Look at me," he soothed. "Be right here with me."

Those beautiful brown eyes opened, and he saw it. He wondered if she knew, if she felt it the same way he did. They'd skipped right over attachment and had already fallen in love. It was right there in her eyes as she stared up at him as he made them one.

A harsh shudder quaked through him as her pussy gave gentle twitches, urging him deeper. "That feel good, sweetheart?"

"It's amazing," she assured him as she laced her arms around his back and held him to her. Her soft skin melded into his rough edges. She took him all and smoothed out the pieces he'd wished he could rid himself of. She seemed to want them.

Unable to help himself, he pressed deeper, lost his rhythm. It was too much to try not to take all she offered. The spasms of her pussy cinched tight around him. Her body milked his release. It shot through him like wildfire unrestrained.

As he bathed her walls with hot cum, soaking her down with his seed, nonsensical words of promise and of love flew from his mouth. To his surprise, her body bore down so strongly on his that another climax overtook her. She seized, and just like before, he held her tight and coaxed her through it until she lay sated and calm against him.

All his.

———

As the sun struggled to burn away the last of the storm clouds, Callie knew it would be a sunrise she would never forget. A few of her brain cells tried to remind all of the others that she should be panicking, but she just didn't have the energy. Most of her simply didn't care that she was likely making the very same mistakes she'd made with Derrick. She was getting all wrapped up in Ford's world so she wouldn't be alone.

Only, that wasn't at all how she felt lying on his chest and letting him soothe her back to sleep. That sense of belonging she'd felt when he was deep inside of her hadn't vacated when he'd eased himself out of her. She still belonged right where she was.

Contentment was a heady sensation for a girl who'd never belonged anywhere.

"Where's my girl?" Ford's gruff tone sounded particularly sweet after all they'd shared.

She chuckled. "I'm right here."

"Part of you is, but where's your mind? I know you've got dozens of questions going on in there. Ask me."

"I was just thinking about how amazing that was." That wasn't a lie. It was the single most satisfying experience of her entire life. She'd had sex before, sure. But she'd obviously never made love before. Sex with Derrick was rare, obligatory, and highly unsatisfying. Always her on top which she hated. Just like everything else in his life, he didn't ever want to put forth much effort.

"It *was* amazing," Ford's vow wiped away all thoughts of Derrick's lackluster bedroom skills. "Are you hurting?" Concern tensed in his words.

"In all the best ways," she assured him. His responding growl was more than worth it.

"Now that I've had you like that, I'm going to be insatiable, baby. I'll want more of that constantly. Just promise you'll tell me if I get to be too much."

Grinning at that, she leaned up on her elbow so she could try to show him how truthful her statement was. She needed to look into his eyes. "Ford, you're never too much for me. I promise." His eyes narrowed, and something he wanted to say seemed to be right there on the tip of his tongue. "What?" she urged. He shook his head, and she couldn't stand it. "We promised never to keep things from each other."

"Fine." He drew her head back to his chest and cradled her tightly again. "Pretty sure I've already fallen in *attachment.*"

God, what a stupid word she'd used. So, he was on the verge of panicking as well it seemed. And that drew the truthfulness from her. Saving him was the most important thing in her world. "Me too."

"Really?"

"Yeah, but..."

"I know," he soothed. "It's been way too fast. I pushed too hard."

"No, you don't know because that's not it at all. It's just..." she shrugged, "maybe I don't know either." Defeat robbed her words of her earlier volume.

"Wanna keep not taking it slow and just let life have us, see where it spits us out?"

Spoken like a man who'd been spit out far too often. "What if...?" She tried to think of some way to explain her take on the world.

"What if what, sweetness? Just say it. Whatever it is."

"Okay, so, I've always thought that if you ask the universe for something, a lot of times it will give it to you. You just sort of have to see yourself having it and be aware when the sign comes so you don't miss it. What if we ask the universe for a sign about what we should do? That way we'll know for sure."

"What if we don't get some kind of sign?"

"We will. I promise."

"All right. I'm down. But fair warning, I'm not just going to picture us getting a sign. I'm going to picture exactly what I want to happen. I'm sick to death of letting life beat the crap out of me. I'm fighting back this time."

"What exactly do you want to happen?" She already knew but needed to hear him say it.

"I want what I've got in my hands right now."

And there it was hanging in the universe between them. She just had to figure out if this was what she wanted. A cowboy's wife? She didn't even know how to be that. Not that he'd out-and-out proposed. Nothing about being in his bed was getting her closer to being a successful photographer. And what if he lost interest the same way Derrick had?

As if he could somehow hear her thoughts, he urged, "I've got to get up and go check on the cattle and see what damage that storm did. Come with me. Bring your camera. You're bound to get some good shots this morning."

CHAPTER THIRTY

After Ford helped Callie up into his truck, he wondered what the hell kind of sign it was that she was looking for and how he might go about getting it to her. His mind was still addled from the awe-inspiring sex they'd had. He wasn't at the top of his game. Idiotic thoughts about paying the Harmon boys to paint one of the old billboard signs with *Ford loves Callie* filtered through his mind. *Dumbass. That's not what she meant, and you know it.*

So, he did the only thing he knew how to do at that moment while she was watching soggy prairie land slowly pass in his windshield. "You still haven't asked me all of them questions brewing in your head, sugar? Let's have it."

She grinned up at him, and he doubled down on his determination to find her some kind of sign. Maybe he would talk to the Harmon boys.

"I shouldn't ask anything I want to."

"You should, and I'm gonna answer."

"You're sure?" She slipped that lip back between her teeth, and he swore his cock awoke from its sated slumber at the sight.

"Ask," he ordered.

"Well, I mean how exactly did that happen with...you know...Meritt telling you she was pregnant? Had you been dating a while? And why did she do that? Did she tell you she lost the baby? I have a friend in LA who had a miscarriage, and they're so awful I can't imagine someone pretending to have one. That's just..." she shuddered, "And if she didn't tell you she lost it what happened when you found out she wasn't? Were you already married? Oh my gosh. It's just so manipulative and awful. I want to claw her eyeballs out, but I know that isn't nice."

When she finally drew a breath, Ford was chuckling at her. "You got any more up there you want to get out first, or should I start at the top?"

Heat bloomed across her face and out of the top of the T-shirt of his that she'd borrowed. She was draped in the thing, and he'd never seen anything more beautiful. Her hair was still mostly a mess from their lovemaking, and he loved that she didn't care. "Sorry." She cringed.

He shook his head. "There you go again. I'm gonna turn you over my knee the next time you do it, and that's a promise. You've got nothing to be sorry for. After everything I told you last night, you've got every right to ask all that and more. Just humored me at how quick they come outta you. You're so damn cute."

She rolled her eyes. "Are you sure you're not trying to get out of answering because you don't have to."

"I'm not trying to get out of anything. But after I get a full day's work pushed into a few hours, I will be trying to get back in your panties, fair warning."

"I'm not wearing any," she teased.

His growl of appreciation echoed through the cab of the truck. Hell, his brothers probably heard it from their houses. "All right, let's see here. Remember when we were up on the water tower and me telling you about how I ran hog wild for way too long?"

"I take it Meritt was a part of you sowing your wild oats, so to speak?"

"Pretty much. I was an idiot. If I could go back and beat the piss outta myself back then, I would. Or maybe what I really wish is that I could go back and beat some sense *into* myself." His head dropped under the weight of the shame.

Her hand found his, and she laced their fingers together. "We've all done things we regret. It's okay."

"It's not okay. I barely even knew her. I barely even remember sleeping with her. I was drunk. She probably was, too, but like I said I don't remember. It was in the back of my truck. I was twenty years old living high and mighty on the Holder name, just like all my cousins and my brothers. We fucking thought the world owed us. For what it's worth, I hated myself back then. I was rebelling against my daddy and all of my uncles. They kept telling me it was time to settle down. That I'd taken it too far. I told them they were all crazy, that I knew what I was doing." He shook his head and prayed that he could somehow show her that he wasn't that asshole anymore.

"It's okay. Keep going," she urged.

"I'm so fucking ashamed I'm not sure I can." The raw truth burned his throat.

"You don't have to."

"No, I want to answer all the questions. I'm determined. Anyway, so I hooked up with Meritt at the Renegade Rodeo that was in town that night. She'd started flirting with me during the first events and was throwing herself at me by the time they were handing out ribbons. I hope to god at some point I thought she was pretty, but I don't remember ever feeling that way. All I can see is what she turned into. It's colored all of the days before the bitter end."

"I feel like that about Derrick, too. I'm so angry at him. I resent all of the years I gave him, and it makes me hate even the occasional good things we probably had at some point. I think love and hate both distort vision. They're a stronger sense."

"You're so damn smart," he vowed. He'd never heard it put like that, but she was spot on. His cousin Meridian topped a hill in the distance on her horse, Kagan. Ford pointed to the silhouette she'd created. "That's a decent shot with the cattle at the bottom of the hill like that."

"Oh my gosh! That's an amazing shot. Can you stop for a second?"

Ford pressed the brake and let her take several dozen photos, but she caught him off guard when she turned the camera on him. "What are you taking my picture for?"

"Because you're gorgeous and amazing and I want to." He appreciated the compliments, but he doubted he was model worthy. "If I weren't prone to thinking otherwise, I'd say you might be sweet on me," he teased, trying to brush off her praise. But she just snapped another photo.

"You're really cute when you're embarrassed," she informed him.

"I do not look embarrassed."

She lowered the camera and stared him down. "I don't ever try to take pictures of how things look. The only thing I care about capturing is how they feel."

CHAPTER THIRTY-ONE

Ford longed to ask her if she could see in the photo screen how much he cared about her because that was how he felt. He kept that to himself and continued on with his confession. "There's only one part of that whole night I have a distinct memory of."

"When she told you she was on the pill," Callie stated succinctly.

"How'd you know?"

"It was the way you froze last night when I said the same thing. The hurt in your eyes. I'm so sor—"

"Do not," he growled.

She gave him a doleful smile. "But what if I want to be turned over your knee."

Holy fuck. That statement caused him to have to readjust his cock lest the zipper of his Wranglers leave permanent teeth marks. "Yeah well, we'll get to all of that later. I won't have you apologizing for anything that has to do with me and her. I don't want you to have anything to do with her at all. Ever." She'd gone as far that morning as to make sure he saw her popping a birth control pill out of one of those spin-dial pill packages and taking it with her coffee. He couldn't stand that she thought she had to prove herself to him. He wouldn't have it. "A few weeks later she showed up at my house pretending to be crying."

"She couldn't even muster real tears?" Callie gasped.

Ford huffed out, "You have to feel bad for something you're doing to be able to cry, I guess. Anyway, she said she was late and that I was the only guy she'd been with in months. I don't know why I never questioned it. I never even asked to see a pregnancy test. I told myself that it was a shitty thing to ask to see after what I thought I'd done to her."

"Do you know why you never questioned it now?"

"Yeah." He cleared his throat and tried to figure out how to explain where he'd been in his life all those years ago. "I think it's kinda what you were saying earlier about the universe giving us signs. I thought that was a sign that my old man was right. I was supposed to settle down. Part of me thought it was a well-deserved punishment, to tell you God's honest truth. Instead of pushing back against the kind of man my parents wanted me to be, I decided maybe I could become that man. Dad knocked Mama up with me a few months before they got married, and they'd made it work. I thought maybe that's what I needed to finally get my shit together. Plus, I was kinda excited to have a little plowboy I could teach to be a real cattle rancher."

"If you barely knew each other, why do you think she trapped you like that?"

Of all the things she'd asked, that one was going to be the most difficult to answer. There were so many things the Holder name stood for. The reason Meritt had chosen him was his least favorite reason. "Her daddy was hard on her," he tried but knew he was stalling. "She grew up in a double-wide in Odell out on the other side of the tracks. She went to Maxwell with me, but she's a couple of years younger. Her family never had much."

Callie squeezed his hand. "She did it for the money." She completed the puzzle with just the few pieces he'd handed her.

"Yeah, but see it's not like that exactly. It's not what she thought it was going to be, and that really pissed her off. I'm not saying I hurt for anything at all, but most of the money Holder Ranch makes goes right back into Holder Land and Cattle. It's not mine to spend. We all work together. We all take a nice salary, but cattle ranching is a crapshoot. In the years that we're hurting, we dip into the business accounts. But the years that turn a nice profit we put it back in the company. There's a season for everything, and I've seen 'em all."

"Oh, so you're saying that she got into the marriage thinking that she could have all of the money that all of you make, but most of that money isn't yours alone."

"Precisely. A couple days after she showed up on my front porch fake crying, I asked my daddy for my grandmother's ring and gave it to her. She got what she wanted. We were married three weeks after that."

"When did you figure out she wasn't really pregnant?"

"She told me she lost the baby a few weeks after we spent the weekend at our family's chalet in Telluride. Only, she never acted like she was hurting or sad or anything. I didn't know much about how all of that worked other than when I'd seen it happen to cows. It always kills me to see 'em go through it 'cause they hurt with it. It never made any sense to me that she was so flippant about it, but I kept my mouth shut. A few months after that, I asked if she wanted to try again. She said she didn't want kids anymore."

Callie shook her head. "I'm about to make you mad at me," she whispered.

"I could never be mad at you."

"Well, I am so sorry that she did that to you. I'm sorry you never had kids."

"I'm going to let that one stand with one reservation."

That got him a broken smile. "What's your reservation?"

"That you don't think I'm falling for you because I'd like to have kids someday."

"I don't think that at all, but I'm glad you told me that."

"I went from wanting to be the exact opposite man from my daddy to wanting to be just like him. I didn't get either."

"Did you ever think about being exactly who you're supposed to be?"

The girl wasn't lying about asking the tough questions. "I'm not sure I know who that is, but since she's gone I'm thinking maybe I can finally figure it out."

CHAPTER THIRTY-TWO

Callie always tried not to hate people, but she was willing to make an exception on Meritt's behalf. If she ever got the chance to tell Meritt exactly what she thought of her, she wouldn't be able to hold her tongue.

Ford parked the truck at a massive barn where there was a gathering of lots of other Holder men. Callie snapped a quick picture of the men in cowboy hats and Carhart jackets. Determination and resign seemed to be frozen in their pose.

She climbed out of the truck and watched Ford take his place in the pack of well-built cowboys. "We got water gaps down in at least three ponds. Have you checked the bred heifers we had out near the creek by your house? he asked his brother Jamie.

"I checked the ones I could find. I'm worried. I'm about to go out in a feed truck and see if I can round up the others."

"They're fine. Just got spooked last night," Ford reassured him.

Callie only understood bits and pieces of what they were saying, but she didn't care. Trying to remain unnoticed, she lifted her camera again and snapped a photo of Ford's face as he consoled his brother. He was so steady and sure. The entire group settled in his presence as if they sensed his calm as well.

She also snapped a quick pic of his gorgeous ass caught up in leather chaps. That would not be a difficult thing to look at every day.

Two men, much older than Ford, approached. Both were in mud-laden boots.

"Dad, Uncle Gentry, there's someone I want you to meet, " Ford gestured for her to join him in the group. A dozen questions immediately sprang into her mind. Were they to the meeting parents part yet? Well, he had met her father, but Abe wasn't really much of a parent. Certainly not like Barrett Holder was, anyway. "This is Callie Monroe, my girlfriend." Oh, okay then, apparently they were not only to the parent-meeting part, but they were also to the girlfriend part. That was a bit of a problem considering that Derrick still hadn't responded to her lengthy email, and none of Ford's brothers or cousins looked particularly pleased with his announcement.

Callie tried frantically to smooth her tangled hair before she accepted Mr. Holder's hand. "Um, it's so nice to meet you, sir." She stopped short of curtsying and called herself a dummy for even thinking about it. She repeated the gesture with his uncle. Both of the men gave her kind, fatherly smiles. Not something she'd ever gotten from her own father, but she knew what they looked like when they happened. Warm breath swirled in her lungs despite the cool, crisp morning.

Ford's father took in the infinite horizon. "You as well, sweetheart. I promise the ranch isn't usually in such a state. We'll have to get you back out here once we get it all cleaned up."

"Oh, it's still so beautiful. I mean," her head fell, "no one's at their best all the time, right?" She hoped he understood that she did not always look like she'd just spent a wild night in his son's bed.

Barrett Holder's chuckle was just a little lower than his son's. He turned to Ford. "Forgive me for saying so, son, but your taste in women has vastly improved since the last one you brought to meet me. Callie, dear, would you mind riding out with Ford and Jamie? We've got a few calves bogged in mud. They're all right for the time being, but there's enough it's going to take all hands."

"Yes, sir. I'm happy to help. I just...don't know how to ride a horse."

"Oh, I bet Ford'll be happy to teach you how to *ride,*" one of the cousins or maybe it was one of his brothers teased.

"Shut the fuck up, Maddox," Ford snapped, eliciting laughter from everyone else. "We can go out in the truck, baby. You can take some pictures of us pulling them out if you want. Nobody ever wants shots of real work on a ranch. Everybody wants the sunset pictures."

"Instead of the work that went into owning the land to take the sunset pictures on," she concluded for him. Suddenly, those sunrise pictures she'd wanted to add to her portfolio felt a little shallow.

All of the other cowboys, who'd just looked concerned that she was Ford's girlfriend, seemed to reassess her. It was almost as if she'd unlocked some old, secret safe of knowledge that they all shared. Okay, so maybe figuring out how to be a cowboy's wife wouldn't be quite as hard as she was thinking.

"Something like that." He brushed a kiss on her cheek.

Mr. Holder cleared his throat. "After that I need someone to check the mustangs."

"I'll do that, too," Ford volunteered. "Callie's wanting to see them."

"I'd appreciate it. Let's get the calves out of the mud, and then we'll start in on those water gaps."

"You and I can get the calves out, Dad. Let Jamie and Wes gather so we can make sure there aren't more out there bogged," Ford suggested. "Then we'll get the gaps."

"Sounds like a plan."

Callie wondered if Ford could see how like his father he was. How the entire ranch looked to him for how to fix a bad situation. Her heart swelled out its pride. He was hers. And unless she got some kind of sign that he shouldn't be, she was going to think about sticking around. Maybe.

Only she had no idea how to even ride a horse or how to do anything else on this massive ranch. She didn't even know where the gates were, or how to drive anywhere. Surely, she couldn't possibly fit in here for very long.

Self-doubt sliced through her, severing the reassurances she'd had a moment before. She was the girl who didn't really belong anywhere. At that thought, her phone rang in her pocket. Deeply regretting the

Britney Spears song she'd made her ringtone, which had seemed appropriate at the time she'd done it, she answered before the song could draw any more attention.

"Nana, hi." Crap. She was going to have to lie in front of Ford's daddy and all of his family. Racing back to his truck she heaved herself inside and shut the door. "Remember I told you Ford was picking me up super early this morning. I'm taking pictures on the ranch." There. None of that was untrue.

"I've been up since four. Your window was open and things in your room got damp from the rain. Please stop lying to me. Sneaking out is precisely something your—"

"Mother would do. Yeah, I know." Shit. How could she have forgotten to shut that window. Well, maybe her mother had felt trapped. Maybe that's why she'd rebelled just like Ford said he had. Callie honestly had no idea, but just then she wasn't going to sugarcoat things for her grandmother anymore. "Ford and I have decided to start dating while I'm here. He's such a good man. I might stay out here with him sometimes. Overnight," she spelled out exactly how this was going to work.

"I don't think that's appropriate. People will talk. It's sinful."

"I know this is going to be hard for you to hear, but I don't care."

"He'll break your heart. That's what all of those Holder boys do. He ran wild in his youth, and he's much too old for you."

"Pops is eight years older than you," Callie defied.

"Your Pops is a good man."

"So is Ford."

"If this doesn't work out, it will hurt both of you. Is that what you want?"

"Of course not." But there was no stopping it. It would be like trying to hold back the wind. If they were going to get hurt, there was nothing she could do but throw herself face first into the pain. Nothing about leaving Derrick had hurt her. Not really. It had scared her a little. She'd been scared of leaving the security and of being alone, but fears aren't enough to hold a relationship together. Eventually you run out of fear and you're left with nothingness. Nothing to cling to. Nothing to wish for. Just barren land that grows nothing. She cleared her throat. "I know your heart is in the right place, Nana. I know how much you love me, and that you're always trying to take care of me, but I'm going to see this through. If I get my heart broken then so be it."

"Calico Anna Monroe, you need to come home so we can discuss this."

For the first time since the night she'd climbed the water tower when she was a teenager, Callie openly defied her grandmother. "No."

"Pardon me?"

"No, I'm not coming back to your house. Not now."

"I've never heard you sound so much like Willow. That should say something to you."

"I have to make my own mistakes," choked from Callie.

"So, you admit he's a mistake then."

"No. Maybe. I don't know but I'm going to find out, and you're not going to stop me." God, that felt good. In that moment, Callie understood that she was going to have to make people listen to her on occasion. No matter who she upset or what the ramifications might be.

That particular time her grandmother, the woman who'd largely turned Callie into the woman she'd become, hung up on her. Well, that was fine.

Power surged through her, and she touched Derrick's name on her phone. She was going to be heard. He finally answered on the third ring. "It's four fucking o'clock in the morning. What do you want?"

Nice way to talk to the woman who'd devoted four years of her life to his dreams. "Did you get my email?"

"Yeah, I got it but that was...way too many words."

Some very odd, almost inhuman, seething noise managed its way out from between her clenched teeth. "We are breaking up."

"Yeah, okay. Whatever. Mom's expecting you at that gala this weekend, and I still need you to shoot our spot for Twitch. Whenever you get over whatever it is you're so pissed about, come back so we can get back to normal."

"NO! I am not coming back. I am not going to any more galas for your parents or shooting you playing video games ever again. We. Are. Over!"

"Right. Okay. I'm going back to bed. I told you I wasn't dealing with you when you're PMSing anymore." And then Derrick hung up on her as well.

If it wouldn't have potentially harmed Ford's truck and her phone, she swore she would've thrown it at the windshield. When she was able to see beyond her own rage, she noticed that every Holder male standing outside the truck was staring at her like she'd lost her mind.

Ford eased the driver's side door open. "You okay, baby?"

"Sorry. I was just really frustrated."

"Sounded kinda like you were drowning a cat. It's several miles to the bogged calves. You can tell me what got my girl so ornery while I drive."

CHAPTER THIRTY-THREE

That afternoon, Callie adjusted the focus of her camera on the impressive tug and tensing of Ford's bicep while he pulled baling wire with something called a fence stretcher. He was standing in the creek with muddy water up to his knees, but he didn't seem to mind. The job had to be done. Callie had never seen anyone work with such focus and intensity. She tried to capture that in her photos along with the times he turned to her and winked while he worked.

She swore a swarm of fireflies erupted from her belly every single time he did that. The warmth eased all of the problems that existed just outside the high gates of Holder Ranch. When she was in his presence on his ranch, the rest of the world was just too far away to worry over. Derrick and Nana and Nina Morales and everything else couldn't touch her there.

As if to mock her newfound security, her phone buzzed in her pocket. She lowered her camera on the strap around her neck and ground her teeth at the text from Derrick demanding an apology from her for awakening him so early in the morning.

You are such an asshole. She shoved the phone back in her pocket and debated texting him exactly what she thought of him or just ignoring him altogether. He'd ignored her for over a year. Maybe if she just stopped trying to get through to him, he'd fade away into whatever his next obsession would be. All she knew is that she would be photographing snowmen in hell before she'd apologize to him for anything ever again.

When Ford finished repairing the gaps, he ran a handkerchief over his face and told Callie to hop back up in the truck. "You're mighty bossy," she teased.

"And you like that, sugar."

She certainly couldn't argue that. She didn't just like it. She loved it. Loved that he was always looking out for her and had her best interests at heart. She loved it in his bed as well.

If she'd known where he was taking her, she wouldn't have bothered teasing him so they could've gotten there even faster. "Oh my gosh!" she gasped as he drove his truck along a fence line. The pounding of hooves at full gallop shook through the truck as he followed the mustangs. Their manes flew out behind them from their speed. "They're amazing."

While they were the very same kind of animal as the ranch horses Ford had shown her, you could tell they were different. Their wildness was alight in their eyes. None of them seemed to mind Ford's truck, but they also weren't going to stop to let him love on them the way Ford's horse, Chief, had done. It must've been incredible for them to still be mostly unrestrained but also to know they were safe.

"That one there foaled a few weeks back. We only keep mares here, but sometimes they send 'em to us already knocked up. The mares won't let us help them, of course, but she pulled through. She had me worried for a while."

Callie grinned at the small foal trying to keep up with his mama. "How long have you had them here?"

"Since I was a kid. The government has to control the overpopulation, so we stepped in to help." He stopped the truck and let her video the horses dancing in the field. "Hey, are you ever gonna tell me what got you up in arms this morning?"

"Nana said you were a sinful mistake." She rolled her eyes.

"I've been called worse I s'pose." He gave her thigh a reassuring squeeze. "Anything I can do to change her mind?"

"Marry me, I guess," burst from Callie's lips without her permission. She turned her frantic gaze to Ford wondering if the comment would bring on panic or revulsion. "Sorry. That just...came out."

"Get outta the truck." He didn't seem to be kidding. To emphasize his point his boots hit the ground a half second later.

Callie scrambled out of his truck. "I'm sorry. I was teasing."

He grasped her shoulders and pulled her into his body. "What did I tell you was going to happen if you kept apologizing when you didn't do anything wrong?"

The dread evaporated in the sanctuary of his embrace. She grinned against his chest. "I just was worried you would panic if I said that."

"That wasn't what I asked you." A fierce protectiveness coupled with his irritation and radiated from his arms to her back.

"That you'd turn me over your knee." She giggled.

But the firm smack of his hand on her ass both shocked and enlivened her. It certainly didn't hurt, but she couldn't believe he'd followed through. What she really hadn't expected was the rush of wet heat that dripped between her legs and the way her nipples tightened to stiff points of raw need. He took another three quick pops and then drew her pussy to his crotch and massaged away the sting. "You do not owe me an apology for anything. I want you to say whatever comes into your head anytime. You're not going to scare me or shock me. Just say it. Whatever it is. You understand that?"

She lifted her head, certain that the sizzle of heat apparent in his eyes was a reflection of the fire in her own. "I do understand that, but I don't understand how I loved what you just did so much."

"Then we'll talk about that, too." He continued to rub away the barely existent sting. "I get that there's a host of complications to the two of us, but I decided I don't care. If your nana hates me, then I'll figure out how to fix that. If you want to get married, say the words."

"Ford, you just got divorced. I like you a lot. I might even love you, but I'm not ready to get married."

"Then we'll go on living in sin. I'll buy Nana some flowers. Maybe that'll help."

"I don't really think she believes flowers are an appropriate sacrifice for sin."

"She want me to slaughter a calf or something because that's just a waste, and as I recall Jesus ain't too good with waste either."

Callie shook her head at him. "No slaughtering necessary, but maybe you could come over and show off your gentlemanly side."

"Now, that I can do. Does that mean I have to keep my hands off your ass because that's going to be a hardship. Not gonna lie."

Callie erupted in another round of giggles. "Just until Nana goes to bed."

"Fine, but you go to bed with me."

"She's not going to like that."

"She'll get over it."

It was almost dusk when Callie followed all of the cowboys back into the barn.

"You know, if your mama gets wind that I met Callie before she did, I'll never hear the end of it," Barrett goaded Ford.

He turned to Callie and raised his eyebrows in question as he scrubbed more mud than Callie had ever seen off of his hands. "Are you good with having dinner with my folks? After that, I want to take a look at that folder of yours."

"Is that what you're calling her snatch?" Maddox chuckled at his own joke until Uncle Gentry popped him on the back of the head.

"So help me, son, I am not too old to take a switch to your behind. I thought the army might beat some manners into you, but I swear they made you worse."

Callie covered her mouth to keep her giggle at bay. Ford just rolled his eyes. She debated having dinner with his parents. So far, she liked Mr. Holder very much, and she was sure Ford's mama was just as kind. But as her defiance had burned itself out, guilt had rolled in on the smoke. She felt badly for how she'd spoken to her grandmother that morning. She needed to apologize. "Could I take a raincheck on that? I need to talk to Nana. I feel kinda bad," she tried to explain without having to clue his family into everything going on.

"Sure, baby. We can do that. You can meet Mama in the morning."

Apparently, she was spending the night with Ford again. He was right. Nana was going to have to get over it.

Before they got in the shower, Ford settled at his kitchen table with the folder of bank documents. Callie wondered what he might be seeing there. Hopefully, something she'd missed.

"Are these the only records they have? Most everyone does everything online nowadays."

"I'm sure Pops prefers them this way."

Nodding at that, Ford flipped through the pages. "I don't see any local contractor's name anywhere, but they've been writing checks to your daddy an awful lot."

"It's supposed to be for things on the farm." Callie had no idea how much money it really took to take care of the land.

"They're still growing wheat and soybeans, right?" Callie nodded. "That ain't cheap, I s'pose. But they need to keep records of everything they pay him and what he says it's for. Something about all this isn't right. They don't have enough land for it to be costing this much to keep."

CHAPTER THIRTY-FOUR

Ford had pulled Callie into the shower with him both for the purposes of cleaning her up and then getting her filthy with his cum, but he'd reminisce on that later. Right now, he had to impress her grandparents.

"Are you ready?" Callie was more nervous than a June bug in July.

"Deep breaths for me, sugar. It's not your job to make your family happy. It's my job to make you happy, but that's a whole other thing. Nana will survive being pissed, and you will survive her anger. I promise. I know you don't like the way it feels, but she doesn't get to dictate your life. You gotta stop this killing yourself trying to keep other people from being ornery."

"Wow." She stared up at him like he might've been her hero. If he could just keep her looking up at him like that, then he was going to get her to stay. He could feel it. "No one's ever said anything like that to me before. I just...always felt like I was in trouble when I upset someone."

"I know. But what other people feel isn't up to you. Now, let's see if I can't win Nana over." He gestured to the front door. Callie filled her lungs with the wet-grass-laced air that surrounded them. "Good girl" he whispered and grabbed a handful of that lush ass to tide him over until this blessed dinner had been eaten.

She shot him a mischievous grin as she pulled the screen door open with a quick screech. Ford let it slap behind him as he stepped into the only place his baby had ever felt at home. The house was much smaller than any they had out on the ranch, but it was comfortable. Just like most homes in the area, they stepped right into the living room.

Mr. Simpkin beamed at Callie as he rose off of the sofa. "There's my girl." He pulled her into a warm embrace that made Ford appreciate the man even more. "Lord, you got your nana all wound up. I've been telling her to simmer down all day."

"Sorry, Pops. I'll try to talk to her."

Her grandfather shook Ford's hand and slapped him on the back. "Her nana just worries you know."

"Yes, sir. I understand that, but I want all of you to know that I have nothing but the best of intentions for Callie. I'll always take care of her."

Her grandfather nodded. "Suits me just fine, Mr. Holder, but you're gonna have to talk taller for Delphia."

"Please call me Ford. My daddy's Mr. Holder."

Before he could respond, Mrs. Simpkin was upon them.

Callie took an audible breath. "Nana, I'd like you to officially meet Ford Holder. He's pretty much the best guy I've ever met. Definite Disney prince status."

Ford chuckled at that analogy, but her grandmother's scowl only deepened.

"Yes, well, we do have to live in the real world, *Willow*."

Ford wondered if the woman was losing her memory or if that was some kind of dig at Callie.

She rolled her eyes. "Oh, that's not passive-aggressive at all, Nana."

Okay, so that was clearly supposed to be an insult. "Who's Willow?" Ford spoke between his teeth.

"My mother." Callie made no effort to hide her answer.

That was a low blow in his opinion. Jesus, this wasn't going to be easy, but nothing worth having ever was. "It's an honor to meet you officially, Mrs. Simpkin. I know we've seen each other around town, but thank you for having me in your home." His mama had raised him right. He knew what to say. Handing over a bouquet of wildflowers, he offered her his kindest smile. "Callie thought you might like these."

Delphia accepted the flowers. "Yes, well, Callie should know that I don't hold with wasting money."

Ford choked back a chuckle. "It's not a waste if you enjoy them, right?"

"Enjoyment fades just like flowers, Mr. Holder."

Callie and her grandfather both rolled their eyes at the same time.

"Del, I really do like him," Mr. Simpkins vowed. "Now, why don't we get to supper? I bet Ford's been out taking care of a wet ranch all day."

"Yes, sir. We fared okay, but the thunder spooked a few calves, and the rains took out three of our water gaps in the creeks."

"My barn roof held up. I was worried. Callie's daddy says we need a new one."

"I'd be happy to check it for you, sir. Give you my opinion on that."

"That'd suit me just fine. I like him a lot, Del. A whole lot."

If Mr. Simpkin wanted to talk shop all night, Ford was game. Maybe if he could keep her granddaddy liking him, her grandma would come around.

He took care to compliment every dish Mrs. Simpkin had prepared, including the store-bought rolls, and kept up with Mr. Simpkin's questions about the Holder cattle ranching operation.

"Mr. Holder," Delphia interrupted his explanation on spring shipping versus summer shipping.

Ford wiped his mouth with his napkin. "Yes, ma'am?"

"I think that tattoos are crass, not to mention sinful. Would you agree?"

Okay, so when he'd reached for the second helping of corn, she must've seen the Holder brand on his arm. "Well now, I'll be honest with ya. I can't reason how Jesus would care all that much about them. Seems to me he's got bigger bulls to move."

"Yes, well, Callie certainly doesn't have any."

Ford schooled his features and refused to shoot his baby the naughty smirk that threatened to erupt on his face. Nana obviously didn't know about that sexy-as-fuck little daisy chain of wildflowers that he loved to run his mouth over. He cleared his throat. "I wouldn't know that, now would I, Mrs. Simpkin?"

"I saw you two on the porch last night. Do you really expect me to believe that you are not practicing sexual immorality?"

"Nana!" Callie screeched. "We are having dinner. Could you stop interrogating him? You're being rude."

"I would like an answer to my question."

Ford debated telling her that he didn't have to practice sexual immorality. He was already pretty damned good at it. But he squared his shoulders, reminded himself that Nana was trying to take care of Callie the only way she knew how, and went on with his answer. "Ma'am, I hope you'll forgive me for saying this, because I am going to forgive you for being nosy. I know you love your granddaughter and want what's best for her, but the things that I share with Callie are between her and me. I would never disrespect her by allowing someone to pry into our relationship. And that is all I will ever say about what we share, so I'd appreciate it if you'd use better manners since I am a guest in your home. Your remarks and questions have been far from hospitable."

"He's right, Delphia. If Callie cares about him, then we should, too." Mr. Simpkin had his back.

"Thank you, sir. I do care about her very much."

Before any more could be said, Callie's father burst through the back door. The hair on Ford's arms rose. Callie instinctively scooted closer to him, and he longed to pull her into his lap until he could get her out of the house and away from the man who clearly frightened her. *You ever hurt her, motherfucker, it'll be the last thing you do.* Ford shot that warning with the daggers from his eyes.

Delphia stood and fixed Callie's father a plate of food. "Abe, we weren't expecting you tonight."

"I don't expect to need an invitation to eat with my own daughter," he came right back.

Callie wilted in her seat. "Uh, how was...work today?" She cringed as she asked. Ford made a mental note to ask her about that later.

"The same way it is every day working for a dumbass. I don't guess you'd know since you don't work." Abe Monroe purposefully slowed his words as if Callie was too stupid to understand him when he spoke in a normal cadence. Ford crushed the napkin in his hand.

"I do work. I work really hard, actually," Callie huffed.

"She's an amazing photographer. She got some great shots of the ranch today along with helping me fix water gaps and tend calves," Ford aimed that right between Abe Monroe's eyes.

He just rolled them. "Yeah, well, she's just like her mother so when she gets bored, she'll take off again."

Callie dug her nails into Ford's thigh. It took him a minute to pry them out of the denim to try to soothe her. "And what is it you do, Mr. Monroe?" As far as Ford knew the man never held a job down for any length of time.

"I'm a maintenance tech out at the power plant. My job is pretty much trying to keep idiots from killing us all. We got a service call this morning from some chick over in operations who couldn't figure out that for the system we designed to work, you have to plug it in. Then I went to McDonald's for lunch. I bet Windell a ten that they'd screw up the order. Should've bet him a twenty. But you know some of us have to actually work for a living, Holder. We weren't lucky enough to be born into the right family."

And Callie's nails were right back in Ford's thigh. "Are you seriously insinuating that Ford doesn't work for what he has?" she gasped.

Ford narrowed his eyes and used most of his strength to ease her grip. "He's not insinuating it, sugar. He's saying it outright, but I'm not offended. If I've learned anything in the last few years, it's that small minds and big mouths have a way of hooking up. That isn't as easy to fix as plugging something in." He did not want to be goaded into an argument with Abe Monroe, but Ford's temper was up. He downed a long sip of the iced tea in an effort to drown out the flare of anger.

"Uh," Callie's grandfather cleared his throat, "Ford, would you mind coming out with me to check that barn roof? I'd appreciate it."

He wasn't leaving Callie in there with her father, but as long as she was coming with them, he'd take the lifeline he'd been offered, if for no other reason than to keep himself from knocking Abe Monroe's teeth down his throat. "Yes, sir." He stood and guided Callie towards the door.

Much to Ford's irritation, Abe followed them out. *You can sack shit up in a pretty bag, but it still stinks.* Ford kept himself between his baby and her father as they walked.

"I don't know why you need his opinion. I've been telling you for two years the barn's gotta be reroofed," Abe smarted.

"Can't hurt to get a second opinion," Mr. Simpkin countered.

Ford prayed the roof was in good shape, but as he studied the rafters and climbed in the hayloft to get a closer look he knew his prayer had been denied. Abe looked far too pleased for anyone's good. Ford refused to let him win.

He hopped down from the fifth rung of the ladder. "I'll tell you, Mr. Simpkin, it does need to be replaced. I think it'd see you through another winter, but I'd feel better if we got it done, so my brothers and me will replace it. No charge."

"Ford, you don't have to do that," Callie's shock perforated her tone.

"I know I don't have to, baby. I want to. It's the neighborly thing to do, and it won't take us more than an afternoon. It's not a problem."

The relief on Mr. Simpkin's face and the ire on Abe's was all the payment Ford would ever need.

Callie's grandfather shook Ford's hand. "Thank you, son. I can't tell you how much I appreciate your generosity."

"We'll get it taken care of soon. You have a preference on what wood we use?"

"I don't have a preference, but please don't put yourself out on the cost."

"I'm happy to get it done for you. Like Abe here pointed out," Ford slapped Callie's father on the back much harder than was necessary, "we've been mighty blessed. We never mind helping a neighbor."

Abe Monroe was visibly seething. Ford laced his fingers through Callie's and made no effort to hide his smirk.

"You're absolutely amazing," she whispered. "Thank you so much." When she dropped his hand in exchange for wrapping her arms around him and burying her face in his chest, he decided that day just couldn't get any better.

. . .

"Can I say something not too kind?" Ford asked Callie as he drove her back to his house.

"Do you remember what you told me when you paddled my backside this morning?" She beamed at him.

"That I wanted you to say whatever you were thinking."

"Same goes, cowboy."

"Makes me harder than a railroad spike every time you call me that, by the way."

"Then I'll have to do it more." She snaked her hand over the bulge in his Wranglers making him growl. "What were you going to say?"

"I understand why your mama left."

Callie nodded. "Yeah, I get why she left Dad and even why she won't speak to Nana. I just wish I knew why she left me."

CHAPTER THIRTY-FIVE

A few weeks later, Callie sat on the worn leather sofa in Ford's living room and opened her laptop. He'd gone out to check on the calves that had been born that morning. Oddly, sitting there in his living room with a warm mug of coffee, he'd fixed for her before he left, Callie didn't mind being alone for the first time in her life. The sweeping green fields that surrounded the house settled her soul. Once again, she was certain nothing could touch her there. Holder Ranch was just too expansive, too safe, for anyone to be able to hurt her.

She popped the SD card out of her camera and pushed it into the computer. She wanted to see the pictures she'd taken of the brand new calves. An email alert popped up on her screen as she opened Photoshop.

Her heart thundered in her chest, and her throat went oddly dry. It was from Nina Morales's assistant. Callie shut the laptop. If she didn't read it, she wouldn't ever have to know what it said. She couldn't quite decide if she wanted to be rejected from the internship, which would be a pretty clear sign that maybe she should stay in Holder County and see what became of her and Ford, or if she wanted to be accepted which would prove that her photography didn't suck. Would that be a sign for leaving?

Her stomach soured at that thought. Was that a sign unto itself? She didn't know. Ugh. Why couldn't the universe send text messages about what she was supposed to do or something? That would be much more clear.

With shaking hands, she opened the screen once again. "You asked for a sign," she sighed out. Clicking on the email, relief immediately swept through her. It was only a request for the second portion of her portfolio. Apparently, Nina had liked the first set of images she'd sent. Okay, so maybe the universe just wasn't certain yet. It needed some more time to think. That was okay by her. More time with Ford was all she really wanted anyway. It wouldn't be all that odd for her to take several more days, heck maybe even a few weeks, to send more photos.

She shut down the email and went back to the calves. They were the cutest things she'd ever seen, and she loved watching their mamas bathe them and nurse them instinctively. Too bad human mamas didn't always know what their babies needed.

———

"Where's Callie this afternoon?" Uncle Gentry asked Ford as they checked the babes to make sure they were taking to nursing.

"Back at the house. I think she's working on the pictures she took this morning. I want her to get good and comfortable at my place, and I knew I wouldn't be out here long."

Gentry smiled at him. "I couldn't be happier for you, kiddo. I wish Maddox would find somebody that'd keep him settled the way you seem to be the last few days."

"He did, didn't he?" Ford reminded. "But he got scared and ran her off."

"Yeah, well, he's got more balls than brains. Always has. It's a dangerous combo."

Ford couldn't have said it better himself. "Are people talking about me taking up with Callie so soon after the divorce?" The question had been brewing in his head for too long for him not to ask someone.

"Would it bother you if they were?"

"I don't know yet. Maybe. I guess it depends on what they're saying."

"Cows are gonna shit. People are gonna talk. Most of it's worth about the same."

Ford chuckled. "That's God's honest truth, but I know this whole thing has to come off as...unusual."

Gentry shook his head at his nephew. "I 'spect what's got you worried is that the people saying it all happened too soon, or a dozen other things, might be right. But that ain't how things work. People have all of these ideas in their heads about how they think life oughta work. If they just follow all of their made-up rules, then nothing bad will happen. If you'll take a second and really think about it, you might notice that life dishes out good and bad with precious little regard to who followed the rules or not."

Ford certainly couldn't argue with that. "Can I ask you something else?"

"I wish you would. You always were my favorite nephew."

"You say that to all of us," Ford reminded his uncle as they watched one of the calves take to his hooves and give bucking a try. They tried not to laugh at the poor fellow when he collapsed back in the grass.

"Did you ever think that maybe whoever is about to ask my advice is my favorite at that moment?" Gentry teased.

"How'd you know I was going to ask for your advice?"

"Cattle ranchers don't much like having to ask for advice, so we do it real quiet like. You got quiet on me."

Shrugging at that, Ford went on with his question. "If I never loved Meritt, how do I know if I'm in love with Callie? It can't be as simple as it feeling different than it ever did with Meritt."

"How did Meritt make you feel when you spent time with her?"

"Like I was chained to rumbling railroad tracks, but I couldn't quite see the locomotive heading my way just yet."

"Apt description. And Callie?" Gentry grabbed a rag from his back pocket and mopped some fluid from one of the calf's heads that her mama had missed.

"I don't know. I just kinda feel better whenever I'm with her. I...like the way she sees things. It's different, ya know? Kind of refreshing. Most of the time she makes me feel like I'm sixteen again."

"Then you just answered your own question, didn't you? Everybody feels sixteen when they're falling in love. That's how it works. Even if you're forty-two."

"You think I'm too old for her? She's mighty young when it comes right down to it."

"You got something against her being young?"

"No. I just don't ever want her to resent me."

"Ford, son, there ain't ever a time or a place for love. It always seems to happen on accident. You weren't out looking for her sitting in Rusty's the day you signed them papers. God saw forth to put your ass on that barstool. You ever think maybe He's trying to make up for all the shit Meritt put you through?"

"Maybe, but that doesn't answer my question about me being too old." Ford braced for impact. In his experience, his Uncle Gentry would always shoot straight with him and never cut the edges. That's why he wanted his uncle to answer the question.

"It does, but you didn't listen. You don't get to decide. You don't get to change how old you are or how young she is. You just get to hang on and keep it good until the Lord calls you home. If it bothers people, let it bother 'em. Sometimes they need something to get all fired up about. Makes 'em feel better. Most of the time it ain't anything that means more than a hill of beans. Why don't you stop trying to figure out if you're breaking some kind of arbitrary rule and just fall in love with the girl? Stop trying to figure every single thing out and enjoy her."

"I am enjoying her," he vowed. "Enjoying her probably too damn much." That morning alone he'd snuck back into bed after turning the horses out to enjoy her a second time.

His uncle promptly doubled over laughing. "That ain't exactly what I meant, but good. Take it a day at a time. See what comes of it."

"Jamie keeps saying she's got leaving in her blood 'cause of what her mama did, but I've met her daddy. I don't blame the woman for leaving."

Gentry thought on that for a few minutes before he shook his head. "People don't leave because they've got something in their blood. They leave because there isn't anything left worth fighting for. When you walked in your house and found Meritt in bed with some shitlicker, that's when you threw her out. Your marriage had been over for years, but you had to see with your own eyes that there was nothing there to fight for. I 'spect her mama found herself in the same place after Callie was born. From the outside looking in, it seems she stuck around until Callie was up and toddling. She must've tried to fight for something with Abe. She was a whole lot younger than Callie at the time, too. Might be good to know if she was running to something or from it. No matter how flat you fry a pancake, it's always got two sides. Before you accept your brother's belief, it might do to hear Willow's side of the story."

Ford couldn't have agreed more, but according to Callie she hadn't seen or talked to her mama in almost ten years. "I'd be happy to hear her side of it, but she left Callie, too. Right after she graduated from high school and took a job at one of those mall photographers."

"Now, that I don't hold with, but there still has to be a reason. Plus, if anybody's got anything in their blood, your little brother has saving in his. He is a part-time firefighter after all. He's got a hero complex several counties wide. All of you boys do. He don't want to see you get hurt again. We can't mind that too much."

Knowing he had no business searching out Willow Simpkin Monroe and knowing that Gentry was right about Jamie, Ford resigned himself to his worry. He couldn't just slap a ring on Callie's finger. He didn't want to tie her down. He wanted her to choose him, to choose Holder Ranch as her home.

She occasionally still talked about that photographer out in New York. If that's what she really wanted, he'd never keep her from it, but it would kill him to watch her drive away. He moved on with his next order of business. "I told her I'd try to be old-fashioned about this, but that went out the window a while ago."

"Do you really think people back in the day didn't like fucking as much as you all do now?"

Ford cringed. "Do I want to continue this conversation with you?

Because if you're about to start talking about you and Aunt Leigh, I'm going to cut you off now."

Gentry shot him the customary Holder smirk. "I don't kiss and tell, boy. All I'm telling you is that there's nothing new about enjoying being with someone you love. Take it from a man who lived all of those good old days y'all talk about. The only thing good about 'em is that they're gone."

Before his uncle could start in on feeding cattle by throwing hay bales out the back of a pickup in the snow instead of having a feed truck, or having to drive cattle all the way to the train station to ship them, Ford came out with the thing that bothered him most of all. "She wants a sign."

"JD Metalworks in Tulsa runs that three for the price of two deal. I need a few new ones for the north side of the ranch. She wanting one with your names on it or something?"

Ford couldn't help but chuckle. "Not that kind of sign. She wants something from the universe that tells her she's 'supposed to stay with me."

"Humors me that you're standing there trying to figure out how to order the heavens around but also still wondering if you're really in love with her. I'll tell you this though—there is one problem with asking the universe to tell you what to do."

"What's that?"

"The way the universe tends to speak ain't in our native tongue."

CHAPTER THIRTY-SIX

"Oh my gosh, that's a lot of pickup trucks." It seemed every time Callie blinked, there were more parked out in front of Ford's parents' home.

"Yeah, I know. I'm sorry. The whole damn family wanted to meet you officially. You want some kind of safe word or something? If you say something like *I want to go ride a horse*, then I'll know you want me to get you the hell out of the fray."

"I will eventually learn to ride a horse if you promise I won't land on the ground, and you'll teach me."

Ford brushed a kiss on her cheek. "You don't have to learn to ride, baby. I was being serious. We need a safe word."

"Those are for sex." Callie giggled.

"Have I ever done anything in bed with you that you wanted to put a stop to? Because all you have to do is tell me to quit and I will."

"Never, and I don't need any kind of safe word for this either." She eyed the trucks again. "I don't think."

"They're all relatively harmless. Mama loves to cook, and she wants to get to know you better."

"The biscuits she made yesterday were outstanding. Do you think she'd teach me how cook like that?"

"Trust me, nothing would make her happier." He opened the truck door. "Let's get this over with."

Half of Callie was excited. The other half was mildly terrified. She'd never be able to remember all of their names. What if they didn't like her?

She stayed tucked close to Ford as he opened the screen door.

"Knock the shit off'a your boots before you come in my kitchen," Sara Holder called.

"I swear that's been her battle cry since I was four." Ford took care to wipe his relatively clean boots off outside.

Callie nodded. "I can't really blame her."

Ford introduced her to the two uncles she hadn't yet met, Wyn and Landon, and an aunt she didn't even know existed named Betsy. Then there was the slew of cousins and his baby sister. She tried her best to remember the cousins' names, but knew it was hopeless.

Thrill lit through her when she spied a collage of framed photographs up the stairwell that she'd missed when she'd been there before. "Is that you?" She pointed to a very young Ford missing both of his front teeth and holding up a blue ribbon.

Ford squeezed his eyes shut and cringed. "Yeah, that's me."

"Oh my gosh. You're adorable."

"I wouldn't go that far."

"What did you win the ribbon for?"

"Calf roping at a ranch rodeo. I got lucky that year. Wyatt's the competition roper in the family." He gestured to another cousin who lifted his hat to Callie. "And Jace rides broncs in the PRCA."

She slowly climbed the stairs and studied every single photograph until one hit her like a brick in the face. A panicked Ford was standing outside the Holder County courthouse with a red head on his arm dressed in a white gown.

Ford gripped the wedding photo in an effort to remove it from the display, but Callie caught his hand. "Don't," she whispered. "Try not to hate the things that turned you into the man you are."

"Why?" he grunted.

"Because I'm pretty sure I love the man you are."

Astonishment shimmered in his eyes. "Does that mean...?" He wrapped her up in his arms. "I love you too, baby. So damn much."

"Are we sure?" she couldn't help but ask.

"I know I am. Are you still waiting on a sign?"

"Not about loving you. I know I love you. I just need the universe to okay this, you know? Holder County is an awfully long way from New York." Callie wondered what more she needed to know. Maybe she really was a flighty as her mother.

Ford was such a good man. He loved her, and she loved him. What more did she need? She kept those thoughts to herself. She just needed a sign. Surely something major would happen and then she'd be sure that she was right where she was supposed to be. Nina Morales would decline her application and portfolio, or some other thing would happen to let her know that in Ford's strong arms was right where she was meant to stay.

Relief at the certainty that she knew what the future would hold washed over her. She just needed a sign.

Ford positioned himself beside her at the table full of his cousins and a few of his siblings.

Callie loved how protective he was of her, even though his family all seemed so great. They'd been nothing but welcoming, but she could feel the slight hesitation in the room surrounding her. Callie wondered if that's because she was somewhat of an outsider, or if they were worried she was going to hurt Ford. Wondering how to prove herself, she waited until everyone was seated and started eating to make sure she followed all of the manners her grandmother had instilled in her.

Ford's mother joined them at the table, and Callie offered her a kind grin. "This all looks delicious, Mrs. Holder."

"Thank you, honey. I didn't make half of it. That's the beauty of having such a big family. If everybody brings something, we have enough food for this ranch and the one next door. But eat up and tell me about the pictures you've been taking of the ranch. I'd love to see them."

"Really?" Shock resonated through Callie's question.

"Of course. Ford can't stop talking about how talented you are," Sara reassured her.

———

Callie promptly turned ten different shades of pink. Ford loved her in every color. "It's just people don't really ask to see stuff that I took on my own. I mean, other than Ford, but I'd love to show them to you. I got some great shots of Ford taking care of the sick calf yesterday. You can see how worried he is and how much better the calf felt when he was there." The way she beamed up at him kind of made him want to see about getting fitted for some kind of superhero cape. Yeah, he could definitely get used to that.

Jamie rolled his eyes. Their mother shot a glare at Jamie that had him trying to hide his next eye roll.

Then she went on and soothed the moment as she always did. "Well, I may be a little biased, but I do happen to think all of my young-gins are photogenic. Barrett and I tried to make the good-looking kind," she teased.

Callie's laughter eased Ford's momentary irritation with his brother.

But Jamie studied her. "How long have you been a photographer?"

"Pretty much ever since I could hold a camera. My grandfather gave me an old Polaroid when I was like five, and I've always wanted to have a camera in my hands since then. It's the only thing I've ever wanted to do. I sold my first image to my grandmother when I was eight. I spent all of the money on bubble gum, but it was the best gum I'd ever tasted." She wrinkled her nose and tucked closer to him. Ford found himself forgiving her nana for her judgmental comments. Callie just made him a better person. That was all there was to it.

"Do you do weddings and stuff like that?" Meridian, one of the few Holder female cousins, asked in a kinder tone than Jamie's.

"I've done lots of weddings, but I think I prefer more natural times in people's lives." A harsh swallow tensed her delicate neck, and she lowered her head. Ford set his fork on the side of his plate wondering what she was about to confess to his family. "My first formal training was with a photographer out in LA who specialized in maternity and boudoir shots. They're so sensual. I loved it. I love connecting women to their natural beauty. You don't have to be all made up in a wedding gown to be beautiful. It just feels more real, don't you think?" Then Callie's eyes widened with panic. "You don't have to answer that. I'm always asking weird things. Sorry."

Meridian, a prosecuting attorney by trade, looked perplexed. "I make my living asking tough questions, so no apologies. I get what you're saying. It's more about the life than the day of the wedding kind of thing. That's a cool philosophy. What made you stop working with that photographer?"

"She went out to the Serengeti to capture images of pregnancy and birth from her homeland. She lives in South Africa now. The images she posts online are breathtaking. Plus, she told me I was ready to go out on my own."

Ford sat up and took notice at that declaration. "I agree with her."

Callie shook her head. "I'm definitely not. You should see the shots Apio gets. I'm not even close to that good. I went back to pictures I hate taking after she left."

"Bullshit," he countered.

"Ford, mind your language at my table," his mama didn't even look up from her mashed potatoes to correct him. Callie shot him a mischievous grin at his scolding.

"I call 'em like I see 'em. You're an amazing photographer. You don't need more training. You need more trust in yourself and your skills."

Meridian decided to help him out. There was a reason she was one of his favorite cousins. "If I wanted to have boudoir shots done, could you do them at my house or do you need some kind of studio?"

Callie's fork clanged on her plate when it slipped from her grasp. "Is that a hypothetical question, or are you really interested?"

"I'm really interested. I think it'd be fun."

Sara Holder chuckled to herself. "I wouldn't let your daddy know you're doing that."

Meridian smirked. "Oh come on, Aunt Sara, sometimes it's fun to make that vein in Daddy's neck stand out. I've done nothing but work lately. I deserve some fun."

"Well, I do like what Callie said about connecting women to their beauty. That's a calling, and you ought to answer the phone when it's ringing."

"Thank you," Callie sounded flattered, "I can take them at your house or out on the ranch if there's somewhere private. I can make anywhere work. I already have a ton of backgrounds in mind for when I eventually open my studio, but that's a long, long way away."

"Why?" Ford demanded.

She turned to stare at him like he was shoving the mashed potatoes in his ears or something. "I still have a lot of training to do. There's so much I haven't learned. I have to know everything before I start. Besides, I don't have the upfront money or a location."

"Why not do it in town? There's four or five vacant buildings near the square."

Now, Jamie looked at him like he clearly didn't have anything under his cowboy hat but hair. "Do you really think the commissioner is gonna let her open up a studio taking pictures like that in Holder County?"

Callie defended the idea, but Ford knew it was in defense of him and not herself. "I wouldn't actually put that on the door or anything, but I still can't open a studio here." She turned back to Ford. "I don't have enough experience. I love that you think I'm that talented, though. That's so sweet."

"I don't think it. I know it," he vowed.

Every female seated at the table all shook their heads at him at the same time. He offered them a collective eye roll. Fine, he'd shut up about it for now, but come hell or high water, he was going to convince Callie that she was good enough to stand on her own two feet. He'd just really love to be the guy holding her hand while she did it.

CHAPTER THIRTY-SEVEN

Out of guilt mostly, Callie had stayed at her grandparents' the night after Ford and his brothers had finished the work on the roof. She hadn't been able to sleep without him beside her. She'd missed those arms, and that chest, and the quiet contented sound of his light snores.

The space between her legs was feeling shockingly vacant, since that was the first night in weeks she'd gone to bed without being with him. She hadn't woken up with that delicious rubbed sensation from his force. She didn't care for the lonely, empty feeling.

Her grandmother tapped on her partially opened bedroom door. "Peace offering." She held up two steaming mugs of coffee.

Overwhelmed with thankfulness, Callie sat up in her bed. "Thank you."

"I think maybe we should talk." Nana joined her on the bed. Callie drew her legs up to her chest. The unease that had existed between them resurrected itself at those fateful words.

"About what?" She hated how childlike she sounded. She was a grown woman for heaven's sake. At some point the fear of disappointing someone was going to get old. Surely.

"Ford."

Clearly, Nana was going to play this close to the apron so to speak.

"What about him?" Now, she just sounded like a surly teen.

"Where do you two see this relationship going?"

Wouldn't her whole life be so much less complicated if she had an answer for that question? "We're very much in love, but beyond that we haven't discussed all that much. I'm good with just love for right now. I don't need more than that."

"What about Derrick?"

"I have made it perfectly clear both to Derrick and to you that we broke up." At least now she sounded her age. Easing into a more adult-like posture, Callie sipped her coffee.

"Yes, well, two years ago you swore you were in love with him, and you said that was enough for you. You didn't need more than that then either. Now, it seems you do. Don't you see how you're repeating your mother's destructive habits?"

"Uh, my mom got pregnant with me when she was nineteen. How does that have anything to do with my patterns? Which are not actually patterns by the way. It's normal to have more than one relationship. Sometimes things don't work out."

"What makes you think things will work out with Ford? Things didn't work out with him and Meritt." Disdain dripped off of every word her grandmother voiced.

"Meritt is legitimately an awful human being, Nana. Like basically despicable. She tricked him into marrying her."

"If Ford hadn't been promiscuous with her, he wouldn't have been able to be tricked, which is what I wanted to talk to you about. There is a time and a place for everything."

Oh, here it came. Callie had received the life seasons lecture every summer from the age of fourteen on. Nothing more than kissing before marriage. Sex after the ceremony. Blah, blah, blah. Clearly her grandmother had no idea what it was like to be with a man with Ford's supreme...talents. With that wicked thought, Callie set her coffee mug on the bedside table. "Are you really telling me that you and Pops never had sex before you were married? That things never got out of hand. You never had...urges." Truthfully, the thought of her grandparents having *urges* was disconcerting to say the least, but she was determined to make her point.

"Well, I..." Nana grasped for words.

"Ah hah! No lying. Remember, lying is a sin."

"I've not said anything," she insisted.

"It's all in what you didn't say," Callie exulted. "Now, thank you very much for my lecture. I'd really like it if we could spend some time together that didn't include you trying to scare me away from Ford."

"I'm trying to keep you from making the same mistakes I made, Calico."

"Even when you use my full name it's still not going to keep me from being with him." Defiance felt awfully, awfully good.

———

By mid-morning, Ford was so restless, his brothers had begged him to go pick Callie up so he'd calm the fuck down.

Her grandpa had made a few comments about missing her, so Ford tried not to complain about her staying with them the night before. Callie wanted to make everyone happy. It was a noble goal even if it was impossible.

Sleeping in a cold bed didn't suit him. He parked the truck in her grandparents' front yard and headed to the door. Callie flew out and raced into his arms before his boots ever hit the porch. Now that suited him just fine.

He lifted her off of the ground and spun her around in his arms. Apparently, he was that guy now. He'd been a cynic most of his life, and here he was spinning a girl fourteen years younger than him around like he'd never been broken. Like he actually believed in love at first sight. Like he really was back in high school. Like he was an idiot.

The thrill in her eyes when he set her back on the ground made it more than worth it. He sank his lips into hers and drank from her like she really was his fountain of youth. "Missed you," grunted from between his teeth when he lifted his head and then returned his lips to hers.

She grinned against the kiss making it even better. "I missed you too," she hummed.

He finally allowed her to breathe. "You're not staying over here anymore. I want you in my bed." When he finally got a visual inventory of her, he noted the hint of a lacy bra tucked between the few open buttons at the top of the denim shirt she was wearing. Clearly, she was trying to kill him.

"I see me being away has brought out your bossy side."

He studied her. "You still like that?"

"Most definitely."

"Good. I'm too old to change my ways."

She rolled her eyes. "Would you stop saying you're old? It's getting on my nerves. We're a sunrise, remember? It doesn't matter how old we are."

Ford made a mental note to keep his mouth shut about it. "I remember. Are you ready to go?"

"I need to grab a few of my tripods for the shoot with Meridian, but then I'm ready."

"Then let's get. My family says they can't stand me anymore when you're not around."

"Do you boss them around too?" she teased. Ford laced their fingers together trying to quell the constant itch that occurred when he wasn't in contact with her.

"Yeah, but in a different way. Mostly I'm just an ass."

"Well, we can't have that. Maybe I shouldn't be away from you anymore."

"That's precisely what I'm saying."

While Ford balanced two cases of camera equipment and a box of the clothes she'd brought with her from California, her father showed up. A knot of irritation cinched in Ford's gut. When Callie tucked herself closer to him, he doubled down on his loathing of her father.

"So, now you're moving out?" Abe sniped.

Callie considered the question long enough to make Ford hopeful, but ultimately he was disappointed. "No, *Dad*, I'm not moving out. This is just some camera equipment for a shoot I'm doing." She injected disdain into every word of her reply.

"Guess who called me last night?" her father matched her defiant tone.

"Who?" She continued to gather random items from the living room and added them to the stack in Ford's arms.

"Derrick."

That stopped her in her tracks. "How did you talk to Derrick? He doesn't even have the number here." Her father's nasty smirk noted his lie, but he seemed to love that he'd gotten a rile out of her. Bastard. "I just thought someone should remind you he does still exist," Abe sneered.

"I'm well aware of his existence. I just don't care. Let's go," Callie urged.

"After you, sweetheart," Ford shot one last *try anything and I'll shove my right boot so far up your ass you'll spit manure* look at her father before he followed her out the door. But while he was staring her daddy down, Abe's phone buzzed in his pocket. When he lifted it out, Ford got a quick glimpse of the caller's name—Willow.

He burned a path to his truck. Callie deserved to know that her parents were talking, but it killed him that this might hurt her. God, he never wanted to hurt her. But her parents seemed damned and determined to, so his job was to shield the blows by taking them on himself. He'd always be there to hold her if she needed to fall apart. He'd sworn he'd never keep anything from her, and he had no intention of starting now.

He set the equipment and the box in the back of his truck and joined her in the cab. She was balled up in the seat with both her arms and legs crossed like she wasn't allowed to take up too much earthly space.

Ford held out his hand. She grinned and unfurled so she could lace their fingers together.

"I need to ask you something, baby."

Her face fell. "What?"

"Do your parents still talk? Or does your daddy know someone else named Willow maybe?"

"What?!" she gasped. "No. I mean, I don't think they do, and how many people in this world are named Willow?"

"I'll give you it's not a name like Bob Smith, but I'm sure there are other Willows."

"Yeah, but not that he was married to. Wait—how do you know they're talking?"

"I saw his phone screen when she called just before we were leaving."

Utter heartbreak was laced in her breath and betrayal-soaked tears filled her eyes. They shattered what was left of Ford's heart. "So, she'll call him but not me." Her tone was haunted now. He'd never heard her sound this way.

"Come here, sweetheart," he whispered. He lifted her into his lap. But after a quick moment of accepting his comfort, she wiggled out of his embrace.

"I want to leave. Please."

She's got leaving in her blood. Jamie's warning pounded against Ford's skull, and he hated himself for hearing that over her sadness. Where had that even come from?

"I'll take you anywhere you want to go."

"I want to go to the ranch. Please. I just want to be behind those gates."

And that was music to his soul. She didn't want to run away. She wanted to run *to* him. He was going to make this work. He could feel it.

Why the hell was her mother phoning her dad? To Callie's knowledge, they hadn't spoken in years. But maybe she was wrong. No, obviously she was wrong. She rolled her eyes. She'd tried phoning her mother for a few years after Willow had moved her to California. Finally, she'd just given up. The pain was all-consuming. And this latest betrayal pricked at the vacant hole in her chest that nothing had ever been able to soothe. Nothing until she'd met Ford.

As he drove them under one of the *Holder Ranch Est. 1889* signs, a little of the knife-twisting pain eased. She was safe here. Her parents couldn't hurt her here. No one could.

"And what was my father playing at, telling me he talked to Derrick?" erupted from her as they made the approach towards Ford's home.

He squeezed her thigh. "I 'spect he wanted this reaction from you."

"He's such a jerk," she seethed.

"Come on, now. You can do better than that. Where's my country girl?"

That, at least, made her grin. She tried to remember a few of the names she'd heard him and his brothers use when they were discussing someone they didn't like. "He's a shitlicker, isn't he?"

"Of the highest caliber, baby doll."

"He was a shitty dad, I know that. What kind of man just lies to his kids to purposefully provoke them? That's just mean."

"He is that. But my daddy has a saying—never corner anything meaner than you. I want you to stay out of Abe's path. He's pissed about me replacing that barn roof. I don't want him taking out his irritation on you. If he wants to talk to somebody about it, he can come find me."

"When I was a little girl, he generally took his irritation out on me." She made that admittance mostly under her breath. She'd so carefully packed up all of those days and buried them deep. She didn't want to unpack them, and yet, they'd forced their way out of her mouth.

Ford gripped the steering wheel until his knuckles were pale. "Callie, baby, I'm so sorry for what you went through, but I need you not to tell me that. I'll kill him. You understand that. I'd put anyone in the ground who dared lay a hand on you."

Nothing about his demeanor said he was exaggerating. Callie laid her hand on top of his trying to ease his brutal grip. "I'm fine. He's an ass. He's the splinter remember. He'll never be more than that. I don't want to talk about him anymore anyway."

"No. Dammit, I shouldn't have said that. I want you to tell me anything you need to. I just..."

"Never want anything to hurt me?"

"Exactly."

"I love that and you. But I really do not want to talk about my father or my mother or anything at all. I want to get lost with you."

Ford grinned at her. "Now that I can do."

He made quick work of unloading her things into the living room and then grabbed a few quilts, a thermos full of coffee, and her hand.

"Where are we going?" Her heart warmed at his preparations and that warmth brought the smile back to her face.

"We're getting lost, baby doll. If I have my way, no one will be able to find us for several days, so I better grab some more provisions."

"Are you serious?" Nothing in the world sounded as good as that to Callie.

Ford planted a kiss on her forehead. "If that's what you need, that's what we'll do. My brothers would try to whip my ass when I get back for taking off on them with work to do though. Notice I said try." He winked at her.

Disappointment sank through her, but she didn't want to let him see it. He was so good at reading her. "I'll take whatever time I can get. I don't want your brothers to be upset with you."

"Let's see where the day takes us. It's a little chilly to sleep outside at night anyway. No one's going to bother us here, either." He gestured to his home.

Callie glanced around and asked the question she'd been wondering since her first morning there. "I like your house just the way it is, but if you want, I could help you pick out furniture to replace what Meritt took."

Ford nodded. "I've been meaning to get to Tulsa to get new stuff, but I'm shit at decorating. The only things I know I want are a recliner and a bigger TV, which I get probably isn't anything you'd want. If you'd help, that'd be great."

"What makes you think I don't want to cuddle up with you in a big recliner while we watch the Pokes cream the Sooners?"

The utter delight in his eyes made her vow to do that very thing with him at some point. "Pokes have only won Bedlam twice in the last decade."

"I'm telling the universe what I want, remember? Plus, I think Gleeson's going to put on a show with the offensive line in coming years. He was a good hire, and Sanders just needs to get a little more experience under his helmet, so to speak. Next year, we're going to dominate."

"Marry me," he blurted out.

All of the vital organs in Callie's body seemed to freeze at that demand. "What?"

"I'm serious. You're perfect. Just marry me now."

"Ford, I...can't do that."

"Why?"

Oh my god, he was serious. Her mouth gaped open, and it took her entirely too long to remember how to bring her lower jaw back in contact with her upper.

"Wait, never mind," he shook his head, "let me get you a ring first."

"Ford!"

"What?"

"I'm not...ready to get married. I don't think. Maybe. I...don't even...I just...oh my gosh. Are you sure you're serious?"

"Maybe." He shrugged.

"Can we go back to before you proposed because I'm a Pokes fan?"

He chuckled and drew her into his arms, which admittedly made it much more difficult to turn down his semi-proposal. "I know that wasn't a real proposal. I guess I just wanted to see what you'd say. If you'd said yes, I would've driven you out to Tulsa to pick out a ring now, but I don't ever want you to do anything before you're ready. And I don't want to marry you because you like the greatest football team in the history of the sport. I want to because I love you."

"I love you, too. I know I keep saying not to take things slow anymore, but maybe let's just slow down on this point if you don't mind."

"Done. You ready to go get lost?"

Relief washed over Callie with such force it made her dizzy. She clung to him until all of her bodily functions returned to their jobs.

———

Okay, so Ford didn't know how not to go after what he wanted. He thought he'd recovered from that slip fairly well. Maybe. If he could just keep his mouth shut and work her into the idea slowly, this would still work. He just had to keep all thoughts of marriage to himself. But god, he wanted it.

He wanted her safe in his bed for the rest of his life. Wanted to see her beautiful body swollen full of his babies. Wanted to be there for every single thing that life would inevitably hurl at them. He just wanted her.

"Whose house is that?" she asked as he drove them slowly across the ranch in a different direction than he'd taken her before. He was determined to let her see all of its glory.

"That's Jamie's house. He wanted the view from the ridge and wanted to be close to the gates in case he gets a call in the middle of the night, so he built it here. That's Charlie Tilson's Chevy parked out in front though."

"Why would he get a call in the middle of the night?"

Ford genuinely loved how curious she was about all things. "He's not just a cattle rancher. He also works for the Holder County Fire Department."

"Oh wow. And who is Charlie Tilson?"

"Friend of his. They've been friends since they were kids actually. Her daddy's the preacher of the Methodist church. He don't much like us, but that never kept the two of 'em from being friends."

"So, Charlie is a girl?" She grinned at that.

"Short for Charlotte. Sorry, I forget you didn't come up here."

"I always used to wish I did. I always felt like an outsider when I visited. Like I was the only person in the whole county who didn't get the inside jokes or something. Plus, it seemed idyllic, until my dad walked in the room anyway."

She'd been fairly adamant that she did not want to discuss her father anymore, so Ford took a long moment to consider, afraid of sticking his boot in his mouth again. "It was a pretty good place to come up, but it had its issues, too. I don't guess anywhere is perfect."

She gave him that grin that eased the jagged edges of their relationship that he'd rubbed raw earlier. "Right here, right now it feels pretty perfect."

"Just have to keep you thinking that way, sugar."

"So, why doesn't Charlie's daddy like you?" Her teeth sank into those perpetually pouty lips, and Ford pressed the truck faster. He needed to get her where they were going so he could get her in the back of his truck and make up for his missteps.

"He thinks the Holder boys run too wild too often. He ain't necessarily wrong. He also isn't the only person with that opinion. Your daddy alluded to it the other night. There's a fair amount of resentment about my family. We've tried to improve our image since my great-granddaddy passed. He encouraged the wrong things both from my grandfather, my dad, all of my uncles, and then us, too. Always wanted his boys to think they were the shit. Now my daddy's in charge of damage control, I guess. Great-granddaddy Holder was destructive."

Callie visibly considered that. "Maybe that's why Nana keeps trying to warn me off."

"Maybe." But Ford doubted his family's reputation was all there was to it though.

"Is that why you replaced the barn roof?" Disappointment tugged at her tone.

Ford laid her hand on his thigh and squeezed it. "No, baby. That was because it was the right thing to do to help a neighbor out, especially the neighbor who helped bring up my girl."

She grinned at that. "Is it bad that I kind of wish my dad had been wrong? It's like I've always wanted to have him dead to rights on something. I feel like he always skates by, never getting called on all the things he does wrong."

"Nothing wrong with wanting people who did you wrong to pay, but sometimes the peace that comes from just keeping them out of your life is worth more than the payoff from seeing them suffer."

"Is that how you feel about Meritt?"

"Most definitely."

She asked more questions as they drove, and he told her everything he knew about his ranch. Whose families had lived where and when they'd lived there, a few stories his daddy and uncles reveled in, and then a few of the stunts he and his brothers pulled back in their day. "One time when I was about ten or eleven, Jamie and I had the great idea that him and Wes and Dalton could all sit in the loader on the tractor, and I could lift them up on the barn roof. The plan was that they could run to the other side and jump into the hay bales. There ain't much reasoning with a ten-year-old who just learned to drive a tractor. Anyway, I almost drove them into the side of the barn, which woulda torn up the tractor and my brothers, before my Uncle Wyn caught us." He shook his head at the memory.

By the time he pulled up to the creek bed on the far side of Holder Ranch, she was beaming. "I love how much you love this land and your family."

"I never wanted to be anything other than a cattle rancher. I'm so damn lucky to be doing what I do, but I didn't think that six weeks ago. All of that came from you."

"Wow," she whispered. "Thank you for saying that."

"Thank you for being here with me."

"What are we going to do here in this extremely romantic spot?"

Ford had hoped she'd think the views from the creek were as pretty as he did. Pleased, he opened his door. "I'm going to spread those quilts out in the back and then I'm going to try to talk you into letting me get to second base."

Her infectious laughter mended so many of his ragged edges. "I might let you get further than that if you're lucky."

He gave her the growl she was after. "Oh honey, I'm about to get that way. Trust me."

CHAPTER THIRTY-NINE

Callie let Ford lift her onto the tailgate beside him. It was so easy to be transported to the past here where time seemed to have left no mark. She imagined that the bed of this particular creek, tucked away in the cypress trees, had looked the same way ten years ago or maybe even a hundred years ago. It was unfathomable to her that this ranch had been right here for even longer than that. The permanence of it contented her much the way being near Ford always did.

"Where's my girl?" he whispered.

"I was just thinking about how long your family has owned this land. I don't know if it would be reassuring to have grown up here, knowing that right where you stood would still be yours for another hundred years, or if it would be intimidating to have the whole county relying on you."

"It's both," he assured her. "We try to be everything to everyone, and that ain't easy. But not having to worry about how you'll get along in the world is worth more than every dollar we have in the bank. The peace here—I wouldn't trade it, you know?"

She cuddled against him. "I do know. That's how I feel when you hold me."

"Yeah?" He still didn't fully understand what he did to her. Maybe it was high time she showed him.

"Definitely."

"Then let me do it right, sugar." He scooted back in the bed, leaned up against the back window, and beckoned her.

He wasn't going to have to ask her twice. She crawled to him as seductively as she could manage in the bed of a pickup.

Something about the way he held her in those massive capable hands and the way the water lapped at the shoreline, the way time existed in that moment just for the two of them, gave her not only contentment but confidence. No one knew where they were, and there was something she wanted so much she couldn't help but ask.

"Hey Ford," her voice was barely a whisper.

"Ask me, sugar bee," he coaxed.

"How did you know I wanted to ask something?"

"You get this little inquisitive glint in your eyes, and you get hesitant for a minute. Cutest thing I've ever seen. I love getting to answer your questions. So, ask me."

Callie debated exactly where to begin. The fantasy had formed slowly in her mind over the last few days until it had overtaken her ability to talk herself out of it. It had stirred in her dreams the night before when she'd been alone, strong and insistent. She'd awoken grinding against her mattress sweaty and wet with need, but he hadn't been there. The absence had only strengthened the desire to have him fulfill this particular fantasy.

Drawing a steadying breath, she swallowed down the tangle of nerves in her throat. "Do you ever...fantasize about us...about me, I mean?"

"I love where this is going. Hell yeah, I do. Most of them are filthy, so I hadn't brought too many up."

Pleased to hear that, she nodded against his substantial chest. "What if I wanted you to bring them up? What if I wanted to fulfill them?"

With one of his hungry grunts, he eased them to their sides so he could stare into her eyes. His intensity filled the air around them. She'd had sex with him so many times, but she wasn't sure anything had been as intimate as having this particular conversation.

He caressed her cheek and then tucked a wayward strand of hair behind her ear. "What is it you're needing from me, baby doll? What are you so afraid to ask for? You know I'll do anything you want. For fucksakes, I'm incapable of telling you no."

He really was, and that only made this more difficult somehow. "It's kind of scandalous maybe." Wishing he really could read her mind so she didn't necessarily have to speak this aloud, she paused and let the gentle breeze fill her lungs.

"I doubt you're going to shock me. Like I said, most of mine are pretty damn filthy. Say it. Whatever it is."

She couldn't look at him anymore. Not when she was about to ask for this particular thing. "What if you're appalled or something?"

His rough-hewn fingertips lifted her chin back up so she had nowhere to look but in his eyes. "How about if I swear to you it won't throw me? I'd say Scout's honor, but that seems like the wrong choice for this particular topic." He brushed a tender kiss on her lips and then took another, longer exploration of her mouth.

His ability to always put her at ease, even when she was at her most awkward, drew the confession from her in bits and pieces. "What if I had grown up here?" Her heart pounded out a frantic SOS in her throat, but the need kept her talking. "What if I'd been friends with Dalton or maybe Meridian in school so I'd gotten to hang out here on the ranch when I was younger? What if everything had been different?"

A harsh swallow contracted his throat as he stared her down.

Her words sank through him drowning him in unadulterated lust. She was only two years younger than Dalton and was the same age as his cousin. *If everything had been different* most certainly meant *what if Meritt had never existed.* "Keep going," rumbled from his chest. "Tell me." He ran his thumb along the delicate skin of her neck, watching as she debated so unnecessarily. "What if I was just eighteen?"

Holy fuck. He highly suspected she'd made herself legal in this particular fantasy so he wouldn't shut it down. As if he would be capable of turning her down on most anything. "It still would've been wrong," he forced the words from his ashen throat. Hell, he would've been in his early thirties. It would have been very wrong.

"I know, but it's just a fantasy, right? We could just pretend."

Holy mother of god she was killing him. He was going to hell just for the thoughts rapid-firing in his brain. There was no saving him now. "Pretend what exactly, honey?"

She ran her fingertips down his chest inflaming him at the barest touch. "What if I told you that I thought your brothers were great, but that I'd had a crush on you for a long time? That you made me feel things I didn't understand. That I needed you to help me understand."

The beast housed in his soul tore at the chains he tried to keep it dammed in. A half-starved growl rumbled from Ford's chest.

She kept going, stoking the flames of the inferno she'd ignited. The embers danced in her eyes. "What if I told you I hurt? That I need you to make it better?"

"Show me where you hurt, baby," he demanded, gruff and urgent. He'd deal with hell later. Satan could have his way with him when he was done. He was going to heaven first. Healing the wounds from her past was most certainly something he'd wished he could do. That might've been impossible, but giving her this, fulfilling this naughty little fantasy she had, well he sure as fuck could do that.

Her eyes closed, and a breath hitched from her lungs. She placed a small, timid hand on top of his and guided him to her pussy. She was fevered to the touch, even through her jeans. When she rocked against his seeking hand, he damn near lost his mind. Her eyes blinked open a moment later. "What if I told you that I didn't know how to touch a man, but that I spent all of my time imagining you teaching me to touch you?"

A rush of hunger tore through him, violently stripping away all notions of right and wrong, all precedence, every foundation he'd ever clung to. There was nothing left but her needy questions and his desperate answers. He was shamefully hard, making it impossible to try to turn this wicked game to a slightly tamer version. And her triumphant grin said she knew he was going to give this to her, to be this for her.

Somehow, she reached through all of the bullshit he'd endured and managed to resurrect both the man he'd thought he was supposed to be and the one he really was. She united him, aligned him, and inflamed him. He was woefully gone, and there was no coming back.

"Is that what you need, sweetheart? You need me to teach you how to be with a man?"

"No," she whispered. Her eyes were suddenly alight with truth. A coy grin turned up the corners of that beautiful mouth. "I need you to teach me how to be with a cowboy."

She rocked that cocktease body of hers against his own. He knew fulfilling her fantasies would be the single most satisfying thing he'd ever do. She palmed his painfully stiff erection, somehow managing hesitation and temerity. Perhaps a better actor than he was.

But he'd sure as hell make do. Slipping into a slightly younger and far less moral version of himself, he tucked her to him and cradled her head in the crook of his neck. Her hot breath taunted and teased his skin. "It feels so empty doesn't it, but it doesn't just hurt there does it, baby?" He dragged his rope-worn fingertips over the top swells of her breasts. She shuddered for him. Her body pitched as wild as a midwestern storm. "They're swollen aren't they. Sensitive for me?"

"Yes," whimpered from her deliciously.

"Let me see. Let me make it better." Keeping his eyes locked on hers, making certain they were both grounded in this moment of the fantasy, he slipped one button of her shirt through its loop watching the juxtaposition of her shiver under the heat of his gaze.

Another harsh grunt vaulted from his throat as he revealed her deliciously innocent white lace bra. Another button. Another pitch of her body. She was so needy for him he was going to lose what was left of his mind.

"Please, please," she urged. Her hands pawed at him like a kitten frantic for his affections.

"Let me enjoy this, sweet baby. I know it hurts." He knew his part. Hell, he'd been with more than one virgin. Girls who'd ponied up their cherry just to be one of his conquests had been the name of his game in his wild youth. That was yet another reason he'd deserved what Meritt had done.

He wondered momentarily if Callie had planned this. The white lacy bra protecting her from his roving hands was innocence personified. He parted the last button and eased her out of the shirt. "Let me see you, honey. Let me see that sweet little body you're needing me to take care of."

The wind rippled across the creek, splitting a shallow crevice in the water, and shook the leaves of the trees surrounding them. He pulled her closer, blocking her from the chill, protecting his baby always.

Restless waves of need continued to break over her body. She squirmed against him. Calling on skills he'd perfected decades before, he popped the back clasp of her bra with one hand. Her breasts spilled forward pulling the straps of the bra off of her shoulders. "Fucking love your tits," he groaned out pure truth. His taut control continued to slip gradually out of his grasp. "I wanna unload all over them. Mark them all for me."

Those dark brown eyes widened with a hunger all her own. "Then do it. Show me who I belong to."

"Not for your first time, baby." He traced his fingers over her diamond-hard nipples and then trailed them downward and teased at her navel. He took care to remind her of the particular fantasy he wasn't going to let her deny. "Once I know you're ready, I'm gonna ruin you for all other men. It won't be something you can wash away."

Another hungry moan was the answer to his warning. "Then get me ready," she urged.

"So impatient for me. Simmer down and let me take what's mine." He flung the bra away and spun his tongue over the turgid peek of her right breast and then the left. The wind taunted her wet flesh making her whimper. He drew her nipple into his mouth and soothed her while he closed his hand over her other breast, giving it equal attention.

Her nipple pulsed against his palm to the rhythm he'd finally been able to recognize as his own. The erotic harmony they created together was the siren call neither of them seemed able to resist.

He understood what she was trying to recreate. He got that she needed to be the girl in the back of his truck because she was the only one he'd ever had back there that would ever matter. If she wanted a moment to recreate the past they would never have, then by the might of his own two hands he would build it for her.

Her head fell back pressing her tit deeper into his mouth. Ragged possession scorched his blood. Ford grabbed another quilt from beside him and draped it over her. Only he would see her bare. He would keep her warm. He would own her so thoroughly she wouldn't think of leaving ever again.

"Let me feel how wet you get for me, sweet baby? Your body already knows how to beg for me, doesn't it?" Popping the clasp on her jeans, he stroked his fingertips over the patch of soaked satin. The fabric amplified his touch making her shiver restlessly. He continued to taunt the overly-sensitized skin of her mound. Lust tore through him at the feel of just how aroused she was.

"Ford, please." She clawed at his back so desperate for this he had no choice but to comply.

"I'm trying to go easy on you," he warned. "But you're not gonna let me, are you? You're too damn beautiful, too damn needy for me. I'm gonna have to fuck you so hard I leave marks when I take that cherry, aren't I?"

CHAPTER FORTY

Pleasure speared through Callie at his question. She could locate no words to reassure him that being left with marks would only scratch the surface of this particular fantasy. Until she'd met and fallen for Ford Holder, she would've thought badly of any kind of objectification. She certainly would never have admitted, even to herself, that she longed for it. But that was before his bruising reverence, his brutal adoration of her when they made love. Now, she wanted to be used. She needed to be his possession. She needed him to grant her this the very same way he needed to own and accept that demanding facet of himself.

Pretending to be a virgin was only one element. She required his dominance more than she required the next pounding beat of her heart. She longed for there never to have been anyone else but the two of them, even if only in her fantasies. And it had all gotten tangled up in her mind together in a storm of forbidden pleasure.

Praying he would understand what she wasn't certain how to voice, she begged, "Please, please. That's exactly what I want. I need to be yours. I need every part of you." She most especially needed all of the parts Meritt hadn't wanted.

He stared down at her half-naked in the bed of his truck like he was afraid she was just a figment of his imagination. Terrified that she would float away on the wind if he didn't hold on tightly enough. She tracked her hands up his thighs again and palmed the thick, tantalizing promise of his erection. "Please," she whispered and battled the shame over her own needs.

He gently lifted her head before she'd realized she lowered it. "Mean what you say, baby." That raw carnality she loved rode hard in his voice. "You want my marks? You want me to cover you with my cum? Are you fucking saying that I can be rough with you, that that's what you want?" He trembled. Callie knew it was with the need to own the man he'd fought for so long to keep from being. Another round of sticky wet heat gathered between her thighs as her body begged for those very things on her behalf.

Her eyes closed under the weight of desire. "I don't just want them. I need them." Her breath hitched with the burning hunger. "Do you want to hear me beg because I will?"

"I'm gonna make you beg, but it won't be for this."

A dangerous flash of depravity flared in his eyes. Callie longed for him to lose control. "Fuck me," she purred. "Hard."

With frantic motions, he yanked her jeans and panties down her legs and then popped the snap on his well-worn Wranglers. The jangle of his belt buckle rang with warning. "Get up on your knees," he commanded.

Callie took her time, taunting his resolve, pushing Ford close to the edge of his control. She wanted to relish in every ounce of his hot-leaded determination. She stared up at him through her lashes and attempted to appear salaciously seductive. His wounded breath said she'd gotten her wish. He shoved his boxers down and freed his engorged cock. Her eyes traced down from his broad shoulders to his dangerously muscular torso. They followed the trail of dark blond hair that led to her prize. He was so thick, so full, so potent. A technicolor display of raw need that rose proudly out of the thatch of hair at his base. A pearlescent drop of need sat temptingly at his slit. She licked her lips.

"Do you see what you do to me?" he snarled.

She gave him a gentle nod.

"Make me so fucking hard for you I lose my goddamn mind."

"Then let me make it better this time."

"You hungry, naughty girl?"

"Yes." She reached for him, but he grabbed her wrist and held her arm away. She pouted for him, poking her bottom lip out for the full effect.

"You put those fingers between your pussy lips, get 'em nice and slick for me, and then show me the cream you make so good. You run that all over my cock, and then I'll let you taste us together."

That wasn't at all what Callie was expecting him to say. The shock only amplified the need pulsing between them. Her nipples were drawn to stiff peaks of painful hunger. She traced her fingertips around them trying to soothe the ache. That drew a guttural growl from Ford. She continued on her trek until she ran her fingers back and forth between the swollen lips of her pussy.

"Damn, that's pretty, baby girl." His gaze burned so intense Callie felt the warmth lick at her naked body. She withdrew her hand from her pussy and traced the thick veins of his cock. Then she spun her fingers around his crown mixing the physical proof of their hunger. "Clean it up," he snapped. "Let me hear how good we taste together."

He laced his fingers through her hair and guided her to his cock. She lapped her tongue over him and moaned at the salt and earth flavors of her cowboy. "You taste so good." She took more drawing his head into her mouth. When she released him, he stared down at her. Intrigue and disbelief battled in his gaze. If he thought she was lying, she'd prove him wrong.

Wrapping her hand around his shaft she took him deep. In a rush of hunger, she pressed him to the roof of her mouth.

"Put your hands behind your back and take me deeper."

Yes. Her body shook like he'd pressed her hands to a live wire. This was what she needed. This was what she'd always needed and had never known. She complied. Clasping her hands behind her back, she drew him deeper and deeper into her mouth.

"Fuck, that's good." His head fell back in ecstasy. If she could've grinned at that moment, she would've. "So damn...good."

Before he'd fallen in love with Callie, it had been more than a decade since he'd had a blowjob. And all of the ones that had come before her had been jokes compared to the fervency and intensity she always used. She wiggled her legs back and forth trying to give herself the friction she wanted. That slick honey she made gathered obviously at the lips of her snatch. Damn, she was perfection. She was everything.

He tried not to choke her, but his hips thrust of their own accord. He had to move. It was just too damn good. Her lips were drenched in the mix of their precum and glowed red from her work.

Suddenly, she freed her hands and dug her fingernails into his ass drawing him deeper. The slight pain only served to flood him with pleasure. "Where'd I tell you to keep those hands?" He gripped her hair hard enough to make his point and pulled her face away from his cock.

She pouted deliciously. He dragged his jeans low enough for his purposes and laid her out before him on the quilts. "So damn beautiful." He ran his fingers from her swollen clit down to her taint. She shuddered, unable to contain the jagged craving. He understood only too well. He leaned over her and watched as she spread her legs so readily for him. A harsh groan snarled from his lungs. "You don't spread your legs like a sweet girl, do you, baby? No. You spread 'em for me like the naughty little girl you are." Gripping his cock, that was so fucking hard the ache seared through him with every pound of his heart, he ran it back and forth over her clit.

"Yes. OhmygodFordyes," she whimpered out undecipherable carnality.

He pressed himself lower, found that tender little opening hidden away in her hot, wet folds, and speared into her in one long ravenous thrust. That delicious gasp he drew from her tore away the last remnants of restraint. "And you don't mind the pain, do you, honey? Not if it gets you this." Raring upwards, he draped her legs over his forearms and held her hips with bruising force as he pounded inside of her. Deeper and deeper with each piston-pound of his hips.

Her head shook back and forth, and her mouth hung open on an extended moan. He pressed in and withdrew and then thrust in faster this time until her body gave way, and she sobbed out his name. "There it is. So damn tight. You fucking ruined me. You understand that? Can't even get myself off with my hand anymore. Not when I know I could have your naughty little snatch wrapped so tight around me like this." He lifted her hips further and pounded into her with punishing force until his cock raked over her clit with his every pass. She whipped and thrashed still trying to contain the need that would never be controlled. "You love that, don't you, naughty girl? You love that I'm a fucking slave to this pussy. That you own me."

Deeper, harder with each driving thrust. He sought the redemption so deep within her, the only thing that would ever make him whole.

Her body seized. She clawed at the quilts. Her mouth hung open as her pussy began its telltale spasms around him. He fucking growled like the beast she'd summoned, the one he'd always been. She'd sprung open the cage, and she was going to have to live with the consequences. "Don't you fucking make me come," he threatened. "I'm not near finished with you."

His balls drew so tight they were painful. His vision clouded making her appear more angel than woman. His filthy little angel. Despite his warning, she shattered on his cock. The gasped groan that tore from her filled him with such force that he swore his body broke apart. Every fragment of him that had never really fit was carried away on the winds. He pulled out and with one stroke of his fist, he unloaded all over her swollen lower lips and that sweet little belly. He made certain she understood that the ownership worked both ways.

CHAPTER FORTY-ONE

Callie was both breathless and boneless. She was utterly melted in every possible way as Ford cradled her gently under one of the quilts. The sun was fading in the distance. "That was amazing," she whispered as she traced her initials over his chest.

"I still feel like I should apologize."

That was the fourth time he'd said that. "You know," she leaned up on one elbow, "when you keep saying that, it makes me feel like I shouldn't want what we just did."

"Oh fuck, sugar, I never meant that." He guided her back to his chest. "You have to understand that..." She could feel him working his jaw against her forehead.

She knew what it was he wanted her to understand. "That Meritt didn't like that?"

"It's more than that. This want I have for you. It's like you're a requirement for me. I love you so much. I'm terrified that I'm going to fuck something up and lose you. I'd bet my profits on four hundred head of cattle that you can't even stand up right now. That makes me want to beat my own chest and also makes me worry."

Callie grinned. "You don't have to worry. I've waited my whole life for a love like this. I'm not going anywhere, and it's not just because I can't walk."

His chuckle shook through her as well. "If we're talking about waiting our whole lives for this, I've been waiting a whole lot longer."

"Would you like me to make that up to you, too?" she teased.

"I'll put it on the list."

"You do that."

"Are you ready to head back to the house? I'll carry you to the front and put you in."

"Do we have to go right now? It's so beautiful out here. I wish I had my camera."

"If you'd brought your camera, I sure as hell would've taken pictures of your pussy with my cock spreading it wide open."

Triumphant at that admission, she giggled. "That can be arranged, you know? We can have our own personal stash of photos."

"I love that plan, but I don't want you thinking that I relegate your career down to what I can get out of it. You're an amazing photographer. You're just so damn perfect. I don't know how I managed to be the guy who gets to see you like that and then hold you like this, but I swear nothing makes me more proud than being yours."

Cradling her cheek in his hand he guided her up to his mouth. For all of the force he'd used when he was fucking her, this kiss was decidedly gentle. It nourished her and filled her up in an entirely different way. In his arms, she felt whole. She felt accepted. He was proud of her. She wasn't certain anyone had ever expressed that to her before. Delight cascaded through her. The pure bliss of it all made her feel like she was dancing even when she was standing still.

When he pulled back to give her breath, she grinned. "You know this is completely crazy, right?"

"What exactly?"

"That we found each other right when we did, right after your divorce. It's just all so perfect I don't think we could've orchestrated it."

"Does that mean you got your sign?"

She knew he wanted her to say yes, but she didn't want to lie to him. "I feel like something this big is going to have this huge unmistakable sign. Plus, Nana had some friends over after supper last night, and I overheard them talking about us. I think we're going to have to give people a little more time to be okay with us."

Ford's brow creased with tension. "What were they saying that upset my girl enough to want to give people patience they don't deserve?"

Callie wondered when he'd stopped caring what everyone else thought. "They were talking about you and Meritt just getting divorced. Of course everyone wants to think that you were cheating on her with me and that it wasn't just her cheating on you." She rolled her eyes. "Even though I wasn't even in the state when all of that was going on."

"People are going to say whatever the hell they're going to say. I decided I don't give a fuck. God knows I've been a source for the Holder County hen-clacking for the last twenty years. Longer than that, really. You don't get to have the last name Holder in this county and not be a source, I don't think. Let 'em talk. Us being upset about it isn't going to shut them up."

Callie knew he was right but she hated to be thought of like Meritt. "I know. I just hate that people doubt your intentions. You're this amazing man. I want people to know that. I don't like them talking bad about you."

He hugged her tight enough that he stole the air from her lungs. She didn't mind the sacrifice. "Love you so fucking much," he grunted.

"I love you, too. And I love that you grunt out your truth. Did you know you did that?"

"Christ, you always keep me guessing, woman. What does that mean?"

"That when you tell me things that you want me to remember, you grunt them. I like that."

"I'll see if I can't grunt more for you, sugar."

Giggling at that, she brushed a kiss on his stubbled jawline. "I know how to make you grunt."

With that he gave her some kind of combo of a grunt and a growl that she found equally intoxicating.

CHAPTER FORTY-TWO

A week later, after swearing on her favorite mirrorless camera to both Ford and Meridian that she would absolutely never have Meridian in Ford's bedroom for her photographs, Ford had begrudgingly consented to letting his cousin and his girlfriend use his guest bedroom for the photoshoot. The natural light in there was perfect.

Ford told Callie to text him when they were finished. He was going to hide out on the other side of the ranch just to avoid any possibility of ever seeing his cousin in any state of undress. Giggling at his utter disgust that morning, Callie continued to snap photos of the light in the bedroom in order to figure out where to best position the cameras for the shoot.

This was the first photoshoot she'd done in three years that wouldn't involve an animal who was more appalled by the entire experience than Callie always was. A knock sounded on the door right at ten o'clock. Callie told herself to chill out. She didn't need to gush to Meridian about how much she appreciated the opportunity to do this again.

Flinging open Ford's front door, she beamed. "Hey. Good. You're here. Are you excited? I'm excited," came out in rapid-fire succession.

She clamped her mouth shut and grimaced. "Sorry. It's just been a long time since I've gotten to take pictures I really wanted to take, and I really appreciate this."

Meridian gave her a hesitant nod. "Maybe switch to decaf."

"Probably a good idea."

"Okay, so...how do I do this exactly? Ford's not here, right?" She walked into the kitchen scanning the house as she went.

"Nope. He said he was going down to Jace's house. Honestly, I don't really remember which one Jace is, but I know he's one of the cousins."

Laughing at that, Meridian rolled her eyes. "Yeah, the Holders are nothing if not fertile. I swear there are times I forget half of them, and they're my cousins."

Pleased that Meridian was already comfortable with her, Callie gestured to the guest bedroom. "Typically, when I do boudoir shots, I try to get an idea of what the model wants out of the pictures. If they're a gift for someone, I can tailor the photos for that purpose. If there's something specific you want to see, I'll make that happen."

Meridian considered that for a moment. "Can I do like a combo of things? I liked what you said about connecting women to their beauty, so I'd like to see how you do that. And then maybe a few I could use to make a few men drool. I wouldn't mind a few revenge kind of photos either." She gave Callie a smirk that she was certain Meridian used in the courtroom when she knew she'd won the case.

A revenge shoot wasn't really Callie's preference, but she'd make it work. "I can do all of that. Let's see what you packed to wear, and we can go from there." She gestured to the duffel bag in Meridian's hand.

Remembering everything Apio had taught her, Callie worked Meridian through several kinds of photos. They brought out the feathers and pearls, the black leather, and then a few that had an edge of vindictive to them. Meridian seemed pleased with what she saw on the screen of Callie's camera when she flipped back through a few.

When they were finishing up, Meridian smiled at Callie. "I know people are running their mouths about you and Ford, but honest to god I never thought I'd see the man smile again after Meritt dragged him down the aisle. Now, that's all he does. So, for what it's worth, thanks for making one of my favorite cousins happy again. And I'll adamantly deny it if you ever tell him I said that."

"I promise I'll never tell him, but thank you for saying that. I know it's been fast, but your family has been so great. I have no idea how anyone could hurt Ford the way Meritt did. I've never even spoken to her, and I really want to bitch-slap her. I'm normally anti-violence."

"Oh honey, trust me, slapping her would be the least of what I'd like to do to her. I was too young back when it was all happening to realize she was lying to him about the baby, but even when I was ten I knew she was fifty gallons of trouble in a ten-gallon drum."

"I think Meritt being trouble might be why he's so protective of me. Maybe he's worried about her being mean or something."

Meridian gave her a genuine smile that stretched the width of her face. "That's not why he's so protective. His protectiveness is in his blood, but bitches don't change their stripes. For twenty years, he was constantly waiting to see what stunt she was going to pull next. That's probably a hard thing to quit doing. But you don't seem like the kind of woman who would ever hurt him. Just give him a chance to really get over all the shit she piled him in."

"I promise I'm not rushing him into anything. I'm happy just the way things are."

"Yeah, well, don't let him rush you into anything either. I swear that Holder brand he's got on his arm might as well be on his brain. Wanting to do the right thing even when it's wrong is how he got in deep with Meritt."

Once Meridian had gone, Callie got to work on her surprise for Ford. She moved the tripods and her camera remote to Ford's bedroom, stripped off her own clothes, and grabbed a quick shot of the smirk she was sporting. She wanted to prove to him how much she loved him, and this level of intimacy was even deeper than the amazing sex they shared. She knew he would see that in the photos.

———

Ford leaned down to stare into his open refrigerator. He grinned when

Callie traced her hands over his ass and then pinched him. Standing, he raised an eyebrow and shook his head at her. "You're gonna get yourself into all kinds of trouble, sugar."

Unfettered delight glimmered in those gorgeous eyes of hers. "I'm hoping."

He slammed the refrigerator door shut. "I was going to offer to fix you supper, but something tells me you might be hungry for something else."

"I'm hungry for both. Plus, I have a surprise for you."

Wondering what she was up to, he took her hands and jerked her into his chest. "You don't need to get me surprises. I have you. I don't need anything else."

Her grin expanded against his chest. "I wanted to get you this. It didn't cost me money or anything. I promise. I am kinda hungry, though. Can we have supper and then I give you your surprise, and then if you like the surprise it might lead to other things?"

Assuming she'd gotten some kind of naughty lingerie to wear for him, Ford tried to think of the fastest possible thing he could make for them to eat. Cereal? No, that probably didn't count as real supper. Plus, he was starving. He had to figure out how to have some patience, but damn it felt like he'd spent more than half his life waiting on her. Now that she was here, all of his ability to wait for anything at all was gone. "Sure, baby. What do you want?"

"Will you make me one of those burgers you made the other night? Those were so good. I've been thinking about them for days."

Chuckling at that, he pulled a pack of meat out of the fridge and created patties like he was being paid by the burger. "How'd it go with Meridian today?" He sure as hell didn't want to hear about his cousin getting boudoir shots, but Callie had been buzzing most of the evening. She must've had fun taking them.

"It was so great to not be taking pictures of dogs in costumes."

"Come again?"

Callie giggled. "I like it when you say that to me in bed."

"I'll say it again later, but repeat what you just said. Something about dogs in costumes?"

"Yeah, that's pretty much what I did in LA. I used to take pictures of all of Derrick's mom's friends' dogs in awful costumes that the dogs hated. It was terrible, but it paid okay. Plus, his mom wasn't a fan of me taking boudoir shoots. She was okay with me doing weddings as long as it was for the daughters and sons of her friends. I did one on my own, and she got all upset because she didn't like the aunt of the bride. There are all these weird rules out there about who you can talk to and be friends with. Tori only wanted me to be seen with the right people. It's like a whole different planet sometimes. But Meridian was great. I think she's trying to get back at some guy. She asked me to take a few photos she planned to use to make a point."

"Jack Decker," Ford supplied as he flipped the patties on his griddle.

Callie's eyes expanded with her excitement. "Ohhhh, who is Jack Decker?"

"The district attorney for Holder County. He beat her out for the seat, and she's still pissed."

"I thought she was the DA?"

"She's a deputy district attorney. Jack's several years older than her, and people around here get a little uneasy when they think our family holds too many county seats. But none of that matters to Meridian. Girl's got bigger balls than most of the rest of us combined, but never tell any of them I said that. She's a hellcat on fire most of the time. She needs to simmer down, but I'm sure as hell not going to tell her that."

Ford loved to watch Callie when she was fascinated. She did this adorable thing with her mouth where she kind of twisted it to one side, and her eyes held all of the wildfire he loved about her. "But even if she's mad at this Jack guy that doesn't mean she'd let him see the photos I took unless they've already slept together, don't you think?"

Trying not to shudder at that, he shrugged. "I do not keep up with all of Meridian's conquests. I don't ever even think about them. Keeping her out of trouble is Maddox and Canaan's job. But I've been in the room when she and Jack were both there. I've seen more than one prairie fire get away from the ranchers doing the burning, and all of those fires were more containable than the two of them. If they ever do get together, the whole damn state might go up in flames."

Callie seemed delighted with his assessment. "Meridian's hair does kind of look like fire."

"Yeah, well, God knew what he was doing, I s'pose. Girl got a double helping of stubborn and spiteful."

"Can I give you your present now?"

Just like always, his baby jumped to the next subject in a flash. Yet another thing he loved about her. That mind of hers was fascinating.

"I wish you would," he informed her as he laid the patties on the buns and started chopping onions.

She gnawed on that lip while she disappeared to his bedroom. He set the plates on the counter and located the spicy ketchup they both liked.

When she returned looking three parts terrified and one part ashamed, he abandoned their supper. "What's wrong, baby?" He eased the even stack of four by six paper from her hands. It took him a moment to realize they were pictures.

The first was a full-length shot of her standing by the window in his bedroom. She was wearing a sheer robe that showed far more than it concealed. His heart pounded out its adamant approval. "Damn," choked from his throat. "You're so fucking beautiful."

The next photo was her laid out on the bed completely naked. His cock swelled to a standing ovation, and his mouth went dry. "So goddamn beautiful," were the only words that he could produce. "I can't believe you did this for me." His eyes took in every square inch of her pale smooth skin. Those California tan lines were almost completely faded, but they created a stunning frame for her tits and her pussy.

"Do you like them?" she whispered.

"Like them?" He managed to take his eyes off of the photos and forced them to hers. "Baby, these are incredible. I love them. I love you." There weren't words. There weren't any words at all that could adequately describe what this meant to him. He was going to have to show her with his body. But something about the next photo—with her on her side and her right leg covering that wet haven that he needed to fit himself to—somehow managed to stop time. He swore the whole fucking world stopped spinning as his mind screeched to a halt somewhere between delight and panic.

If he hadn't been so incredibly addicted to her body, so intimately aware of her every curve and hollow, he never would've noticed how swollen her breasts appeared cast in the shadows of the dimly lit photos, or how her hips were just a little wider. Her soft sweet belly might've even been just a touch swollen as well. Maybe he was just imagining that part. Maybe he'd seen it in his mind's eye so many times, wished for it, prayed for it, that he was lost somewhere in that hunger. But her hips and her tits, there were definite differences there. He knew. He was staring at the evidence.

Glancing back at her, he debated how to proceed. Did she know? Surely if he knew, then she did. Maybe. Was this how she wanted to tell him? Callie, his sweet precious baby girl who never managed to keep things from anyone, couldn't possibly have kept this from him. Could she? She said everything that came into her head. He stared at her intently. If she wanted to tell him this, he needed her to say the words. "These are stunning, baby. How are you feeling?"

That question knitted her forehead. "I'm fine now. I was just kind of a little bit intimidated to show these to you because I've never done shots of myself. It's good that I did this though. It gives me a lot of empathy for my clients. It's a way bigger deal than I ever imagined it being. I was having a really good boob day, and still I was so judgey about my body. I wanted to give them to you, and I didn't want to all at the same time."

"So, you managed to connect your beauty to yourself this time." He set the photos on the counter and cradled her gently to his chest. She had no idea. My god. She didn't know, and he did. How often did that happen?

"Thank you for saying that." She squeezed him hard enough to make it difficult to breathe, but he sure as fuck wasn't complaining.

He planted a kiss on top of her head. All of the patience he'd been so certain he'd lost since he'd met her returned tenfold. He'd wait. He'd let her tell him whenever she realized it and was ready. His mind tallied out a list of things he needed to do before she finally understood what had happened. He needed to make a trip to Tulsa. He needed a ring. Part of him wanted her to have the ring before she realized that they were going to have a baby.

"Uh," he cleared his throat, "let's eat, okay? And then I'll show you how much I love this and just how much I love you."

She gave him a quick nod. "Perfect. I'm starving."

CHAPTER FORTY-THREE

"Come here to me," Ford soothed as he lifted her into his arms and carried her to the bed.

"You don't have to carry me." She snuggled her face against his neck, which gave her words no credence at all.

"I love to carry you. Now, let me put my baby to bed." *Babies*, he mentally corrected. Standing her on her feet, he painted gentle kisses from the sweet spot behind her ear down her neck. She gave him a delicious shiver and let her head loll to the side granting him a larger canvas.

As he kissed and suckled, he worked through the buttons on her blouse. Gently, he cradled the weight of her breasts in his hands. Fevered heat spilled into his palms. The satin cup of her bra did nothing to ease the heat and nothing to contain their heft.

Using his fingertips, he delicately slid the shirt off of her shoulders and down her arms. He let it spill into a soft flannel pile on the floor. As he freed her from the bra, she sighed in relief. There were harsh red lines from the straps marring her skin, but he said nothing. He just administered his suckling kisses there, trying to ease the pain. He longed to care for her in every possible way.

The roll of her body caused her breasts to sway in a mesmerizing dance all for his eyes. "Please," she whimpered. "Please...they hurt."

Damn, damn, damn. He sank his teeth into his tongue to keep from telling her why and simply cradled them in his hands trying to ease the tender ache. "I'll make them feel better, baby doll. I promise." That's what he would've said if she'd never shown him those photos. For tonight, he needed to be the man he'd been a half hour ago, before everything in his entire world had somehow gotten even better than it had been before. He prayed she'd be as thrilled as he was.

He eased her jeans down her long legs and let his hands explore her hips. The soft, needy moan she gave him erased a little of the gentleness he'd been trying to cling to. He sank his lips to her, devouring the sweet, spicy flavors of Callie. He tasted every inch of her mouth, every plump curve of her bottom lip, every corner, the pull of her cupid's bow. He wanted it all and would never get enough.

Lifting her back into his arms, he laid her out in the bed and stared down at her. The moonlight from the window split her almost in two, but it crossed there at her womb so he began his kisses just over her adorable belly button and trailed down through the light.

He traced his fingers back and forth through the tender curls over her mound that concealed her slit. She shook with the hunger he would feed. "That little honeypot already sweet and creamy for me, baby?" Her breath stuttered from her lungs. "I want my taste," was his only warning before he spread her legs all for himself and let his tongue dance up and down her slit.

"Yes," gasped from her. He spun his tongue deep in her opening and then back and forth over her clit. There was a ripe edge to her nectar tonight. If he wasn't so addicted to her pussy, he never would've noticed, but it was there. Like a starved man set before a feast, he devoured those flavors, that reassurance that she was indeed full of his baby.

Her hips locked around his jaw as he worshiped her with his tongue. All of that spicy cream dripped down faster than he could catch it, and he damn near lost his mind. That familiar impatience churned through his veins, but he banished it. That night he had to be gentle. There was just too much at stake.

"More," she fussed. "Please, please more."

Torn between giving her what she was begging for and being easy with her, he debated. Both. Couldn't he do both? Surely, he could figure that out. "My naughty girl gets so impatient for me. Let me make you wet, honey."

"I'm soaked," she fussed. "Please."

He certainly knew she was soaked, but Christ Almighty he wanted to drown in her essence. That wasn't what she wanted that night, and he would always give her every single thing she needed.

Standing quickly, he shed his clothes and then ascended her body. His fingers stroked over her pussy as he made his climb, but that wasn't what she wanted either. The needy impatience shook through her. Her hand wrapped tight around his cock. A raspy growl rumbled from him. It pleased her. Ford could see.

With a molten look, she licked her lips. "All for me," she cooed.

"Every fucking inch, sweet baby. You sure you're ready for that."

"So ready."

Incapable of denying her anything at all, he swiped the head of his cock through the juices coating her pussy and eased himself inside. She bucked bringing him deeper against his explicit permission, not that he'd scold her for the needy motion.

Her pussy nursed at the head of his cock rendering him mindless and breathless. He pressed himself to his hilt and reveled in her low hum of pure satisfaction. Oh, his baby loved to be full. He knew. He eased back and then sank low again, achingly slow. He picked up pace on the next thrust until he was moving to the rhythm of her.

Catching her hands in his own, he pinned them to the mattress over her head. He swore he could feel every needy nerve ending in her channel. He filled every silky crevice like she'd been made for him alone. He was certain she had.

"Listen to me," he managed in a half-grunted plea. "I love you," he swore.

Her eyes flashed open. "I love you, too," she managed in a tender whisper, while his body made promises all its own.

Another thrust in and out. "I will always be here. No matter what." His voice turned gritty under the choke of arousal. "Fuck...so good."

Before he lost the ability to talk at all, he forced himself to go on. "Always, baby. Always right here."

"I know," she moaned out a soft sound of longing and lifted her restless hips.

He abandoned his vows and mastered her body. Desire and love ran thick and urgent through his veins. "Gonna fill you full," he warned. "So damn full of me."

"Yes, yes." Her body tensed under his. He released her hands, and she wrapped them tight around his back holding him to her so nothing at all could exist between them, nothing but their child.

He pressed until he knew he'd reached that wild, untouched depth of her, the one that belonged to him. She came in a rush of frantic pulses and desperate cries.

The hot tide of cum surged through his cock. He couldn't hold it back. Gripping her hips with more force than he'd planned to use, he slammed inside of her and filled her just as he'd promised. He drenched her in his seed and let that knowledge sate him.

After he'd tenderly cleaned her up, he cradled her on his chest. "I was trying not to be rough with you," he admitted cautiously.

"Why?" She grinned up at him. "I like it when you're rough."

"I know. That's just another thing I love about you."

"You still wore me out though. I'm crazy tired."

Swallowing down a half-dozen things he longed to say, he pulled the covers over them even though it was really too early for bed. "Then let me hold you while you sleep, sweetheart."

"It's barely eight," she yawned out the words.

"Yeah, but," he scrambled for a reason beyond the one that was obvious only to him, "you worked hard today and like you said, I just wore you out."

"I guess I did." She slipped her leg between his knees and nuzzled into his chest, like the final piece of his puzzle to make him complete.

While she slept, he let the worry take hold. What if she wasn't ready for a kid? What if he'd been too rough? She was awfully young. Was she already late and just hadn't thought much of it, or was it really that early? Maybe her cycles weren't regular or something. He didn't know. It had only been a couple of months that they'd been together.

How the hell had it only been that long? It felt like forever in all of the best possible ways. He'd all but forgotten all of the years he'd been with Meritt. It should've been sad that she was so replaceable, but that was how life worked, wasn't it? The bad was easier to wipe away than the good would ever be. No one ever regretted losing the shitstorms when the sunshine itself replaced them.

He let Meritt slip through his hands and made no effort to hold on to any single grain of sand from that relationship.

He and Callie would figure this out together. He just had to prove to her that he'd be there for every moment of the rest of their lives. Beyond that, they'd just figure it out. She'd been asking for a sign. Well, this was one hell of a sign.

Unless he was wrong. The doubt compounded on the worry. He tensed his arms around her. Her breasts were still fevered and tender. But that could be because of something else. Maybe he was dreaming this all up because it's what he wanted so badly. She'd put on a little weight. That was it. Good. That was precisely what he wanted her to do. If she was really pregnant, she'd know, and she would be the one telling him. Wouldn't she?

CHAPTER FORTY-FOUR

Endlessly thankful that Dalton and Wes were running his feed trucks that morning, though Ford knew he'd owe them a week's worth of feeding at some point in the future, he turned slightly in the bed and grinned down at Callie still sound asleep in the crook of his arm. Sweet baby. Her hair was in a wild mane covering her bare breasts and shoulders.

He longed for her just like this—warm and sweet and natural. She was tucked up in a ball against him. He let his hands caress and awaken the descent of her spine and her bare ass. She grinned but kept her eyes shut tight.

Overcome with the need to prove to himself that he could be gentle, almost achingly tender with her this time, he brushed a kiss along her hairline. "I want you."

"I love the way you sound in the mornings," she informed him.

"How do I sound?"

"All gravelly and even more sexy than normal."

"I'll have to remember that." He continued to try to coax her awake, but his mission was interrupted when her cell phone buzzed on the side table. It was just after seven. Ford couldn't remember the last time he'd slept that late, but who the hell was calling her?

Huffing out her irritation, Callie slid upwards in the bed, yanked the sheets up over her tits, and stared at her phone. "It's Nana." Ford tried to listen in to determine what was going on. "Wait. What?" She paused long enough for the answer to that question. "But why? You've owned the farm since Mom was a kid."

Not much he could make out of that, and he couldn't hear whatever Delphia was saying. A knock on the front door had him lumbering out of bed and yanking on his Wranglers. Clearly, his sleeping-in time was over, and his brothers wanted some help.

Scrubbing his hands through his hair, he swung open the door with an apology pinned on his lips, but he stopped before any words could fully form. Clint Garcia, one of the sheriff's deputies, stared back at him with a frightened expression. "Uh, Mr. Holder, sir..." he held up an envelope.

"What the hell is this?" Ford demanded. Barbed wire twisted in his gut. Every hair on his body stood on end. Somehow, he knew whatever that phone call was about it had something to do with what was in that envelope.

"I'm here on behalf of the Holder County Superior Court."

"I know who you work for, Clint, for Christ's sake we went to school together. Just give me the envelope and stop calling me Mr. Holder."

Ford jerked the envelope out of Clint's hands and tore it open. His heart pounded out a vengeful war-drum cry. *Sonuvabitch*. He read the words *spousal support modification request* and *falsified information* before he closed his fist around the paperwork. "How fucking many times can she do this? I signed the papers eight weeks ago. She isn't getting one red cent from me. She was the one that was cheating," he seethed.

Clint shrugged. "Guess the judge thinks she has a case. I'm not sure."

"Ford, what's wrong?" Callie rushed from the bedroom in one of his T-shirts and her jeans. She had her purse slung over her shoulder.

Clint visibly took his time staring at her appreciatively. An odd growl kicked up from low in Ford's gut. "I'll talk to my lawyer. Get off my land," was the only warning he gave before he slammed the door. Turning to Callie, he tried to count to ten before he spoke but only made it to four. "It's Meritt. She's suing for alimony again. I'll talk to Dale Miller. He handled the divorce. I'm sure she won't get anything, but the woman loves to make my life a living hell."

Callie's already worried features fell. "I'm so sorry."

"Not your fault, sugar. Tell me what Nana wanted and why you think you're leaving." He gestured to her bag.

"I have no idea what's going on. Apparently, there's an assessor out at the farm along with some kind of doctor who works for the state or something. I don't know. I have to go see what's going on. It looks like my *father,*" she spat the word, "is trying to take full possession of my grandparents' farm without having to pay for it or something. Nana is confused and upset, so I have to go out there and see if I can make sense of this. He's always been an asshole, but this is extreme even for him."

"I'm coming with you," Ford informed her.

"No, you don't need to do that. You have to handle this," she gestured to the paperwork. "I'll be fine. I just need to calm Nana down and get through to my father."

Ford ground his teeth. "Callie, baby, he's furious with me. If he decided to take it out on your grandparents, then I'm the one who needs to talk him out of it. Now, I'm coming with you. I'll call Dale on the way."

"I'm sorry about all of this," she fussed.

He cradled her chin in his hands. "What am I about to say?"

She managed a slight grin. "That I didn't do anything worth apologizing over."

"Good girl, now keep telling yourself that while I get a shirt on."

———

Callie tried to listen in on the phone call Ford was having with his lawyer as he drove them off of Holder Ranch. The only thought that remained centered in her head was that Meridian had been correct—Meritt was nothing but trouble.

"I haven't even seen her in months, Dale," Ford huffed. "How the hell would I have given her the impression I'd come into more money than I had when she left?"

Feeling guilty for using Ford's problem to distract from her own, Callie recounted the things Nana had told her. There was some farm assessor out on the property who was supposed to be drawing up paperwork on how much the farm was worth. Had her father somehow come into money? That seemed unlikely. And even more importantly, did he really believe that her grandparents would sell the land they'd saved so long to purchase? A spark of hope remained ignited in her belly. Now her grandparents would see what a wretched human Callie's father really was, and they'd kick him off their land for good. She just had to make sure her father didn't get his way. But he couldn't possibly. This was one of his get-rich-quick stunts again. She was sure.

With that thought easing the tense set of her shoulders, she tried to discreetly adjust her bra. She wished she'd just start her period because her boobs were killing her. Of course, with all of the sex they'd been having lately, they'd likely scared Aunt Flo off. But surely, any day now, she'd show up with all of her crampy, bitchy glory, and Callie would be miserable. At least her periods were super light since she'd been on the pill so long.

She was already halfway through the placebo pills in her birth control package. It likely wouldn't be any day now, it would be any minute now. Dammit, she probably should've put on a pad before they left Ford's house. It would just be the icing on the cake of this horrendous morning to bleed through her jeans while she was trying to talk to a tax assessor and yell at her father.

CHAPTER FORTY-FIVE

Ford handed his phone to Callie when he ended the call to keep from hurling it against the windshield.

"What did he say?" Callie asked.

"For me to bring the papers to his office and that he'd take care of it. He seems to think something must've happened that made Meritt believe I'd come into money. I have no clue why she'd think that, but god knows she's only happy when she's making me miserable."

"Ford, I'm really..."

"I know you are, baby, but this isn't your fault. Let's just go see if we can't get through to your daddy and then I'll deal with my ex."

"I'm sure this is just one of Dad's get-rich schemes. Either that or he's trying to get back at me for something. He's such an ass, but his bark is always much worse than his bite. I'll get through to him. Nana said he's trying to get Pops declared unable to care for himself or something. She said that the doctor said they were going to have to get evaluated by the state to prove that they're healthy."

Ford had no doubt that her daddy was an ass, but he'd done more rounds with greedy vipers than Callie ever had. Abe didn't want the land. Not really. He wanted attention, and he wanted money. Ford had his checkbook in his back pocket. If he had to pay off her daddy to shut this all down, he would.

He knew that's what Abe was after anyway. Ford had circumvented his plan to bilk her grandparents for more money for that barn roof, and now Abe was pissed. This was yet another reason he sure as hell would not be giving Meritt spousal support. The words rolled into a rock in his throat making him gag. She'd had all the support she wanted until she got caught with her pants down, literally. Now, she was going to have to lie in the bed she'd wanted to be in for years.

When Ford saw the black Nissan Frontier parked in front of the Simpkins' house, a half-dozen cogs in his mind turned slowly until they locked into place. Even he would never have believed that she'd do this, but once again, he'd failed to see just how mean his ex-wife could be. He'd taken his father's advice and tried not to corner her, but it hadn't worked. Not when she was the master puppeteer and had an idiot like Abe Monroe caught up in her strings. Ford had cornered the marionette, and now he was going to get the manipulator.

Too angry to speak or move, he glared at her truck. When Callie opened her own door and slid out of his truck, he jerked back to life. Stomping to her side, he wrapped his arm over her shoulders and pulled her close. If they were going to step into one of Satan's rings, he'd keep her safe.

"What's wrong?" Callie shivered against him.

"I'm not sure yet, but I have a good idea. That's Meritt's truck," he spat.

"Why would she be here?"

"We're about to find out." Too far gone for manners, he flung open the front door without knocking. "What the hell are you doing here?" He spared no pleasantries for Callie's grandparents. He'd talk with them later.

Meritt narrowed her eyes into a vicious sneer, precisely the expression she'd used for the last year they'd been together. "My god, you are so predictable."

Abe looked far too pleased for anyone's good.

Ford spared her an eye roll, and pulled Callie tighter against him.

"God knows how much you love to run your mouth, Meritt, so get to it."

"I knew you'd do this. I'm honestly almost disappointed it was this easy."

Callie's fists clenched against Ford's thigh. His baby narrowed those pretty brown eyes, and Ford was momentarily concerned he was going to have to break up a cat fight.

Meritt continued. "You always have to be the hero, don't you? I knew you'd come out here to save your little jailbait slut. Too bad your brain isn't as big as your dick."

Ford lunged for her, but Callie gripped his hand and managed to pull him back. "Don't," she ordered. "That's what she wants."

"No, that's not what she wants," Ford snarled. "She wants me to pay your daddy off and then what, Meritt? If I pay him off, you have some kind of deal worked out with Abe so you get half or something like that?"

She gave him a simpering smirk. "That and proof that you do have access to the vast Holder Land and Cattle checking accounts when you need them. That looks very good for me in court. I told you a long time ago not to cross me, but you did it anyway. You just never learn."

Panic cinched in his muscles, but he'd be damned to hell before he'd let her know she'd gotten to him. "You can take me back to court all you want, but you'll never get a dime of Holder money. I wasn't the one having an affair. As you'll recall, that does matter in the state of Oklahoma."

"Really?" Meritt laughed in his face. "You expect everyone to believe that you just happened to find her right after I left? Get off your high horse. I wasn't the only one messing around."

"That isn't true," Callie huffed. She shook her head and turned on her father. "Dad, how could you do this? To me? To Nana and Pops? How can you seriously sit there and be working with...*her*."

"You're such a spoiled brat," Abe scoffed. "Like I told both of you, not all of us were born into the right families. The Holders have more money than they have sense, and I think it's high time the rest of us get our share."

Rage ignited in Ford and unhinged his temper. "Call her a brat one more time and it'll be the last thing you say."

"Ford, stop," Callie soothed. "This is ridiculous. You're not giving them anything because Nana and Pops aren't selling the farm, and you," she gestured to Meritt, "just told us your whole stupid plan. Go ahead and take us to court. We didn't start dating until after those papers were signed."

"Good luck proving that. Your grandparents aren't able to care for themselves anymore, little girl," Meritt slithered like the viper she was. "The farm rightfully belongs to your father since he's the one who stayed here to care for them all these years."

"Bullshit," Ford snapped. "Get out. Now."

———

Callie sat beside Ford on her grandparents' old sofa and tried to understand what Dale Miller and Meridian were explaining. The pain and disbelief seemed to have rendered her deaf. She couldn't quite make out what was being said, or perhaps it was the shock of it all that had created the barriers.

Ford shook his head, "So, if I buy the farm and return it to Harold and Delphia, Meritt can use that as evidence to get alimony, but if I don't then Abe could take their land?"

Dale gave him a somber nod. "Your hands are tied, which is precisely what Meritt wants. She's gambling on the fact that you'll break down and purchase the farm if Abe pushes hard enough and then she grants herself access to the company accounts when your net worth is being calculated."

Meridian cut across him, "But none of this works Meritt and Abe's way unless they can get a judge to rule that the Simpkins are incapacitated and in need of guardianship. Then the courts would have to appoint Abe as the guardian. We can stop that from happening."

Dale shot her a long-suffering glance. "From what I was able to deduce from my earlier conversation with Abe, the claim is that the Simpkins are unable to manage their financial resources. Because there are two loans against the farm, the property itself is the resource they seem unable to manage. Mr. Simpkin, you did try to secure a third loan two months ago. That combined with the lacking funds in your checking and savings accounts does make my job more difficult."

"I'm lacking funds because he constantly asks for money," her grandfather vowed. "I've given him thousands over the years. Half of the time I don't see the improvements he said he was making."

Her nana alternated between crying and praying.

Ford stood and started to pace. "Mr. Simpkin, I am not going to allow Abe to take your land from you. We'll figure something out so that I can buy it and give it back to you. There has to be some way to prove Callie and I weren't dating until after my divorce. Once I figure that out, everything else falls into place."

"If you buy this farm it will be even more difficult to get a judge to believe that you weren't with Callie before the divorce papers were signed," Meridian cringed as she spoke. "You've only been dating two months. It's a significant enough purchase to make it appear that you two were together for years. We're going to have to handle this a different way."

Suddenly, a hesitant hope cleared Callie's muddled mind. "There is. There is a way to prove that. I just have to call Derrick. I'll be right back."

Ford grabbed her arm as she whisked past him. "You are not calling Derrick."

The ego and pain in his eyes wounded her. She'd seen it before, but it had been almost gone completely the last few weeks. "Ford," she tried to beg with her eyes, "I am not Meritt. You know that. Derrick can help us if he will. You can't fix this on your own. I deserve the chance to help. Honestly, maybe even more than that, I deserve the chance to make Derrick hear me. I need you to understand that."

CHAPTER FORTY-SIX

Ford was furious, mostly with himself, but if he were being brutally honest, he'd admit he was ticked with Callie, too. Every fucking time she called Derrick, a bolt of betrayal tightened in his chest. He needed to be the one that saved them, dammit. How did she not get that? All he'd ever wanted to be was her hero.

He went back to calling himself an asshole for good measure. The only saving grace was that Derrick had yet to pick up his phone. Some hero.

"Ugh!" she tried to growl and sounded a great deal more like a pissed-off kitten.

"What is it you think he's going to be able to do?" Ford finally asked.

She leveled him with a cool glare. The chill twisted up his spine. He really was being an asshole, but he had no idea how to stop. "I wasn't even here in town until the day of your divorce. He can corroborate that I was in LA."

"Meritt had an affair a decade ago with some fucker that lived in Dallas. You don't have to be in the same state to screw around. That doesn't prove anything."

"It's the only option we have right now, and I'm going to figure this out. Meritt and my father are not going to win. I refuse to let that happen." Shaking her head, she went back to her phone and scrolled through her contacts. When she landed on one, she slammed her finger down hard enough to redden the tip. "Mrs. Devers, uh, hey, it's Callie." Her entire face contorted in a deep cringe. "How are you?"

It killed him to see her so miserable. He reminded himself that this was entirely his fault. In an effort to make up for being a douche most of the afternoon, he laced their fingers together and mouthed, "I'm sorry."

She gave him that sweet broken smile that had twisted him in knots all those nights ago at the bar. They'd figure this out. He just needed to get his head out of his ass, and she had to stop calling Derrick. Ford would figure out some way to save her family's farm and to get Meritt's claws out of his family's bank accounts.

"Listen, I know Derrick and I broke up, and I'm so sorry to bother you, but I really need a little help." Her head dropped at the woman's reply. "Derrick didn't tell you we broke up." Callie nodded. "Well, we did. That's why I haven't been back to LA in months." She rolled her eyes. "No, I wasn't on an extended vacation. I'm not coming back, but if the past four years have meant anything to Derrick I really do need a favor."

Ford loathed every word of this conversation. If he clenched his jaw any harder, his molars were going to turn to dust. He told himself to be a better man than he'd been with Meritt, but dammit, how much more was the biggest mistake of his life going to continue to cost him? Life had already beaten the shit out of him. Couldn't he catch a break?

It was late in the night with Callie sleeping with her back to him that he finally grasped why this scared him enough to make him resent everyone and everything. What if Callie thought this was the big sign she'd been asking for? What if Meritt cost him the only thing that had ever really mattered? What if Meritt cost him Callie?

———

By Friday night, everything was locked in a stalemate. Ford couldn't buy her grandparents' farm, and the hearing on their ability to prove that they were capable of caring for their assets loomed on the horizon.

Seated at Ford's mother's kitchen table, surrounded by his brothers and sister, Callie tried to eat the meatloaf. She really did. It smelled so good, but she was sick to her stomach over all of the insanity going on around them.

Ford's father, Barrett, tossed down his napkin. "Son, there has to be something we can do. I've got a call in to a few other lawyers out in Tulsa and to my accountant. They'll come up with something. I've a good mind to go out to wherever it is that Meritt is staying nowadays and say things I've wanted to say to her for years."

"It wouldn't do you any good," Ford summed up the general defeat that draped the table like a lead tablecloth.

"It'd make me feel better. That's better than nothing," Barrett countered.

His mother squeezed Callie's hand. "Things have a way of working themselves out. You'll see."

"I'm not so sure about that this time, Mrs. Holder," Callie whispered. "I'm so..."

Ford shot her a pleading look, and she sealed her lips. But she really was sorry. It was her father's fault this was happening. If her grandparents had made him leave the farm instead of her mother, everything in her whole life would've been different. Everything would've been better. And now, her father was going to cost them everything.

Barrett continued to stare down at his plate as if the answer everyone had been searching for was there in the recesses of the mashed potatoes. "It boggles my mind that she existed around this family for twenty years and never grasped that the money is in the land. It's not in our bank accounts."

An odd huff of irritation from Ford had Callie grasping his hand. "It would make her whole day if I sold off part of my land to buy that farm and then granted her access to the business accounts. She lives to make me miserable. She has since day one. And to be fair, Dad, it ain't really like the Holder Land and Cattle accounts are empty or any of us are hurting for money."

"Cattle ranching is a crap shoot on a good day and a direct route to destitution on a bad. The only way to make a little money in cattle is to start out with a lot of money. We've been very fortunate. You know that. I know that. But we've had our lean years as well. And we will again. Meritt has never been able to think past the end of her own nose."

"She's a brat. No one's denying that," Ford said. "But I'm the fool who married her." He stood from the table, tossed his napkin into his plate, and stormed out the back door.

Sara shook her head at her husband. "He's tried so hard for so long, Barrett, could you please save the lectures for some other time."

"I wasn't lecturing him. I was trying to talk through to a solution."

Callie stood to go after Ford. "I'll talk to him."

But Jamie caught her shoulder as she made her escape. "Let me. I owe him an apology anyway."

CHAPTER FORTY-SEVEN

Ford knew someone would come after him. That's why he hadn't made it further than the back deck. He stared out at the lands his family had owned for more than a hundred years and wondered if any of his ancestors had ever felt as stupid and defeated as he did at that moment.

He'd thought it would either be Callie or his father. He wasn't expecting Jamie. "If you came out here to remind me that you told me not to get involved with her or to tell me that she's got leaving in her blood again, save it. My patience is thin enough."

Jamie leaned against the rail beside him. "Guess I deserve that. I was actually going to apologize for saying that shit."

Turning to stare down at his little brother, he narrowed his eyes. "Why?"

"Because I was wrong." He shrugged. "Even with all of this shit Meritt's dished up, you still look happier than I've ever seen you. I want that for you."

Ford attempted to swallow down a little of his irritation. "Thanks."

"You know, Dad wasn't trying to be an ass. He was working his way around to asking Callie what she thought about moving her grandparents out here to the ranch, and just letting her daddy have that farm."

"Yeah, well, he needed to get there a whole lot faster." Ford shook his head. "Besides her granddaddy's every bit as proud as ours was. He's not going to sell that land. You never sell the land," Ford stated the foundational belief that farmers and ranchers lived by. Most cattle ranchers would vow that they sold grass not cattle. After all, you couldn't raise one without the other. If you wanted to survive in this business, the future was in the land.

Jamie chuckled. "You think I don't know that?"

"You're the one that said it."

"I'm going to let that one go instead of popping you in the mouth for being a fuckwhistle right now. You do know that you don't always get to be the only hero for her, right? I honestly can't figure out if you're so pissed because you've decided this is your fault, or if it's really just because you can't figure out a way to save her all on your own."

Being called on the carpet only served to make Ford angrier. "I don't need a lecture from Dad, and I sure as hell don't need one from you."

"Fine," Jamie huffed, "but if you want her, and we all know you do, then you're going to have to sacrifice a little of your ego and swallow some of that pride. Take it from me, hanging on to who you thought you were supposed to be ain't worth it if you lose the only chick on this planet who clearly gets the guy you really are. Besides, you ever think that maybe the Holders just can't save everyone in this town? Maybe we aren't even supposed to. Seems people hate us when we do and when we don't. I'm not sure it even matters anymore."

Ford was aware that Jamie was no longer discussing the issue with Meritt and Abe Monroe. The look in his little brother's eyes held far too much raw pain and rejection.

"Jamie," Callie's tender voice pricked the cool night air. Both men turned to stare her down. "Can I talk to him for a minute?"

"Be my guest." Jamie and Callie exchanged places, but Jamie turned back before he returned to the kitchen. "There's shit worth holding onto in this life, man. Your pride ain't it."

"Hey," Callie wrapped her arms around him. Instinctively, he folded her into his chest and let her bury her face in him.

"Hey, baby. I'm sorry I'm being an ass." Jesus, how many times had he apologized for that in the last week.

"You're not." She lifted her head and gave him that grin that undid him. "I really do love that you want to be able to fix all of this for me, but I want to help. I wish you'd let me."

"I'm trying. I swear. I just...I don't know..." He knew what he wanted just not how to say it.

"You want to be my knight in dirty cowboy boots?" She sank her teeth into her lip to keep her smirk at bay.

Chuckling at that, he gave her a begrudged nod. "Is that so bad?"

"No, but you're already that. You solving this whole thing all on your own won't make you a hero any more than not solving it would knock you off of the throne I have you on in my head."

"I don't deserve a throne."

"How about a really tall horse then?"

"I might could agree to that. It's better than like a gold-plated tractor or something," Ford teased her. She just always made him better. Maybe part of what Jamie had said was right. Ford didn't have to be the hero every time. He just really wanted to most of the time.

Her giggling was interrupted by the buzz of her phone between them. She fished it out of her pocket and stared down at it in disbelief. "It's Derrick." She answered before Ford could protest.

His muscles vibrated with possession. The word *mine* seared in his skull. She did more listening than talking but then leapt into the conversation. "You're here? Like here in Oklahoma?!"

Every curse word Ford knew and a few he made up on the fly paraded through his head, but he kept a tight lock on his lips. She wasn't Meritt. He knew that.

"No, we don't have personal drivers out here, and I'm not surprised Uber doesn't come to Holder County." She sighed. "Okay, fine. I'll come out to the airport. I'll be there in a couple of hours." She ended the call and then immediately held up her hand. "I need to go talk to him. He came all the way out here. I need you to trust me."

"I do trust you." Ford wasn't entirely certain that was true, but he knew it was a product of his marriage and had nothing to do with Callie. "Answer one question for me—do you want to go talk to him or do you just think you have to because he flew out here? I won't have you doing things out of guilt."

She considered for a long drawn minute. Ford ordered himself to be patient. "I want to go talk to him. I deserve to really be heard." She stared down at the wooden planks beneath her ballet flats like she was worried the foundation was going to splinter into pieces at any moment.

"Can I come with you?" There. He hadn't demanded to go with her. That was something, even if he wasn't going to take no for an answer.

Her head jerked back up. "I didn't want to ask you to do that. If you don't mind, I'd really appreciate it. I can handle it on my own, but I don't want you to worry."

"I trust you." If he said it enough, surely he'd get it cemented in his head.

"You're trying to, and I'm trying not to resent that you don't. On the other hand, if Meritt wasn't the wicked witch of the Midwest and she flew two thousand miles to see you, I'd want to be there, too."

"I'm sorry that I'm still letting her ruin this," he choked over that admission. Instead of apologizing for being an asshole, that's what he'd been trying to say for days.

"She only gets to ruin this if we let her. I have no intention of giving her that power. Now, let's go see if I can talk Derrick into coming up with some proof that I didn't even know you until the day of your divorce."

CHAPTER FORTY-EIGHT

Two halves of her existence were about to collide, and Callie swore she could hear the impending explosion. The last thing she ever thought Derrick would do was to come all the way to Tulsa. She was certain his mother had sent him, but why she'd sent him remained to be seen.

He was the only person who could testify on her behalf about when her and Ford had started dating, so just then she needed him. She was going to have to put up with his toxic levels of self-absorption. The desire to put on a pair of wading boots before they entered the airport continued to taunt her.

"I don't think you ever told me what Derrick does for a living." Ford interrupted her thoughts.

"He doesn't really do anything. He tells people he's a pro video game player, but that's not really true. Mostly he just lives off of his parents' money and does what they tell him to do. His father is Steven Devers, the movie producer. Part of the reason I left was that I was so sick of his parents and of him spewing on about dreams that were never going to come true. He never wanted to put any real work behind the dream. That's not how people make things happen."

"I guess I owe the idiot my thanks. Maybe he'll let me buy him one of those tiny bottles of wine or some airport shit."

Shaking her head at that, she leaned across the console of Ford's truck and brushed a kiss on his cheek. "Why do you want to buy him a drink?" She already knew but wanted to hear him say it.

"Because I got you," he supplied readily. "Would you mind telling me about the cheating? You told me he'd done it but never really elaborated."

Callie cringed. Ford had been open about Meritt's cheating. She knew what that had to have cost him, so she went on with the story. "I caught him more than once jacking off to some chat room woman on his computer. He'd rather do that than be with me."

Ford shook his head. "That had nothing to do with you."

"How do you figure that?"

"He knew all along that you deserved better. Helluva lot easier to get your rocks off to something on a screen than pull your head out of your ass and put forth effort to be someone even close to the kind of man that you deserve. Like you said, effort ain't something he's got in spades, and work is worth more than want every fucking time."

"Well, then it did have something to do with me at least a little. Besides, you still partially blame yourself for what Meritt did. It seems like you could take your own advice."

"I blame myself for falling into Meritt's trap. I'm letting go of the affairs. The brilliant and beautiful woman sitting right beside me proved to me that none of that was my fault. She needs to learn the same thing about her ex. Let's get this over with." Ford pulled into the parking lot and made it to her door in record time.

Callie's heart tripped over the next few beats. Tension roiled in her belly, and she still hadn't shaken the nausea that had come on earlier in the week from her father's stunt. It felt like a decade since she'd had to exist in Derrick's world, and she had no interest in having to return to the misery if only for a few minutes. But this was for her and Ford. She'd endure as long as she had to.

The Tulsa airport was relatively empty that evening. It was so different from LAX Callie was certain Derrick would be appalled at the quaint midwestern passthrough. She saw him before he noticed their approach. He was standing there looking both lost and annoyed. Of course, he almost always bore that expression. As he turned towards them, the almost comical difference between the man holding her hand and the one holding a bouquet of flowers struck her. What had she ever seen in Derrick? Ford was all rough edges and work-worn hands. Solid, substantial security was housed in the very marrow of his bones. His thick muscles were ranch earned and used for more than being impressive, although he was certainly that as well. Mostly he looked like hers. Her cowboy, her love, her life maybe.

Derrick's weekly manicures and lean body made it clear that he paid a trainer a lot of money for nothing more worthy than the vanity that drove him.

"Who are you?" Derrick demanded of Ford, but he also took three rather large steps back making him appear to be a child who was about to be scolded. Callie reminded herself that Derrick really was a child, a rich spoiled brat much like Meritt only with money. In typical fashion, he ignored Callie altogether.

She cleared her throat. "This is Ford Holder, my boyfriend. Why did you fly out here?"

"Mom told me I had to," he admitted.

Ford's eye roll seemed to clue him in as to how asinine that sounded. "For what purpose?" Ford demanded.

This time Derrick turned his attention on Callie. "Mom said you needed a favor or something, and I'm supposed to bring you home."

Ford's mouth opened, but Callie shook her head. "LA isn't my home. I'm not coming back. If you ever listened to me, you'd know that."

"So, what? You're going to move in with him and do your picture thing or whatever? And eat, clearly." He gestured to her hips. "They obviously don't have yogalates fusion classes out here in the asscrack of America."

Before Callie could even gasp over his insults, Ford had him by the collar of his Hugo Boss shirt. "If I were you, I'd turn around and walk, douche-whistle, before I fill your fat mouth full of shit straight out of the asscrack of America."

She watched Derrick's face tinge of purple before she touched Ford's massive forearms. "Let him go."

When Ford released the shirt, Derrick gasped for breath and stared at him. "I could have you arrested."

"Oh, I wish you'd try," Ford spat.

Callie rubbed her temples. "Derrick, I'm sorry you flew all the way out here. I am not coming back to LA, and I'm not accepting those flowers either. We're over. I don't know how to make that more clear for you. I've tried everything I can think of." She took Ford's hand. "Let's just go." She'd never seen Derrick angry about anything. She didn't like that side of him any more than she liked his typical laidback complacency.

But as they were walking away, Derrick called, "Callie, wait!"

She knew she probably shouldn't have, but she turned back. "What?"

He made it to them in a few strides. "Mom said something about a lawsuit or something. What's that all about?"

"Ford's ex-wife is making a spousal support claim against him by insinuating that we were dating prior to his divorce. I thought maybe you'd be willing to help me prove that it isn't true. I didn't even come out here until two months ago. But you don't seem like you'd be interested in helping us, so," she shrugged, "never mind."

"You're divorced?" Shock furrowed Derrick's brow.

"Is that all you got out of that whole story?" Ford clearly wasn't in the mood for more small talk.

Derrick rolled his eyes, but then he pulled his phone from his pocket. "When is she saying you two started dating?"

"Over the summer," Callie refused to hope. She'd been disappointed too many times.

"I don't know why I'm doing this, but I have the pics the press took of us at all of those events Mom and Dad made us go to over the summer. It would've been hard for you to be cheating on me since we were out most every night at one thing or another. The photos were on all of the gossip blogs so they'd have a timestamp tied to the IP addresses."

———

Never in his life had Ford wanted to hug someone right before he kicked their ass. "May I?" He gestured for the phone.

"Don't break it. There are only fifty in existence. It's a prototype my father got from Apple."

Ford ignored the warning and scrolled through the pictures instead. Relief washed over him with such force it made him woozy. An odd reaction to seeing the woman he wanted to make his wife out with another man, but it wasn't just that he was going to get to shut Meritt's mouth once and for all. It was so much more than that. *I never try to take pictures of what it looks like. I try to capture how it feels.*' Callie's words replayed in his head. The photographers must've used the same methodology because in every image his baby—stuffed into designer gowns and jewelry that would never be her—looked absolutely miserable.

Swallowing down that pride his brother had referenced, Ford handed the phone back. "I can't thank you enough for helping us. Can you send those to her so we can show the lawyer?"

"Yeah. No problem. Turn your AirDrop on, Callie."

She retrieved her own phone and waited on the pictures to download. "Why are you doing this?"

"I don't know." Derrick sighed. "I guess because...you look happy." The next words rang with irritation. "I guess I don't want you to hate me."

"I don't hate you," Callie assured him. "Thank you for this." But when she gave him a gentle hug, an odd strangled growl erupted from Ford's throat without his permission.

She released Derrick and shook her head at Ford. "Not Meritt," she reminded him quietly.

Callie tugged at the scarf she was wearing as Ford drove them back to the ranch.

"Baby, what's wrong? You're going to fray that thing if you yank on it any harder." He eased her hand away from the scarf.

"I'm just retaining water. My period's a little late because of all of this stress and everything. I can't believe he pointed out my weight. That was low."

Carefully measuring his words, he squeezed her hand. "He's an idiot like I said. I've got no interest in being with a shovel handle in a dress. I like your curves no matter what size they are. He was just trying to get to you. You're fucking beautiful, and he knows it." She'd shoved a box of tampons and pads under the sink in his bathroom. Ford had assumed that he'd been wrong about the pregnancy, and that she'd started. But maybe not.

It had been three nights since they'd made love, so he wouldn't know. That was yet another thing he'd let Meritt take from him. No more. Tonight, he'd fuck her until she understood how addictive her gorgeous body was and how much he appreciated those intoxicating curves.

"The pictures only solve half of our problems though," she lamented. "My father can still try to get guardianship of my grandparents and take their farm."

"Yeah, but it frees me up a little bit to make a move. Once Dale can prove to the superior court that Meritt doesn't deserve alimony because she was the one that was cheating and not the other way around, I can purchase the land, pay your daddy off, and make sure that land stays with your grandparents."

"I can't believe you'd really do all of that for me."

"Hey," he stroked his thumb back and forth over her palm trying to soothe her. "I know I get off on being your hero, and I'll try to get better about it. But more than the fact that I love you, I know how important that land is to your family. I know that it's the only place you ever really felt at home. I won't let you lose that."

"How did you know that?"

"You really want me to answer that?"

"What do I say every time you ask me that?"

"Fine, but you're not going to like it."

"Say it anyway."

"I don't blame your mama for leaving, but when she decided to go she yanked you off of any kind of foundation you ever hoped to have. That's hard to rebuild."

"We did move around a lot, I guess." Defeat tugged at her words.

"It was more than that. Ever since I filed for divorce, people have been asking me why I didn't do it sooner. Hell, for a long time I asked myself the same thing. What was I so afraid of that I'd choose misery over the unknown? I finally figured it out. Once you get accustomed to something, even if it's bad, it's what you know. You get to thinking that's how life is supposed to be because you can't see it being any other way. You figure a shaky foundation is better than no foundation at all, so you just keep trying to stay on your feet and make it through the next day. Your grandparents' farm was the only place that you could always count on. It was the place that showed you that all of the other places you lived weren't really what you wanted."

Callie was quiet for long enough that Ford worried he'd way over-stepped his bounds. But she finally released a long pent-up breath. "I guess I never really thought of it that way. But hearing you say it, that is kind of how my whole childhood felt. I was almost always alone even when my mom was there. Does that make sense?"

"Yeah, baby doll, it does. I just want you to know that you never have to be alone ever again."

CHAPTER FORTY-NINE

The next morning, Ford sat in the Simpkins' living room opposite Callie's father and Meritt. Her old man looked like he was going to burst a blood vessel trying to keep his mouth shut over something. Ford kept his arm wrapped tightly around Callie, still wary of her being anywhere near his ex. They were all waiting on Dale Miller to show up.

At ten past ten, he finally knocked on the door. "Sorry I'm late. I had to do a bit of research on what Ford sent me last night, and I was contacted by another party who is interested in purchasing the property, but let's get started."

Callie's mouth hung open until she turned to stare up at Ford. "Your dad?" she whispered hopefully.

Ford shook his head. "He wouldn't have done that without talking to us first."

Before they could debate anymore, Dale popped open his briefcase.

Callie's grandfather finally found his voice. "I am not selling my land."

"I understand that, sir. I'm just here to present the offer that I was hired to present, but I do have some information for Meritt, first." He handed over copies of the photographs Derrick had given Callie.

"What's this supposed to prove?" Meritt's voice made Ford's skin crawl.

Callie narrowed her eyes. "It proves that Ford and I were not together prior to the day of your divorce. Those photos have time stamps and they were from major events in LA. They couldn't have been altered in any way. I was living in Derrick's parents' home at the time, so it would've been next to impossible for us to have had any kind of relationship before my arrival here."

Dale cut across her, "Before you continue on with this, Meritt, I do have access to all of Ford's banking and credit card records. There are no charges that would make a judge believe that Ford spent any time in California prior to your divorce. The pictures prove that Callie was not in Oklahoma before the end of August. You are free to go on with your lawsuit for spousal support, but you're not going to win. He owes you nothing, and that's precisely what you'll get out of the Holder accounts. Even if Ford does decide to go on with the purchase of the Simpkins' farmland, you have no claim to the money he accesses to buy the land."

Abe decided to leap into the fray. "See, I knew something like this was going to happen. That's why I'm accepting the other bid. It's from some landholding company, so it's more money than I would've gotten out of him anyway." He threw a hand Ford's direction.

"You double-crossed me?!" Meritt screeched, like she was the only one in the room capable of such a thing.

"Well, he certainly learned from the best," Ford huffed.

"I don't care who did what to whom. I'm still not selling my land, and without my signature nobody is selling anything." Harold vowed.

The front door swung open just then and a woman who looked so much like Callie that Ford was worried he was having a stroke stepped into the room.

"Mom!" Callie gasped. "What are you...when did you...oh my gosh, how did you get here?" She stood but didn't go to her mother.

"Actually, Dad, you are going to sell this land. You're going to sell it to me. I own the landholding company. I don't want you two worrying over the money anymore. I want you to retire and enjoy the farm. But in order to do that, Abe, we'll be moving you off of our family land. You can leave. Now."

"You can't just throw me out of my house," Abe spluttered. "I'm not selling the acre my trailer's on."

"You're not selling anything," Willow came right back. "My parents are selling their land to me, and I am removing *you* from my land. I'm not afraid of you anymore. You have no power over me or over our daughter. And now you also have no power over my parents. So, you can move out peacefully, or I can call the sheriff. Makes no difference to me."

Callie seemed to finally locate her voice. "Mom, where did you get the money to do this? And where have you been for the last ten years? How did you even know this was going on?"

"We'll go over all of that later. I've been planning to purchase the farm for years now, so that you could be rid of your father when you're here. I wanted to...try to make up for, well, everything. But then, he decided to jump into bed with this piece of trash, and I had to move faster." She pointed to Meritt.

"We're not sleeping together," Meritt gasped as if that was the most offensive thing Willow had said.

"Give it time," Ford vowed. Callie shot him a horrified expression that had him contemplating an apology, but he only called it like he saw it. As far as he was concerned, they deserved each other.

Callie's grandparents had gone in the kitchen. Since Meritt hadn't been able to come up with another way to get Holder money in the palms of her hands she'd begrudgingly left. But Abe was still mean-mugging his ex-wife and Ford.

Willow kept her distance from Callie which only infuriated Ford more, but he kept his mouth shut. She didn't need her mother. He'd love her enough for both of her parents. Just because Willow had come in and saved the day, assuming Harold and Delphia agreed to all of this, did not mean she was a good mother or even a good person.

Ford knew he'd have to keep that opinion to himself though since Callie seemed pleased that her mother had returned.

When Harold and Delphia joined everyone in the living room, Ford prepared himself for another round of insanity. Her grandfather cleared his throat. "Willow, if you really do want to buy the farm from us, and you're okay with us living here until we can't anymore, then we've decided we would like to just give it to you. You don't need to buy it from us."

Willow shook her head. "Dad, you need the money. I have more than enough. I have no interest in living here, but I want you to be comfortable until, like you said, you can't be here anymore. That wasn't something you ever offered me when I needed help, but I'm not going to make that same mistake."

————

Chill bumps charged down Callie's arms as she watched her mother square off with her grandparents. Shock continued to twist in her belly. She couldn't believe her mom was there, that she was the one who'd saved them.

Nana's lips pursed. "Willow, you know that we do not believe in divorce. When you chose to leave Abe, you left us without any choice as to which side to take."

Willow rolled her eyes hard enough that Callie was certain she'd just gotten a glimpse of her own brain. "Mom, I never asked you to believe in divorce. I asked you to believe in me. In your kid. I needed that belief. I needed you to not have forced me into a marriage I never wanted. But mostly, I needed your help, and you turned your back on me. I'm not certain I'll ever forgive you for what you did, but I also won't make your mistakes. You deserved to have to live with him for a few decades, but you've served your time now. I've been working in real estate for years now. I saw the listing contingent on the property claim when it came up in the area. I tried to call and reason with *Abe*," she spat out his name, "but that got me nowhere. So now, I'm here." She turned to Callie. "I'm sorry I haven't been around much. You never really seemed like you needed me when you were a kid. You had more figured out than I did most of the time. But I know how much you love this farm, so I want you to always have access to it. I was hoping you'd let this be my apology."

Ford eased Callie closer to him which gave her strength. "What am I supposed to say to that, Mom?"

"That you forgive me," Willow all but demanded.

"I'm not sure that I do. Nana and Pops took Dad's side in your divorce, so they abandoned you, but then you turned around and did the same thing to me."

"I'm trying to say I'm sorry, Callie. Don't be so dramatic."

"Stop talking," Ford ordered. "Now."

Tears drenched with betrayal and anger stung Callie's cheeks as they streamed down her face. She was tired of being the one that had to try to raise her parents. She was tired of the shallowest of people cutting her the deepest. She turned and buried her face into the soft denim of Ford's shirt. He filled her ears and her heart with tender, steady reassurances.

"I've got you, baby," he whispered. "I will always have you. I will always be right here. I promise."

Willow joined them on the couch. "She doesn't need anyone to be there for her. I raised her to be strong and independent. She can think for herself."

Before Callie could argue, Ford beat her to it. "She is one of the strongest and most independent people I've ever encountered, and she sure as hell always thinks for herself, but no one needs to be those things constantly. Everyone needs someone to catch them when they fall because at some point everyone falls. As far as I'm concerned, every single one of you dropped the ball on her account. And I'm putting a stop to that bullshit right now. Honey, are you ready to go?"

Callie stood beside him. "He's right, you know. I spent most of my childhood trying to be the person who caught you when you fell over and over again, Mom." She turned on her father. "And trying to stay away from you." And then on her grandparents. "And trying so hard to keep you happy. That's not how childhood is supposed to work. I'll talk to you all later. I need some time to think. But thank you, Mom, for doing whatever it is you think you've done here."

CHAPTER FIFTY

Standing in Ford's bathroom, Callie stared down at the last placebo pill in the birth control package. Okay, something was definitely up. Last month her period had been super light, basically just a little spotting. And now she still hadn't started at all. Her mother had put her on the pill when she was fifteen. She could count on one hand the number of times she'd forgotten a pill in the last thirteen years. None of them had happened in the last two months, so she could not possibly be pregnant.

Great. The stress had gotten to her, obviously, and now she was going to have to find all new doctors in Tulsa assuming she was moving here. Ford hadn't exactly asked her to move in with him yet, but she was fairly certain that's what they both wanted. She'd never even sent the rest of the photos to Nina Morales. The cynical part of her wanted to believe that all of the insanity that Meritt and Abe had put them through was a sign that she should leave, but after listening to her mother talk the day before, it occurred to her just how much her cynical side sounded like Willow.

She was still hoping for a surefire sign, but right now she wanted to get some closure with her family. She went ahead and took the placebo pill for good measure and then went to pour herself another mug of coffee.

Ford grinned at her as she entered the kitchen. "We've got shipping trucks coming in this morning. I've got to be out there. Want to come with me? You'd get some great shots of the cattle."

"I'd love to, but I'm going to go talk to my mom and my grand-mother. I need some peace with all of this." She was also going to stop by the drugstore and pick up a pregnancy test just to ease her mind, but if she mentioned that he wouldn't let her go alone.

He already looked like he was being torn in two. "I can't go with you, baby. I've got to meet those trucks."

"I'll be fine. I love when you're with me, but I need to do this on my own. I promise I'll be back before you're finished shipping."

"Head out to the barn when you get here. I'll probably be out there."

She prepared a travel mug of coffee and kissed him on the cheek. "I will."

"I love you Calico Anna Monroe the first," he teased.

"The first?" She laughed.

"That's what you told me your name was that night at the bar."

She hid her face in his chest. "I need you to never tell me anymore about what I said that night."

"But you said so many good things," he continued to harass her.

"Like what?"

"That you wanted to marry me and have my babies."

She shook her head at him and wondered if he somehow knew some-thing she didn't. *Completely impossible*, she reminded herself. "Did I?"

"Hell yeah. You also nuzzled your head up real close to my cock when you laid on me in the truck. I deserve some kind of medal for being a gentleman. And then you sprawled out kinda like a starfish in my bed that night. You still do that by the way."

"Now, *that* I believe. I'll be back in a little while." She indulged herself in another dose of his kisses before she headed to her car.

No one was in her grandmother's house when she eased the door open. Relieved at that, she slipped to her bathroom and pulled the box of tests from her purse. She loved Ford. She knew he loved her, but she was fairly certain they were not ready to be parents. They weren't even ready to get married. Shaking off that fear, she assured herself, yet again, that this test was just so she could sleep at night. She'd ask Meridian to recommend a gynecologist in Tulsa and make an appointment to figure out why her period was MIA.

She tried and failed several times to get the cellophane off of the box. Cursing and ripping one of her fingernails, she finally freed the damn thing. Sweat dewed at her hairline. "For fucksakes," she quoted Ford as she tore the top of the box off. There were three tests in the box, and they all had different instructions. Deciding on the find-out-six-days-before-your-missed-period version, she finally located the correct set of instructions.

Scanning over the steps, she tried to calm her racing heart before she attempted to pee on the right end of the stick with the results window facing down. "Oh, crap. The timer." Locating her phone she set a timer for two minutes and returned to the position.

But as she turned the test upright and tried to start the timer with her other hand both pink lines were already glowing. Her lungs forgot how to take in air. She made herself check again at the end of the two minutes. Two bright pink lines stared back at her along with an ever so helpful guide on the test indicating that two lines definitely meant pregnant. "Holy fuck." She tore open the other two tests and did those as well. After five minutes, she had four pink lines and a YES on a digital read out.

Meridian's reminder about just how fertile the Holders were tried to reach through the deafening panic in her ears. Maybe the Holder men really were extremely virile.

Oh my god, what was she going to tell Ford? What if he freaked out? What if he didn't want babies yet? They'd only been together a couple of months. This wasn't at all taking things slowly. He'd just gotten divorced, and Meritt was a monster. Oh god, what if she tried to hurt the baby because she hated Ford so much?

A thousand terrible scenarios scrolled like a horror movie through her head. Every pink line seemed to highlight every doubt and insecurity that she kept hidden in her soul. He'd joked about making babies that morning, but he had no idea she was pregnant. She was too young to be a mom, wasn't she? Maybe not. Her own mother had only been nineteen, but she'd also been kind of a terrible mom so that wasn't helpful.

"Callie," Willow's voice rang through the house.

"Crap." Callie quickly cleaned up and washed her hands. She couldn't leave the tests in the trash, and she really did not want to shove pee sticks in her purse. Shuddering at that, she continued to let the ridiculous panic over the stupid things rule her. It was easier to panic over relatively inconsequential things. That kept her from panicking over the fact that she was going to have Ford Holder's baby.

She'd held a baby once for a couple who was having boudoir shots done. The kid had screamed the whole time. Oh god. What if all babies didn't like her?

She wrapped all of the tests and instructions up in the drug store bag and tried to shove them in her overly full purse. More of the bag stuck out of the purse than was in it.

"Callie?" Willow knocked on the door. "Are you in there?"

"Yeah," Callie tried to calm her voice and her breathing, "be out in just a sec."

She gripped the counter as a wave of dizziness washed over her. Having no idea if it was the shock or if it was the pregnancy itself, Callie splashed some cold water on her face and tried to decide what to do first.

Eventually, she could stand without feeling the earth itself move, so she opened the bathroom door. She wanted to sit on something that was not a toilet.

Her mom and her nana were waiting on her in the bedroom. Great. She forced a smile. "Hey. Sorry." She gestured to the bathroom. "About that."

But her mother narrowed her eyes. "What's wrong?"

"Nothing," Callie insisted.

Nana gave her an incredulous look. "Calico, you have always been a terrible liar."

"You look like you're either about to hurl or pass out or both. Now, what's wrong?" her mother demanded.

Before Callie could stop her, Willow pulled the Driscoll's Drugstore bag out of the top of her purse. "That is none of your business," Callie protested, but her mother was determined.

She revealed the tests and looked horrified. "This is exactly my business actually. Now, you listen to me and you listen good. You have to leave."

"What?" Callie sank down on her bed thankful for the soft surface that suddenly seemed to be the eye of the storm. "Why would I do that?"

"Because this town is like stepping back in time. They all but pinned a scarlet letter on me when I was pregnant with you. Ford might be a nice guy now, but that's before he gets strapped with a kid he didn't plan on having. I used to think your father was a great man before, too. I was so sure I was in love with him and look at how he turned out. Ford is the oldest son of the oldest son of the Holder family. He's practically a golden child in this town, and that family is not going to like you marring his image. They'll force you into a marriage to save their image."

"That isn't true," Callie huffed. "They eventually got over it when Meritt..." realization took her by the throat. It had claws. "Told him she was pregnant," she managed in a strangled whisper. What if he didn't believe her? What if he felt trapped again? God, what if someday he hated her as much as he hated Meritt now?

"Just pack your bags and go back to LA. Nana says you were making decent money out there with the pet photography or whatever. You're going to need that money if you decide to keep the baby. And I'll be in Denver so that's not too far for me to come help you when you need me. I swear I'll make everything up to you. I'll be so much better than your nana was when you were born. Men are always ready to jump into bed with you, but they are never ready for what comes of that."

"This is what I was trying to prevent from happening." Her nana was close to tears. "I don't want this to be our legacy."

Callie's brow furrowed. "Our legacy? Wait, does that mean...? You and Pops."

Willow rolled her eyes. "Oh grow up, Calico. Your Pops isn't my real father."

"What?!"

"He adopted me after they got married, but apparently my dad was a real piece of work. Nana let him knock her up."

Certain she was going to vomit, she spoke the only words that made any sense to her at all. "If he adopted you, then he is my real grandfather, so never say that again. I'm leaving."

"Good. Drive far and fast," Willow ordered.

Her mother, her father, and her entire life passed before her as she drove. Her parents had always been broken. Everyone was in one way or another, she supposed. But they always managed to cut her with their shattered edges.

She should've asked Nana about the man who was Willow's father. That was obviously the mistake Nana referenced, but just then she didn't care. None of this was how things were supposed to be, and absolutely nothing made sense.

CHAPTER FIFTY-ONE

"Eight twenty-nine," Ford called out the number on the digital scale as Wes, Jace, and Maddox continued to push the steers through the line. "Eight eighty-one. That's a big'un," he commented to their buyer, but something was wrong. He could feel it. His gut twisted and cinched with every single number.

The buyer continued to scribble down the weights Ford called out. They were trying to get the trucks loaded before lunch. Gentry and Leigh were hosting the buyers for some food before they left with the trucks.

His phone buzzed in his pocket between two steers so he checked the name, worried about Callie. It was a Holder County number but not one he recognized. "Hey, Dad," he gestured to the scale. "Can you take over for a sec?"

Barrett stepped in as Ford exited the weigh station. He tried to block out the low bellows of cattle from one ear with his fingers and answered on the other. "Hello?"

"Ford, it's Delphia Simpkin. I need to talk to you." Every single thing about Callie's grandmother sounded panicked.

"Just one sec," Ford signaled to his brothers who were working the line. "I gotta take this," he called. They nodded their agreement, so he climbed up in one of the horse trailers so he could hear. "Is Callie okay?"

"I don't think so."

"What's wrong?" Ford demanded.

"I tried so hard to keep Willow from making my mistake and now Callie's done it as well. We've been punished for generations."

Rapidly losing his patience, Ford bit back the first dozen things he longed to say. "What are you talking about, Mrs. Simpkin? What mistake?"

"She's pregnant," came out in a choked sob. "She took a test here this morning."

"I know she's pregnant," Ford assured her. "How on earth is that a punishment?"

"What? How do you know?" She sounded so much like Callie in that moment it made Ford smile.

"I could tell."

"Why didn't you say something to her?"

"Trust me, ma'am, the last thing you ever say to a woman you're in love with is, 'hey honey, you look like you mighta put on a little weight.'"

"Willow told her she had to leave—that you wouldn't want the baby. She told her the whole town would hate her for ruining your image. And that your family would force her into marriage. I think Callie believed her. Willow told her to go back to LA and get her job back. She got in her car, and now she's not answering her phone."

"What?!" Ford flung open the trailer door and raced to his truck. "Why the hell would her mother say that to her?"

"Because...that's...well that's what happened to Willow. I made so many mistakes, but you have to believe me, I was trying to save them. Willow won't let me go after her. I told myself that Willow would come back, that she'd bring Callie back to us if we let Abe live here. I had no idea that she'd stay away for so long."

"Jesus, it'll take me a half hour to get off this fucking ranch." Ford wanted to shake Callie's mother but not near as much as he wanted to find his baby and assure her that he was thrilled. "Before Willow got in her head, was Callie okay with it?"

"I don't really know."

"You listen to me, if you hear from her you tell her that I've never been so happy, that my family will be thrilled, and that I'd burn my godforsaken reputation to the ground before I'd let her go on for one minute thinking she's in this alone or that this is some kind of punishment. I don't give a shit what anyone in this town thinks of me. I love her, and I'm going to find her and we're going to have a baby and we'll figure everything else out. Every word. You say every word of that to her. And if I ever hear you refer to my kid as a mistake again, I assure you I'll have plenty to say about it and none of it will be kind."

"I'll keep trying to call her."

"Good." Ford ended the call. Gravel and dirt launched in the air behind his tires as he took off towards the north gates of Holder Ranch.

———

Callie pulled up to the barn, only it looked different than the one she'd been at before. Great. They probably had a bunch of different barns, and she had no idea how to get to the one Ford said he'd be at. Wiping the crumbs from her second McGriddle off of her chin, she climbed out of the car. At least there were trucks up there. Someone must be here, and they would probably know how to get to Ford.

The food had done a decent job of restoring her. Now, she just needed to figure out how to tell Ford what was going on. Heading into the dusty barn, she batted away a few flies.

Ugh, she didn't remember any of the people standing in the barn's names. "Um, hey," she squeaked.

"Callie," one of them smiled at her. "What are you doing all the way out here, sweetheart?"

"I'm really sorry, but I don't remember your name."

"I'm Ford's Uncle Wyn, and this is my son, Beau." Beau tipped his hat to her. "And don't worry, even our own mother called us by our siblings' names more than she called us by our own."

Callie grinned at that. "Do you happen to know where Ford is? He told me to meet him at the barn when I got back, but I'm not sure which barn."

"He likely meant Barrett's barn out on the other side of the ranch. You just turned in the wrong entrance. Ford's not likely to be done with his buyers yet. He won't be back at the barn for a few more hours. I could take you to his house if you'd like, or I can take you out to the pens where they're loading the trucks."

Callie did not want to make her announcement with Ford's whole family there. With a few hours to think over everything that continued to swirl through her mind, suddenly Callie knew exactly what she wanted to do. "No, that's okay. If I wanted to go see the mustangs, which way are they?"

"You're not too far from them out here. In fact, you could walk if you want. We moved them to a parcel about a half mile that way. Just follow the dirt path."

"Thank you."

She wandered along the dirt path in the direction Wyn had sent her and let the serenity of the ranch embrace her. It extended its arms wide before her and soothed her soul. She wanted her child to have a life like this, somewhere where everyone looked after them and loved them. A place to always call home. Somewhere to always come back to when the world got to be too much.

A knot slowly formed in her throat. This wasn't at all how she'd imagined her life, but she had asked for a sign. This was a pretty huge one. She wished she knew what Ford would say. She prayed he wouldn't be upset, and that he'd believe that she hadn't missed a single pill. The package said they were ninety-nine percent effective. She'd never imagined she would fall into the one percent. Ford teasing her about her introducing herself as Callie the first whipped through her mind. Her laughter was hollow.

Half of her heart seemed to have joined that knot in her throat and the other half had slid slowly down to her womb. She'd never felt more divided or more frightened.

She didn't want to give up being a photographer. She didn't really want to give up any of her dreams, but if the baby needed her to she would.

"I'll never ever leave you," she spoke aloud and rubbed her hands over her still relatively flat stomach. "Never. Not even when you're eighteen and ready to move away. I'll never not call you or check on you. And neither will your daddy." She knew that. Ford was nothing like her father, and she would not become her own mother.

CHAPTER FIFTY-TWO

Every rhythmic lurch of his tires on the cement drove Ford more and more nuts. Where was she? He kept constant search of every vehicle he passed on his way to I-40 and hadn't seen her car anywhere. He tried to call her a half-dozen times but got no answer.

"Dammit, Callie, where the hell are you?" He asked the ether, and, to no one's surprise, got no response. Every mile he progressed made him hate her parents even more. He'd deal with them later. Right now he had to find Callie.

The Burger King loomed in the distance. Maybe she'd gotten hungry. She was pregnant after all. He pulled in and searched the parking lot. Then did the same for the Whataburger and the Captain D's. Nothing.

———

Exhaustion and panic twisted up Callie's spine. Surely, she'd walked a half mile by now and there were no horses. In fact, there was nothing but more green pastures. She had no idea where she was. She didn't even know how to get back to that barn and to her car.

Pulling her phone from her pocket, she whimpered at the No Service displayed on the screen. "Fuck." She held the phone up in the air hoping to somehow get a signal that way, not that she'd be able to talk with her phone way up there.

Still determined, she turned and walked ninety degrees from the way she'd been traveling down another dirt path. She tried to remember if she'd made any turns on her path. Maybe Wyn had forgotten a step or something. They all knew the land like the back of their own hands. They didn't even have to think to get where they were going. It was instinctive.

She forced one foot in front of the other for another several yards and looked at her phone again. Still no signal. Gritting her teeth and summoning determination she didn't even know she had, she pressed on, certain she was going to collapse at some point. She had to get some help. It would be really bad for the baby if she passed out.

Another fifty yards, and she turned her phone over. If she'd had any strength left, she would have jumped for joy. She had one single precious bar. She touched Ford's name and prayed he'd be able to come find her.

He answered on the first ring, "Callie! Where the hell are you?" He was particularly growly this morning.

"Hey, could you not yell at me—I've kind of had a day?"

"Sorry." She could hear him taking a deep breath. "I've been out looking for you for an hour. Where are you?"

"What? How did you know I was lost?"

"I didn't...lost...where...you?"

Callie squeezed her eyes shut. The phone was cutting out. No. Please.

"I'm on the ranch," she shouted.

"What?"

"I'm on your ranch," she tried again. "I was looking for the mustangs."

"Keep walking towards the east gate. The signals are better closer to the road." Thankfully that came through clear, but Callie's feet were already killing her. She forced herself to stand and continue on the direction she'd been going even though she wasn't sure that was east.

"Can you hear me now?" she asked the painfully clichéd question.

"Yeah, that's better. Did you say something about the mustangs?"

"Yeah, your Uncle Wyn told me you would be a few more hours with the buyers, so I went for a walk. I wanted to see the foal again, but I must've gotten turned around. I took a different dirt path a while ago, and now I have no idea where I am."

"Thank god," relief washed through Ford's words. "Stay right where you are, baby. I'll be right there. I know where you got turned around. I've got to go get Chief."

Callie remembered going through a few pretty narrow places. Could he really not get his truck through? She didn't want him to have to go get his horse. That would only take more time. "I'm really..." she started to apologize but stopped herself. She hadn't done anything wrong. Everyone gets lost sometimes. She was in unfamiliar land, and it was going to be okay.

"Good girl," Ford chuckled. "Your nana called me and told me. Baby, if you're even half as excited as I am then we're going to be just fine. I know it's not like we planned this, but I love you so much. I want to raise a family with you. I want to take care of you always."

With that, Callie swore even her aching feet felt a little better. "I love you, too."

"She told me what your mom said. I was worried you'd listened to her."

"My mother has always given terrible advice. I usually just let her talk and pretend to do whatever she says then I do what I know is right. I would never have left. I knew we could figure out how to do this, even if it is really soon. I am scared though."

"I know you're scared. Jesus, it kills me that I'm not there with you. I swear I'm coming, baby. Just hold on, and it's not too soon. It's right when it was supposed to be. Does that mean that this is the sign you kept wanting?"

"I never really needed a sign. That was just my cynicism talking. The signs were all right in front of me. Every single time you've made me feel loved. That's all I should've been looking for."

"Good. It's going to take me another half hour to get back to the ranch and that's assuming I don't get my ass pulled over for going ninety. Do you want me to get one of my brothers to come get you?"

Callie tried to weigh how badly she needed to pee again against the embarrassment of one of his brothers having to rescue her. Her pride won out. "I'll be okay. Will you stay on the phone with me though?"

"Of course. I'm going to lose the signal again once I get out near the stables, but when that happens just know that I'll be there in just a minute."

Almost an hour later, the steady sound of rapidly approaching hooves shook the ground. Relief washed over Callie's weary form. Another minute passed before she could see him riding on top of his copper quarter horse heading straight for her. He pulled up on the reins as he got to her, slid off the horse, and wrapped her up in his arms. "Are you okay?" She managed a nod, but he was squeezing her too tightly for her to give him a verbal answer. "Thank god. You walked almost four miles from Wyn's barn, baby. You have to be exhausted. I don't want you exerting yourself especially right now." He ran a gentle hand over her belly.

"I'm okay," she assured him. Truthfully, she didn't mind being fussed over a little.

"Do you want me to take you to the mustangs or back home?"

"Anywhere that there's a bathroom first, and does that mean that I get to call your house home?"

"Make me the happiest cowboy on the prairie if you would." He remounted Chief and then to her shock reached down and pulled her up in front of him. She awkwardly straddled Chief as well.

"Uh, wow, it's really high up here, and there's no saddle."

"I've got you. I didn't want to waste time saddling him. We're going to take it nice and slow. Lean back against me and relax. We'll be home in just a few minutes."

She tucked herself in the crook of his neck as he took the reins and guided them home.

For the first time in her life, she was going to unapologetically do exactly what she wanted to do.

"I love you so much," he vowed again as they rode.

"I know you do," she assured him. "I love you, too. Do you want to know what Nana told me this morning?"

"Of course."

"She told me that Pops is not Willow's birth father." Callie felt Ford tense for just a minute.

"That explains a few things."

"You mean like why she was so hard on my mom?"

"That and something my Uncle Gentry told me."

"What did he say?"

"He said a lot of people like to stick to these rules they have in their head because they think the rules keep them safe. Your grandmother clings so hard to the rules because maybe her mistake cost her quite a bit. She didn't want you and your mom to go through the things she went through, whatever they might've been. So, it comes from a good place, but it's misguided."

"That does make a lot of sense," she agreed. "I think she has in her head that she has to pay for the mistake she made with my mom's birth dad. Instead of seeing the good that came out of it, she only focuses on the rules she thinks she broke."

"Forgiving yourself isn't easy, baby. You and I both know that. I think that's why it bothers me so much when you apologize for everything. I don't want you to live your life trying to make other people happy. I know it soothes you in the moment, but you'll wear yourself out trying to meet expectations that no one can achieve. When you constantly feel guilty for things that you can't change, I worry that it leaves you in a place where it's mighty easy to forget to see all of the amazing things you do because you're so worried you might've upset someone."

"I mostly just want to make our little family happy." She placed a hand on her belly again and tried to imagine it being big and round. She couldn't wait. "I promise I'll always try to remember to see the good and not to worry so much about everyone else's definition of what's good and what isn't."

"You make me happy by just existing, sweetheart."

"When the baby is born, we can just keep showing Nana how good things are. Eventually, she'll see, don't you think?"

"I think we ought to try even if she can't see for a long time, and I think we ought to try to start showing her before our baby is born."

CHAPTER FIFTY-THREE

Lying in bed the next morning Callie had questions she wanted answered.

"Just ask me," Ford prompted her before she'd said a word.

"How did you know I wanted to ask you something?"

"I just know. Now go on with it. Whatever it is, it's bugging you."

"Does me being pregnant remind you at all of...you know...when you and Meritt were first together? It bothers me that I've put you back in the same boat, I guess."

"I'm not in the same boat, and you aren't Meritt," he quoted. "I'm in love with you. I was never in love with her. You really are pregnant. She never was. I'm older, wiser, been through some shit and now I know exactly what I want and she's lying on me in our bed."

"What if people think the baby is the only reason we're together?"

"Like I keep saying, people will think whatever the hell they're gonna think, but I figure in fifty or so years, after our kids are grown and running this ranch and we're still together in our rocking chairs on the front porch, people will figure out that it wasn't just for the kids."

Callie couldn't have asked for a better answer than that, but it brought on another question. "Does it bother you that I'm so much younger than you are?"

"I thought I wasn't supposed to say anything about that anymore."

"Okay, but if you were supposed to."

"No. It doesn't bother me. I just never want you to feel like you gave up any part of life for us. If there's something you want to do, I want to make sure it happens."

"I don't feel like I'm missing anything. I do want to keep taking pictures and maybe open a studio, but mostly I just want to be with you and with our baby. I know I'm younger, but I've lived through a lot of shit, too. You tend to grow up pretty fast when you have a childhood like mine. I was the one who had to raise my parents."

"Yeah, I figured that out all on my own. I think I might've finally figured out something about the two of us as well."

Contentment soothed her, still a heady sensation for a girl who finally belonged right where she was. "What's that?"

"Nobody gets to get out of this life unbroken. That just ain't how it works. So, if you get lucky enough to find the person who has the broken pieces that fit yours then you hold on tight and kind of put each other back together."

"Ford," she choked, "I love that."

"Yeah, well I love you."

"I love you too."

"Is it bad that I hate your parents?"

Callie chuckled at that. "Hate is a strong word."

"Fine, I really dislike them."

"I'm not a big fan of theirs right now either, but holding grudges isn't going to be helpful. I just want to keep the baby away from Meritt and away from my dad."

Ford turned so he could stare down at her. "Honey, I had no idea you were worried about Meritt like that. You know I will never let her get anywhere near you. I will protect you and our kids until my dying breath."

"I know, but I might need you to remind me of that every now and then."

"I'll say it every damn day if that's what you need. And it won't just be me either. There are a whole bunch of Holders who'd go to the mat on your behalf. We take care of our own. Speaking of that," he reached into his bedside table and extracted the ring box he'd purchased a few days before.

"Oh my gosh." She sat up in bed and pulled the sheets up over her naked breasts. "You're doing this now. Here?"

"I can put it back 'til later, but I want you to have it. I'm impatient. You know that." He started to return it to the drawer, but she caught his arm.

"No. I want to be impatient, too."

Smirking at that, he kicked off the sheets and blankets. "You want me to put on some shorts before I get down on one knee, or are you okay with me being nekkid?"

A fit of hysterical giggles broke over her. "I like you nekkid."

"That's my girl." He got on his knee, and Callie tried to remember how to breathe. "I love you Calico Anna Monroe the first, but I'd really like to make you Calico Anna Holder if that sounds good to you."

"It does," she assured him. "It sounds perfect!"

He slipped the most beautiful oval diamond ring she'd ever seen on her finger. "Oh my gosh!" She stared down at it in disbelief. "It's perfect."

"Just like you, baby."

"Thank you." She pulled him back up into the bed with her. "You really are my sunrise, you know that."

"I don't think so," he corrected her. Callie's brow furrowed. "I decided we're the whole endless Oklahoma sky. An unending number of sunrises. We go on forever and ever."

"I love you, Ford Holder," she gushed again as she climbed in his lap and gently placed the hand with her ring over the Holder brand tattoo on his arm. Callie Holder. She grinned at everything that was to come. Every road she'd taken had all led her right here. She didn't need a sign to know she was right where she was always meant to be.

Her whole entire life she'd believed she was nothing more than a thousand questions, but she'd fallen in love with the answer to them all.

———

A week later, Callie was laid out on a cold exam table in a doctor's office in Tulsa. An ultrasound tech was squirting jelly on her stomach. Ford was attempting to hold both of her hands without getting in the tech's way.

"I'm good. I promise," she assured him.

"Okay, let's see if we can't figure out how far along you are," the tech explained.

"I don't think I'm more than a few weeks along," Callie tried to explain.

"Your doctor thinks you may be further along than that."

Callie gasped as the grainy, black-and-white image appeared on the screen. "Oh my gosh. I can see it. It's...real."

Ford stared at the screen in dumbfounded awe.

The tech chuckled at them both. "You appear to be almost ten weeks along."

They turned to stare at each other. "The first time," Callie whispered.

He nodded his agreement. "Guess the universe was listening."

"It always does."

EPILOGUE

Five Years Later

Dr. Monahan grinned at Ford who was busy brushing his wife's hair away from her sweaty face and brushing kisses everywhere he could reach. "Looks like you got yourself a little girl this time."

Callie used her waning strength to lean up from the bed. She was grinning and crying at the same time, but that's what she'd done for several days after both of their little boys had been born, so Ford wasn't too worried about it this time.

"When you told me it was going to be a girl, I didn't believe you," she informed the doctor. Thrill and shock lit her exhausted tone. Ford accepted the tiny pink bundle wrapped in blankets like it was the most precious thing in his world. Other than his wife and his sons, she was.

"I'm not sure I know what to do with a little girl," he admitted in a choke. Overwhelming emotion and protectiveness gripped his vocal cords.

Callie grinned. "You always know exactly what to do with me," she reminded him.

He brushed a tender kiss on his little girl's forehead and then another one on her mama's. "I already bought you a pony," he informed their daughter. "And I'll teach you to ride, just like I taught Mommy."

Everyone in the delivery room chuckled at him. He didn't care.

Apio snapped another picture of the three of them as Ford laid the baby on Callie's chest. Callie had wanted this birth photographed in all of its gory but beautiful detail. Apio had flown in from Johannesburg to do the honors. Connecting women to their beauty indeed. She'd agreed to fill in at Callie's studio on the square in Holder County while Callie took a few months off with the new baby.

Just outside the delivery room there were at least three dozen Holders along with Willow and Callie's grandparents. No family was perfect. Ford was just glad they were there. It made Callie happy, and that was all he ever wanted.

Callie had labored throughout the night. Ford had been right by her side for every contraction, just like always. As he turned to glance out the window just then, he noted a gorgeous sunrise cresting the buildings in Tulsa. He was certain his girls were the only things that would ever outshine the Oklahoma sky.

ABOUT THE AUTHOR

Bestselling author Jillian Neal likes her coffee strong and sweet with a shot of sinful spice, the same way she likes her cowboys. In fact, her caffeine addiction is quite possibly considered illicit in several states as are a few of the things her characters do. When she's not writing or reading, you'll find her in the kitchen trying out new recipes or coming up with ~~excuses~~ reasons to purchase yet another handbag or make an additional trip to Sephora. Though she'll always be a Bama girl at heart, Jillian hangs up her hat and kicks up her boots outside of Atlanta with her hunk-of-a-husband and her teenage sons.

For more information...
jillianneal.com
jillian@jillianneal.com

ALSO BY JILLIAN NEAL

BROKEN H.A.L.O

H.A.L.O. Undone

H.A.L.O. Redeemed

Fractured H.A.L.O.

CAMDEN RANCH

Rodeo Summer

Forever Wild

Cowgirl Education

Un-hitched

Last Call

Wayward Son

GYPSY BEACH TO CAMDEN RANCH

Coincidental Cowgirl

GYPSY BEACH

Gypsy Beach

Gypsy Love

Gypsy Heat

Gypsy Hope

www.ingramcontent.com/pod-product-compliance
Lightning Source LLC
Chambersburg PA
CBHW060912190726

48286CB00002B/476